W9-AVO-610

THE WOMAN
Who Fell Through
THE SKY

SANDIA BELGRADE

THE WOMAN *Who Fell Through* THE SKY

Copyright © 2013 by Sandia Belgrade
Printed in the United States of America

All rights reserved. No part of this book may be reproduced in any form or by any electronic or mechanical means including information storage and retrieval systems, without permission in writing from the author. The only exception is by a reviewer, who may quote short excerpts in a review.

The Woman Who Fell Through The Sky is a work of fiction. Names, characters, places, and incidents either are products of the author's imagination or are used fictitiously. Any resemblance to actual persons, living or dead, events, or locales is entirely coincidental.

* * * *

Cover Art: Tayrawr Fortune
By permission of the artist

Excerpts from "The Corn Mother" by Carol Lee Sanchez

* * * *

Firebear Press.com

* * * *

ISBN-13: 978-1483933139
ISBN-10: 148393313X

DEDICATION

*To Pavita, for all her loving care
of this manuscript and me*

ACKNOWLEDGMENTS

Love and gratitude to Pavita Decorah, Ellen Farmer, Carolyn Flynn, Sugandha Brooks and others who have offered comments and editing suggestions.

Appreciation for Molly Rowan Leach who designed the cover and for Debora Lewis (arenapublishing.org) who formatted the book and finalized the cover for publication.

Thankfulness to Tayrawr Fortune for her haunting cover picture.
To the Pedernal Mountain in New Mexico for the inspiration.

.

ONE

The presence of a woman intruded on the landscape, one of the upright forms. Each hair on her arm inclined west to east moving in the late summer breeze along with las flores de la quebrada, the wild flowers at the base of the mountains. On the meadows higher up, the wheat colored grasses bent in the same direction. The woman panned the surrounding mesas with her binoculars, taking in the monochromatic pattern of meadow grasses and chamisa spread out before her. The lens pulled back. Its owner lay in the long grasses watching the sky which hung suspended just out of reach as it does in New Mexico. The clouds shuttled by and for a brief moment she gave herself over to the blue and white screen that glided passed giving the sensation that both she and the sky were moving. Strong as the pull of the sky was, uneasiness crept in. She stood to see what denied her peace.

The telescopic eyes of the binoculars scanned the cliff opposite her, a good mile away, and half again higher than the place where she stood. The finger-grooved indentations of the base narrowed as they rose up from the earth towards the mesa. The coloration of the rock layers broke into a staircase pattern as she neared the top, and the eyes of the binoculars came to rest on two women standing at the edge of a mesa.

She sucked in her breath. The person facing her was a woman. Surely it was a woman, but there was a thick growth of facial hair on her chin. The woman whose back faced her was retreating from the woman with the beard. Her left foot stepped closer to the round eyes of the binoculars. Alethea moved to readjust the focus, but as she did, the woman fell backward into space, her body suspended in air for a timeless moment.

For a split second she saw both the woman who was falling through the sky and the one who remained on the cliff, frantically reaching for the body, a look of horror on her face. Alethea keyed in on the woman falling, who had lost her hold on the world and quickly disappeared from view.

And then there was no one in her sights, neither the earthbound woman, nor the one who had fallen through the sky. "Oh, my God," cried Alethea. It had happened in a compressed moment in time. Her heart pulsed with questions: did she jump? Was it an accident—her foot could have tripped—the woman could have pushed her. What had she missed while trying to readjust the lens? She jammed the binoculars whose vision she could no longer trust into her backpack and took off to find help.

Alethea was a large woman running in the thin air of high altitude, and soon gasping for oxygen, her feet churning in the direction of a tavern she knew was below the mesa. Though she jogged several times a week, conditioning was of no help now. Natural grace became a clumsy effort to brake on the sharp degree of slope. The momentum careened her forward and she fell, her backpack landing with a sharp blow on her back. Pain flared in her knee. She lay face down, breathing into the pine needles. In her mind, the woman fell again. She leaped up. The knee was scraped and bleeding. She began running again, her lungs gasping for air. Her heart beat, an incessant metronome. "Later, I can rest later."

At a desperate pace on the uneven terrain, she found in herself the kick that joggers experience until the small bar appeared, its sign chipped and a woman with a red bandanna around her head jumped up from her chair behind the counter, startled by Alethea's wild appearance.

"Phone," she gasped. "Por favor, telephone! Urgencia. A terrible accident."

The old woman's wrinkles fell away from her face as she stretched into motion, unnerved by Alethea's face, which was red to the point of alarm. She saw the scratches all along her arms and the one knee bleeding freely. She ducked under the bar counter.

Alethea glanced in the mirror behind the bar. Her face was puffy with exertion, so splotched that an old childhood scar was hardly visible. She looked away quickly as the woman brought out the phone from behind the bar and gave it to her to dial. Alethea spilled out directions to a rescue operator who promised quick response. She hung up the phone and looked again in the mirror. Mirrors threw back an image that always surprised her. Her view of herself was that of a thinner woman though the reflection showed otherwise. She saw the tangled mass of long dark hair, the small down turned nose, the cheeks, angular for a large woman. An attractive 31-year-old head perched on a round body. The bandanna reappeared in the mirror.

The old woman had been watching her. She offered a glass of water in her wrinkled hand. Alethea wanted to stare at the hand, but there was no time. She drank the cold water greedily and handed her the glass, looking directly in her eyes. "Gracias." Outside the glare of daylight stunned her sight after the bar's dark interior. The late afternoon sun dared her to climb back up to the top. It had been cool there. There had been wind. She hurled herself up the trail to the Jemez mesa where the two women had been. Her pack felt heavier as she dodged the discarded beer bottles that lined the trail. In the late afternoon, she climbed in a pattern of walking and running, the falling body as her companion.

At first it had clawed against the sky. And then—was she mistaken—it seemed to relax into its flight down before disappearing from view. The memory of the falling woman became etched in Alethea's vision of the sky. The body fell over and over as she trudged up the mesa, and she nearly believed she'd see the woman still falling when she arrived.

Only the sky met her. She came out of a stand of lodge pole pines, their tall, bare trunks rising above her, the first 25 feet with no branches. On the edge of the clearing she stopped to catch her breath. In the center of the empty campsite was a smoldering fire. The bearded woman was nowhere to be seen.

Alethea ran to the edge of the cliff and peered over. She lay down on her belly and thrust her head over the side until she felt she was nearly hanging upside down. The sheer drop made her stomach lurch. The granite walls stretched further down than the eyes could see at this angle. Below her the canyon was dense green thicket and the scrub oak was beginning to turn red. The sun had already deserted the canyon bottom. There was no body to be seen. Had the woman with the beard also lain there, hearing the wind swirling up from the canyon? She slid back from the precipice and stood up, her balance shaky. In the late afternoon light, the smoke from the deserted campsite was a quiet presence. The fire pit was encircled with a ring of rocks that had been placed to the four directions. Had they been doing some kind of ritual? On one of the stones was a small bundle. She quickly unwrapped the cloth covering as if someone might catch her in the act. It was a journal. Thick and bulky, crammed with pages pasted in, containing the odds and ends of someone's life. She skimmed through for clues, wondering if that excused the invasion into someone's private life. The writing was sprawled, often illegible with personal notes, women's names. The tone came across as angry in several places.

There were also pages of songs, strings of notes and chords. Sometimes just a small phrase. Other verses were longer, complete with repeating choruses. Alethea had little talent for melodies, but some of the words resonated within her. The bearded woman's horrified eyes hovered around her. Alethea turned to the inside cover and saw the several names:

Brenda Firestone
6200 E. Larchmont Drive
Scarsdale, NY. 14217

That had been crossed out and changed to:
Borrasca

Rt. 1 Box 309
Espanola, NM 87533

And a third name appeared below that one:
Bejay Storm
% Siren Productions
PO Box 63884
LA, CA 94720

The name Bejay Storm jarred her mind, but the sound of whining tires below the mesa jolted her attention. Feeling like a thief she inexplicably stuffed the journal into her pack before a large 4x4 Jeep exploded into the clearing. Four men jumped out. "Where is she?"

"She fell off that ledge She could still be alive." Alethea pointed to the outcrop where the woman had fallen. The tallest man got on his belly and crawled out onto the ledge. Two of the men held onto his ankles, so he was able to stretch out even further than Alethea had.

"I think I see her." They began shuttling out rope in the fast dimming light.

"Doesn't look good. You know her?"

"No," Alethea replied.

"I know you."

Alethea wheeled around and looked directly at one of the men.

"Kurt Deming. Right. Right. You do rescue work."

"I'm a paramedic with the Forest Service. You don't know what happened?"

Alethea shook her head, and the binoculars told their story again, how the body fell through the sky. Her mouth guarded one detail: the bearded woman. "I saw her fall from over there."

She pointed to the facing slope where she had been standing. The palisade walls of the cliff were now a bright focus for the dying rays of the sun. The light was fading quickly, yielding to the darkness creeping up the canyon walls.

"Might be impossible to get to her before the darkness takes over," cautioned the tall man.

They lowered ropes and grappling hooks.

"I just happened to look over here."

"You saw her fall?"

"Yes."

"Was anyone with her?" Kurt posed an innocent question.

Her brain fought the answer away. Even to say there was another woman on the ledge implicated her. She didn't know if the woman had been pushed or had fallen, yet she felt an unaccountable protectiveness for the bearded woman. It wasn't like Althea to be deceptive, and the impulse startled her. She stumbled over the truth as if it were a lie.

"I don't know. I saw her falling in midair through the small round screen of my binoculars. It was all I could do to keep the binoculars moving as fast as she was falling. I'm afraid I'm not much help." She led his mind down another path.

"I thought my seeing her was going to be a significant coincidence, that because I'd seen her and run for help, it meant she'd be saved. Now she might die after all, and I won't have mattered."

"That's quite a personalized view of life. Children are alive today because people rushed into fires with their clothes ablaze to save them. Once I saw a man climb a burning tree to rescue a frightened cat. It's what we do for life."

His matter of fact attitude annoyed her. "I'm not so immersed in tragedy as you are. I was looking for wild flowers."

The men did her the favor of ignoring her while they fashioned a hoist. The tall man stepped off the world, like the woman had done, but he dangled securely from ropes. The darkness continued to grow around them.

They waited in the silence while the man rappelled down the cliff. They cursed the sky for not staying lighter, longer. Finally he called up to them. By the time they pulled him back up to the mesa, they were speaking into the sunset.

"She's there all right, but the ledge is barely holding her. It'll never hold two people. We'll need a strong portable light and more cables." They bandied opinions preparing to descend again.

"Getting dark. We might have to wait until morning."

"She can't wait that long--if she's still alive. I couldn't tell. The risk of exposure is too great."

"It doesn't look very hopeful," Kurt conjectured. "Even if she survives the fall, she might not survive the cold in addition to trauma. Night will make a big difference."

Alethea looked over to the other mesa where she had stood hours before. Nothing human was there now. Nothing that revealed the full story. She felt in her backpack for the journal to reassure herself of that reality. In the changing light she folded her arms around herself, trying to understand the impulse that had led her to rearrange the truth.

A layer of clouds was moving in. With cloud cover, it might stay warmer, but there would be no stars to keep her company or a moon to help find her. Darkness began to cover all the shapes.

Alethea climbed into the vehicle with the man heading back to town for the cables. "I'll hitch a ride with you. My truck is just off the highway, a few miles from here."

The Jeep lurched forward. Alethea looked back at the outline of the figures standing on the ledge in the dim light—stone menhirs gathered around a secret place.

TWO

Borrasca reached through space to bring her body back to earth—but her arms were too short. In her mind, Borrasca fell alongside Cade. Passed the cliffs. A scream broke through the canyon walls and echoed in her ears. So intense was her identification with Cade, she didn't realize the scream was her own. She expected the earth to shift. To fall away like soft shoulders. The uneasiness in Borrasca's stomach and the limits of empathy by the living for the dead kept her on the ledge. She leaned over the mesa as far as she dared. Peering through the rocks and the underbrush, she saw Cade face down on a ledge, not moving. The distance between them was a universe, measured one plane to another. Death hovered over that ledge. Borrasca drifted in between realities, one of them trying to cash in a claim on the 39-year-old woman below. The body whose weight she knew so well lay still. Perhaps, ownerless. There was no way she could get down the steep precipice. Panic overtook her. She scrambled back from the ledge, confused. Rudderless. She started to go for help only to return. How could she leave? Cade fell again. "I have to find help." She took off, hysteria rising, her breath coming in short sobs, running away only to come back once more to the ledge trying to sort out the two voices of her confused mind. One was in her brain, rooted in this world, which directed her away from the edge. "Find help," it screamed! From deep within her: "I can't leave her here alone."

The brain directed her to the path. She careened forward on the downhill trail, oblivious to the branches which caught her arms, the cactus that punctured her sneakers. Trickles of blood formed on her arms and legs. She veered from one tree to the other, not seeing the hawk circling overhead. Her vision was blurred from crying as she staggered down the trail and onto the highway now cast in twilight and eerily lit by a small gas station.

The attendant was dumbfounded by her appearance: a big woman with a large mass of tangled hair and a face registering terror. He kept moving backward as she ran towards him gesturing wildly. "Phone. I have to make a phone call."

"Sure. It's over there." He pointed to the wall.

"I don't have change."

"This ain't a bank."

Then he heard her barely audible voice, "It's an emergency. A woman..." Images fell in front of her eyes, and a loud cry came out of her mouth instead of words, pushing the attendant back another step.

"Ambulance," she pleaded. "I have to call an ambulance."

His brain finally caught on. He ran to the office and fumbled in the till for change. Borrasca's shaking hand froze at the touch of the coin.

"Do you want me to dial?"

"Yes. Police. Ambulance. Please find help."

He dialed the 911 number, and she grabbed the phone from him, listening to it ring. A serious man answered. When she asked for an ambulance, he inquired, "Where are you, Miss?"

Borrasca looked around and read the large letters on the sign. "The Sinclair Station... near ..."

The attendant filled in the words. "Abiquiu."

"Abiquiu." A woman has fallen off a mesa."

"Someone just called in, Miss. Are you there? A rescue team is on the way."

Borrasca dropped the phone involuntarily. It swung on its cord as her mind raced to fathom what he said. The dangling phone talked back to her. "Are you all right? They're on their way."

She turned on her heels away from the swaying phone receiver. "Bathroom?" she asked. He pointed.

She ran into bathroom and threw up into a filthy bowl. The water threw back her reflection at her then collapsed into her insides and poured out into the toilet. She stayed on her knees, unable to move or open her eyes, until the stench forced her to her feet. Her eyes were blurred and running. Her limbs became the controlling elements in her body. She fled, leaving behind a bewildered mechanic.

Demons followed, those speedy wanderers on the planet who sense when a spirit is ripe for torment. One demon warned her, "Somebody saw. They're gonna blame you."

She retreated from the highway back into the forest and found the road leading back to the top of the mesa. The trees crowded out the night sky and became background for her nightmare. As the shadows lengthened with the night, she provided her own torture. Borrasca looked up, expecting instant repercussions from the universe. On one limb, partially torn away from the trunk was a harpy like creature with the head of a woman fused into the tree trunk. The other branches became talons which reached out for her. "You abandoned her. They'll think you pushed her," said a demon.

She avoided the sweep of the claws and fell awkwardly on the downward incline. Cade fell along side of her and they landed with a thud into a low pinion tree whose branches broke her descent. "Oh, sweet Cade." Soon only one word, all sensation heaped into one name: "Caaaaade." Into one image: Cade falling. She forced herself to her feet, the brain directing her back into the world. She swerved aimlessly among the trees, alternately weeping and screaming. She stopped in front of a *lodge pole* pine and wrapped her arms around it. A convulsive burst of tears overcame her. Her arms reached above her head encircling the trunk. A short woman and an old ancient tree. She dug into the trunk, and the bark crumbled, falling into her hair. The touch of the tree showering her with pieces of itself brought an inexplicable moment of grace.

She shook the bark from her head, and her feet found themselves running again on a path that took her back to the world of roads.

Before she could decide in which direction to go, a speeding car came around the corner. Without thinking, Borrasca stuck out her thumb. He was young. He saw her breasts. Instinct made her pull back—she could be hitching a ride with one of the demons. "Where to?" he asked.

She threw the question back. "Where are you going?"

"The hospital, you know, the one in Espanola."

Isn't that where they would take Cade? She hopped in and then he saw her beard. Saw her swollen eyes, her face caked with dirt and felt trapped. She was going to unfold a plot around him, and he with a car full of stash. The loud blaring music saved them both from having to talk. He asked if the music was too loud. If she wanted a beer. She took the beer for her parched throat and gave stony silence to the rest of his inquiries. Throughout the long ride, with only the dashboard for light, they held each other at bay.

As they approached town, the sound of squealing tires and cars backfiring could be heard. Saturday night low riders. He dropped her off in the parking lot of the hospital and she jumped out, only to walk headlong into a commotion of people gathered at the front entrance. An ambulance with its red flashers rotating cast them in a red glow. The presence of so many people made her hang back on the edges. She turned to see if he was still watching her, but when she did so, he put the car in gear and burned rubber out of the parking lot. The flash of light bulbs brought her attention to reporters with cameras. She pulled up the hood of her sweatshirt and tightened the drawstring until only her eyes were visible.

A man was holding center stage, and quieting reporters. "The woman fell from a ledge. We do not know the extent of her injuries, and the doctors have offered no word at this time on her condition."

It became clear to Borrasca that what had happened on the ledge between her and Cade had entered the public domain, and the man standing in the middle of the crowd was liking that. He began taking questions.

"Was she alone? Who found her?"

Borrasca strained to hear. The self-important looking man was probably an administrator. As if he could know what had happened. She who had been there didn't know. Why couldn't they say how she was? The drift of the exchange became apparent. "We think another woman may have been at the scene, a woman with a beard." Borrasca panicked.

"How's that? Do you mean a transvestite?" They volleyed him with rapid fire questions.

"Look, this is a first report. Don't pressure me for more answers. We'll know more when we find her. Thank you."

There was little interest in Cade. They were fixated on the idea of a woman with a beard being at the scene, not the woman who fell.

How did they know I was there? No one thought to look for the bearded woman at the edges of the crowd. They were intent on the man who knew, standing in the center. Near him she saw Kit whose height made her stand out in the crowd. How did Kit know to be here? Had she told them about her relationship to Cade? What did everyone know? Borrasca backed up and headed towards the road. In her mind she saw a headline: *"Two lesbians on a ledge.* The demons came out of the crowd whispering, "They're looking for you."

This is exit time, Cade. This is no place for either of us. I can't abandon you to them—she turned around. Cade? Are you all right? She backed up into the night, waiting for an answer which never came. She had already been walking for hours, but there was nothing to do but walk the three miles to La Puebla. It would be safe. There was a road and she was going to follow that road. She moved quickly down the highway and then turned off on a dirt road, feeling her despair in the stones under her feet. A moon would have helped. Oh, Cade, she repeated. My dear Cade. Borrasca fought off the images that besieged her. She was just walking a road.

At the house she paused in the driveway, afraid to go in. The automatic nightlight had come on and its glow riveted her in place. She watched her dog Emma walk into its glow. She had picked up her scent and began barking. Borrasca ran to her to preserve the silence.

"Hey, girl. It's okay." She knelt and hugged Emma, grateful to have something to hold. She went furtively into the house and turned off the light. It would be safer in the dark. Her paranoia settled over every corner of the house as one by one, she walked into each room. "He didn't say you were dead—Cade, are you?"

Hysteria welled up. Borrasca flung herself on the couch crying until some semblance of reason returned.

She made her way into the kitchen where the stillness echoed off the white stove. She fought for focus. The calendar on the wall said it was Saturday. The clock above the refrigerator had moved into Sunday. People survived such falls. The man at the hospital hadn't said she had died. On instinct she picked up the phone and dialed.

"Amyneita," she yelled into the receiver.

"Borrasca?" The groggy voice at the other end had been pulled from sleep. "Where are you?"

"Tell me she's all right." There was a pause. "Please say she's alive."

Amyneita's end of the line was silent.

"She could fall that far and still be alive."

"Borrasca, let me come over."

Amyneita listened to her cry before asking, "What happened?"

"I don't know. She fell. A long way.... I don't know what happened, and if I can't tell you or me, how can I tell the police or anyone else?"

"You weren't there when they found her?"

"I left. I went to get help." Borrasca's voice dropped away. "Oh dear God."

Amyneita waited and then spoke into the silence, "Are you okay, Borrasca?"

"When I called the rescue number, someone else had already called in. Someone had been watching us." Her voice cracked. "I couldn't find my way back up the mesa. Too many trees. Demons. I hitched a ride to the hospital. The place was crawling with people. The man at the hospital said they were looking for a woman with a beard."

The conversation felt like it was happening to someone else.

"I was there, too, but I didn't see you," said Amyneita. "Linda Bressure who works in Emergency called me. When I got there I overheard her tell them you two were lovers."

"Oh, Cade, my sweet love."

Amyneita tried calming her with details. "First they said she was alive, but no one could see her. Then they said they didn't expect her to live, but we still couldn't see her. When her father and step-mother showed up, they stopped giving us information."

"If she dies, she has a will saying she's to be buried on women's land. They won't honor that unless we make them. They don't own her," Borrasca screamed. "They don't own her."

"I can be at your house in 20 minutes. Don't deal with this alone."

In halting words, her breath coming in short gasps, Borrasca pleaded with her, "Don't tell anyone that I was there with Cade. Promise me."

Amyneita hesitated at the gravity of the request. "I promise, but be up front with me about what happened."

"I don't know! You must believe me. I who was there don't know." She jammed the phone in its cradle. Amyneita held the silent phone in her hand, sensing more than grief was happening. Borrasca had entered one of those places where the dark had been given permission to enter. What had gone on between the two of them?

Borrasca wandered from room to room, her arms wrapped tightly around herself, her body unable to light on any surface. She paced the house until she came face to face with the answering machine. It was blinking. She pushed the button and lay on the couch to listen.

Brenda, it's mommy. Call us, honey. Your father and me get worried when we don't hear from you. Come home for the holidays. We love you.

Bejay. Where are you? We get the gig to end all gigs and you don't show up for rehearsal. The Spiral Shell for two weekends is too good to blow off. Get your ass out here.

Borrasca, it's me, Kit. There's a meeting for the Los Alamos demonstration against the Nuclear Waste Project. Call me if you go. I need a ride.

The tape ended and shut off. Borrasca lay stretched out in the dark. There were no more names they could call her. If she was Brenda to her mother, and Bejay was her stage name, if Borrasca was the woman on the mountain who had watched her lover fly off the edge of the world, who was the pathetic woman on the couch? Brenda, she intuited, was innocence. Bejay was midnight glitter, but Borrasca had killed them all. Who was Borrasca without Cade? She cried until exhaustion brought sleep and a respite from the ache in her gut.

In the morning, the desert light blazed through the window. Her bladder needed attention. She staggered up, noticing the front door had been open all night. She could take care of bodily functions, but she was having trouble getting from point A to point B. The thought of a bath and her bladder got her into the bathroom. Her mind raced to make sense of events while she sat on the toilet, yesterday's dust still in her mouth. She drew hot water for a bath while old song lines came to her lips. Bejay is the one who sings, remember? You are Borrasca.

She immersed herself in the steam, coiled within her thoughts. The demons climbed inside. "Fuck off," she yelled. The waters enveloped her. She touched herself all over her sore body, crossed her arms to find comfort until her hands gently found her breasts.

"I love you, Cade."

THREE

IN THE FIRST SECOND
the earth was moving under her feet,
the world was giving way to open space.
Cade saw this in a removed way that at first
shielded her from fright
She stepped out of her body
she stepped   into air
In the first second, she felt free
not of the earth
not of the living
nor the dead
part of that large body of those undefined
who had come before,
who have some relation to divinity.
The lodestar attracts us.
The leylines point the way.
That was it:
She had misjudged her leylne.
Nothing had offered a hint that in her 38th year
she would misjudge the way and step off the world.

FOUR

The man dropped Alethea off at her truck. Las flores de las quebradas could not be seen in the dark, but surely they waved in the evening breeze. Alethea turned the truck around and headed down the highway. A woman lay dying in the evening. Nothing inside Alethea felt life there.

She turned down her dirt driveway. No one was home. In the dark she reached around the door and switched on the light. It filled the room and spilled out into the front yard in little squares. She ran a bath and examined her scraped legs. One knee was caked with blood. Her feet were swollen. She went to the refrigerator while the tub filled and tasted a spoonful of ice cream, but it turned sour in her mouth and she dumped it.

She stepped into the tub anticipating the pleasure of steeping in the waters. The heat caressed her body, but her mind replayed the incident. Alethea saw the woman fall again. She sank lower into the warmth, but when the image persisted, she hauled herself out of the tub to retrieve the journal from her pack and crawled in bed with it.

As her eyes found the first page, she saw the patterns cast by the overhead light in the periphery of her vision. Something in her—reader or snoop—was resisting, holding the mystery at bay. She who was never given much to analysis found herself scrutinizing every detail. A self-conscious reflex had set in. Each gesture mattered; nothing occurred without a questioning echo. It exhausted her. She put down the journal and closed her eyes.

She'd witnessed a woman falling through the sky. The image permeated every fiber of her consciousness. The magnetic pull of the two women on the mesa persisted, their images becoming impressed upon her as nothing ever had. A woman with a beard had stood on a mountain. Another had fallen through the sky, a feminine Icarus. Men usually defined the life and death adventures, but she had witnessed an extraordinary thing on top of a mountain, and it had happened to two women who carried the power of enchantment. The effect it was having on her arrested her being to the roots.

Most of the myths of women that she'd read were from the Indian cultures of the Southwest. She learned about Spider Woman and Changing Woman of the Navajo people. Though their culture was not hers to claim, these myths had become part of her psyche, perhaps the psyche of many women.

There was also a legend of a falling woman. According to the story. the people—no, it had been waterfowl. They had joined their bodies together, so the young woman could fall safely on this platform of bodies. When they grew tired of holding her, it became necessary to provide her with a permanent resting place in the world. Somehow the great Turtle, whom Native people said made life possible in this world was involved, but she couldn't remember the ending of the story.

How did these myths relate to what had happened and in any way explain her actions? Inexplicably, she had lied to protect a woman she had never met. Had taken her journal. Two actions totally out of character and baffling. There no way she could explain what she had done. She picked up the journal again, hoping for clues to understand herself and what she had witnessed.

The journal had been started in February, three years earlier. Many of the entries were personal dialogues with private admissions: the little blemishes of life scrawled only for the mind's relief. There were also songs. Musical verses and lyrics crowded the pages. Alethea's feelings about invading someone's privacy were secondary to an overwhelming sense that some key she needed was here. It struck her that the three names were the same person, a woman with several identities. The shift between them kept Alethea guessing.

Feb 18. haven't been able to sing well the last few weeks. I keep thinking some heckler will be in the audience—waiting for me to make a false move and the papers will mop up the floor with our act. Well what difference does it make who is watching or who writes what review? What someone makes of it is their business.

March 12. The paranoia has gone away. For now. The audiences are behind us. And besides we want people watching, don't we? We're center stage and Bejay is the eye of the storm.

One line resonated within Alethea: "What difference does it make who is watching?" She, Alethea, had been the watcher. Wasn't there some belief that said the watcher and the watched are inextricably connected?

Sept 29 I'm ready for a break. Maybe it'll slow down in winter. I like the band, but it's not like hanging out with the women in the desert. I miss the land. I've gotten on a treadmill and can't stop. Why am I complaining? Good money, good reviews. I swear I'd complain at anything.

Oct. 15 Hanukkah is months away and they're wanting me to come home. My parents will never be at ease in their lives. The Holocaust is still going on for them. My life as a Jew comes only from my connection to them. I can't seem to claim it for myself though the Shoah impacts my generation and me. I'll go home for their sake and light the candles, eat latkes, and when I'm back in New Mexico that world will be miles away. No matter what happens I can't hurt them.

It was becoming clear that Borrasca was the "I" whose persona governed the tone of the journal. The entries in winter described a bleak period in her life. The impetus of pain had forced her to explore herself, though she was a resistant seeker. The intensity of her thoughts overwhelmed Alethea who came from a family closed to emotions. While she herself avoided intimacy and the entanglement of relationships, this woman Borrasca ran headlong into experience.

Jan 17. We have become sex objects for macho men to ridicule. Still, the records sell, the audiences keep coming. The pace increases. Thurs. a recording session lasting well into Frid. morning. Friday night a gig. Sat. we signed albums at a mall. Then I slept with Calypso. Why? I was really needing space. Now I have another entanglement.

As she scanned the journal and songs, it suddenly dawned on her that Bejay Storm was Borrasca's other identity. Bejay, the lead singer of the new indie band that everyone was listening to had been on the mesa. The lyrics popped off the page:

> *Say Free, stay Free one more time*
> *Stay Free don't wait for another time*
> *Love me floating in your bed*
> *Float Free, free one more time*
> *Love is free, keep our love free.*

It was the song that had been on the radio for months, She'd sung along with it driving to and from work with the rest of America. She felt foolish for not having guessed her identity sooner, but who looks for a rock star in their binoculars in Abiquiu, New Mexico? The frantic face on the mesa had been Bejay Storm. That song had been born in this journal.

The journal entries moved from despair into joy, much of it due to a notable event. In Borrasca's words she'd met "an incredible woman" named Cade. The entries became less frequent in the glow of new love. All that Spring the journal lay fallow. By summer, the same magnetism that had brought them together began polarizing, sending them on careening courses:

July 6. This relationship cannot work. We're too different. She is this cerebral person with a reserve about her. How can a hedonist be compatible with a research physicist? She's too academic. When we go to the women's land she looks like she's going on an Audubon Society hike. The land women are more into essentials--no, that's not fair. Cade knows deeply about essence.

July 11. Cade gave me a copy of her book to read. I tried, but it's too linear for me. Still I wish the Codebook were accessible to more women. She's a good role model.

July 24. Saw Cade again last night. We managed to get out of our conceptions of who we are and gave ourselves permission to just be. And oh how she can be. I can still feel her tongue. At one point during the night I woke with my arm asleep under her, but I was afraid to move it for fear she'd wake up and roll away from me.

Was Cade the woman who fell through the sky? When her rational mind acknowledged they were lesbians, a rush of unsettling emotions rose inside her. Their lives were part of a parallel universe running alongside the one Alethea inhabited, mostly invisible to her and outside her point of reference. She couldn't read any section for long when the woman with the beard would appear or the body would float above her. The face before her, the body above, falling through the sky. She leaned against the headboard, recalling admonitions from her parents' generation. Not to touch anyone in gym class or in the showers. Borrasca was a notorious bad girl who ran contrary to all society had taught her about the roles of women. Good girl; bad girl. Virgin or whore. Borrasca was off the continuum. Alethea was more open-minded than her parents were, but she couldn't shake her fascination about them, not just because they were lesbians, but because they'd stepped outside the boundaries. Was Borrasca trying to pass as a man with the beard? And Cade—what did she look like? Clues were missing in the journal and in her own life, which had become a puzzle with missing parts. She turned off the light.

The falling woman must be the Cade mentioned in the journal. Both women brought a vitality into their lives in a way that she hadn't. A singer. A scientist doing research. She imagined Cade alone in the dark on a ledge. And where was Borrasca of the horrified face? Had she run from the scene to go for help or to run away? Alethea fell into restless dreams of two women touching. The black of night curled around her longing. No one touched Alethea. She woke with a start, her feet drawn up in a fetal position. She reached again for the journal in the early morning light with the instincts of a hunter looking for herself in the quarry.

What struck her about the journal were not merely its intimate revelations, but that it chronicled the account of a woman journeying toward herself. Borrasca, the woman of three names, was alternately self-assured or filled with doubt. A sensual woman living at a high pitch of intensity. The raw quality of her thoughts—many of them inscribed in moments of extreme anguish—informed every page. Borrasca was her antithesis. She jumped in and rolled around with life. What had brought Borrasca outside the realm of ordinary? The last entries in the journal were dated only three days before.

What do you know--we're booked at the Spiral Shell in LA next weekend. Calypso says this proves we've made it. I've wanted to play the Spiral Shell forever, but I don't want to tour and leave Cade right now, and she won't come with me. Why can't she understand how much I want to share this part of my life with her? I feel split and don't know how to bridge our lives. This will be my last weekend home for a while. Here there's peace. Calm beneath this sky.

Where was the house of this woman yearning for peace? Borrasca may have returned there last night. Alethea jumped out of bed and threw on her clothes. Under 360° of uninterrupted sky she drove, the sun-drenched light reflecting off her truck. The ungraded, winding dirt road of Rt.1. was just off the Espanola highway. It cut through a wide swathe of high desert land to La Puebla, a sprawling little settlement of a few hundred houses. Strange that its name was feminine—La Puebla. She was sure that the Spanish word for town was el pueblo.

Alethea followed the numbers on the mail boxes until she found the adobe house, set back from the road about 200 yards. The roof was bowed from age, and the sagging adobe tilted the appearance of the entire house. A small tool shed shaded by four neat rows of apples trees was on the south side of the house. No one could be seen except for a cat that stopped licking its paws long enough to watch her from the driveway. There was no vehicle. Perhaps no one was home.

She got out of the truck and surveyed the house, but she could not bring herself to walk up the driveway. What would she say if Borrasca were inside and actually opened the door? "I saw you and your lover on the mesa. What happened? Did you push her? Did she fall?" Is that what she most wanted to know—what had happened? She was uneasy with the other question: who are you to me? She was not ready for either answer. There was one other question, and the hospital would have the answer.

FIVE

Borrasca heard a vehicle on the gravel driveway. She stood by the side of the window and peered through the curtains. Old Emma, who hadn't heard the truck, lay at her feet sleeping. A woman sat in a blue Toyota pickup watching the house with the motor running. Borrasca held her breath.

The woman got out and leaned against the cab. She was a good-sized, zaftig woman. From this distance Borrasca could not see her features, hidden behind the bangs on her forehead. She wore jeans and a heavy chamois shirt. Her presence ignited terror as the minutes stretched endlessly. Finally the woman opened the cab and got back in.

Borrasca's mind sent out messages of alarm while the woman backed up the truck and drove away. People are looking for me. An imbedded fear of secret police and Nazis welled up in her. There could be a story in the Sunday morning paper. More people might come by to stare. To ask questions. Maybe the person who had called in was the woman who had come to stare at her house. How did she know to come here? Only the land women know me. Even the neighbors don't know that Borrasca and Bejay are the same person. Have the police made that connection? Her mind sought rationality as a concoction of fantasies wound about her.

With a sickening realization, she remembered her journal. She flew into the bedroom to her altar. Her worry stone was there. Quan yin. Several amber beads and a large crystal. No journal. Frantic, she pulled out the drawers of the nightstand, sending everything onto the floor, already intuiting where the journal was. She had left it by the fire ring. It proved she'd been on top of the mesa with Cade. They suspected her of foul play. It was going to get blown out of proportion. Her brain fought for control as media headlines flew past her: *two lesbians in tragic struggle*.

"I'll be convicted in the press. No one will believe me—I don't know what to believe!" Her brain reeled off images of Cade's flight down: the body suspended for an infinitesimal moment before it began falling through the sky.

"I'm not waiting around for them to come for me. This is Sunday. I don't have to be in LA until Wednesday. I'll drive out. Get myself together. Sort everything out. I can go from point A to point B."

She stopped in her tracks. I have to see Cade first. I can't leave her like this. I could sneak in a side door at the hospital—no, they'll be waiting for me. Her mind jumped from ledge to ledge. The police will be looking for Borrasca, but not Bejay storm. If I get caught here, the whole world will find out that Borrasca and Bejay storm are one and the same person.

Furiously she began packing clothes. One outfit for rehearsals. Jeans for the drive. Sparkles for the performances. She couldn't know she would not be back. She went to the altar to get Cade's picture, but drew back from its touch. "Cade," she screamed. The words of a partially remembered Kaddish tumbled out of her mouth, then stopped midstream. Someone could fall that far and live if the ledge protected their fall. Amyneita didn't say for sure. She didn't say.

The events replayed in an endless time loop. People will say I left my lover to die. That I killed her. No one will listen to me. They'll want a story. Her mind reeled at the stereotypes the press would revel in. They'll decide what happened. I was there don't know what happened.

"What happened, Cade?" Her voice rose into a scream and roared back in her ears: "I don't know." she pounded her grief into a pillow, "I don't know." She was physically spent, but the thinking mechanism was in overdrive, scurrying in survival mode. She flung more clothes into the suitcase and a large pack and put them in the trunk of her car. She poured out food for the cat and Emma for several days. Two bowls of water. Wrote a note asking Amyneita to look in on them.

She sat in the car, running a debate with herself. I'll never get into the hospital to see her. If did, I'd never get out. What if she's dead? I can't leave her in the hands of her father. Anguish mounted in her chest. Cade will understand if I say good-bye in my own way at Chaco. Funerals are social conventions. Please understand, Cade. I love you, but I can't be there. Cade rushed past her, falling away from her outstretched hands. Her body floated through the air. She heard a scream swirl around a ravine and echo back to her. She put her foot on the gas and peeled out of the driveway.

She had become Borrasca, the sudden storm that comes up. She who runs with the wind, one step ahead of danger. Survival was a growing root inside, an instinct born of her Jewish history, of centuries of fleeing. A history that replayed as she decided to keep ahead of whoever was in pursuit.

Any other day, she could have driven to Chaco canyon without checking a map. Today she took several wrong turns, alternately speeding or becoming so lost in thought that her speed fell well below the limit. She worried about the police stopping her for speeding or going too slow, tracing her license plates—was an alert out for her car? Her friends wouldn't tell the police anything. Country women knew better than to talk to authorities. But now they had her journal. And someone had seen.

It was sundown by the time she got to the unpaved road leading in to Chaco. The sky, which had been ablaze with a dying sun, now became that shade of deep blue black, which held everything in relief outlined against the horizon. When the washboard road forced her to slow down, she became impatient in the growing twilight, wanting to be there before dark.

Borrasca was not prepared for the divine to make an appearance. As the car headed over a bridge spanning a dry arroyo bed, a small herd of four wild horses appeared on her left, leading a colt or filly. They were all white, and their whiteness took on a ghostly presence in the dusk. She shifted down, and in that instant, the horses stopped and looked up at her. They, like her, arrested in flight. She felt the tautness in their bodies. Their white light, like an aura, encapsulated all of them-- horse and woman--in a silent, magical enjambment.

At the prompting of something she couldn't detect, they suddenly turned and ran. Borrasca's eyes teared up—that the universe could still feel her deserving of magic, extending to her an unspoken gesture of life. Her hands trembled on the steering wheel. Around the next turn Chaco Canyon appeared, the oldest ruin of its kind in North America. Its stark stone shapes were silhouetted against the sky by the time she arrived. She turned her headlights off.

The ancient Anasazi, ancestors of the present day Pueblo people, had constructed a sprawling settlement that had lasted longer than most present day structures. Old as the wild stallions. Older than most written histories. Pueblo Bonito stood before her, the largest of the great houses in Chaco, and perhaps the largest ancient pueblo ruins in North America. It was a beehive of apartments where its residents had once dwelled. There were also kivas, large circular prayer rooms built underground with ladders reaching up into the sky as the only way in or out of them. Other larger kivas were used for public ceremonies.

On the north side of the floor of each kiva, small round holes called sipapus were dug into the ground. These were the place of emergence for the spirit. How keen was their understanding of the numinous. In some cases, there were dark tunnels which led to the kivas and if one walked through them, they emerged into daylight. When she had first come here, she entered one such tunnel, and after emerging into the light, she understood how one went from the dark depth of the soul into the realm of light. This is what she hoped for tonight.

She parked the car and furtively looked around to make sure no ranger or stray tourist was around. There was no one her paranoia could detect. She grabbed her sleeping bag, water and pack and climbed over the rocks. The walls of the pueblo hung roofless, the ceilings having disintegrated and fallen long ago. She walked through the rooms open to the sky. They were nestled side by side in a tight honeycomb arrangement with a connecting sequence of doorways, each one representing passage, until she came to a larger room that once served as a storage area. From this familiar place, which had offered her comfort and sanctuary before, she was safe. No one was going to swoop down on her for having violated a historical ruin. Her paranoia diminished.

She turned on her flashlight to scan the mud floor unwilling to share the space with reptiles or scorpions. Spirits, yes. Creepy crawlies, no. Satisfied it was clear, she spread out the down sleeping bag and lay on her back, encompassed in the vast panorama of the sky and stars, free of humans. Her mind became still in the black void until she heard a coyote in the distance. Its call summoned her.

Borrasca prepared a makeshift altar and sat cross-legged in front of it, waiting until the moon was directly overhead. Isolated from everyone else alive, she reached out in desperation to the spirit world. She cedared herself off, cast a light around her for protection and prayed, acknowledging the four directions and the powers around her. She didn't attempt to take on Indian tradition as her own, but its grounding in earth and spirit resonated within her. Like many women she knew, her own spirituality was a blend of Dianic wiccan beliefs and indigenous traditions. It didn't escape her notice that she could more easily call on these traditions than those of her own Jewish roots.

As the daughter of holocaust survivors, she'd inherited a legacy of loyalty as well as a painful, imbedded reminder about the past. It was through pain that she bonded with her parents and their history. Judaism's spiritual dimensions were obscured by the one central fact of the camps and their effect on the survivors, her parents, and their children, she and her sister Mimi. Being a Jew for her was rooted in a familial definition.

Borrasca opened her mouth, and something reminiscent of a wail called out Cade's name. It echoed off the layers of walls and reverberated back to her. Nothing made fathomable what had happened in that moment of bright sun on the mountain, in an irrevocable split second. "Blessings, Cade. Forgive me for whatever I might have done." She moved back and forth between the part of herself holding on to rationality and the other grasping a ledge. She said a prayer of Metta for Cade and all sentient beings, knowing she had to begin by extending compassion to herself. After several aborted attempts, her voice cracking, she intoned:

May I be happy and peaceful.
May Cade be happy and peaceful,
Free of pain and sorrow and suffering.
May all people and creatures everywhere
Be free of pain and sorrow and suffering.

The solace she felt was short lived. She was exiled from Cade, from herself, her family and the lesbian community, from all people who had suffered. Hers was a private diaspora—no that wasn't it. Jews were a people undeserving of the horror meted out to them. She had no right to compare her plight to theirs. She covered her face in her hands, filled with the guilt and sadness that had constellated in her. As a little girl she had sat with her grandmother, her bubbe, in a synagogue saying Kaddish for the dead. She began the Kaddish prayer. The words, unspoken for many years, echoed off the walls of the ruin: Yit'gadal v'yit'kadash-sh'mei raba...

The comforting sound of the ancient words reverberated through the maze of the ruins long after she stopped singing. She offered gratitude to her teachers: Jamilla, Wallace, and Ayya Khema. Only then could she find enough peace to close her circle of one and lie down. Her head facing north, she fell into the sleep of the lost and disconsolate.

The next morning, before the ranger made his inspection, she was gone, leaving no traces anyone could detect. She was learning to walk on the face of the earth without leaving an imprint. Her car flew across the great American desert. She floored the gas pedal, and after a burst of a 100 miles an hour, the sense of urgency left her. She slowed to a more manageable speed, but the calm she had experienced at Pueblo Bonito had vanished. The landscape swept by her unobserved except for one cluster of leaning rocks which jutted out against the sky. She saw Cade fall from them and jerked her head back to the road in front of her.

She practiced being Bejay and sang. Her voice gave her reliable footing. "I give thanks for this band. I can get up on stage and forget everything else. I stand in the spotlight and the audience thinks they're looking at the genuine Bejay. Could fool even me. If I don't get this voice in shape, I won't fool anyone." She began another warm up. Her throat cleared, her larynx eased. She took a few hits from her water bottle and savored the moment. She sang most of the play list. An hour later despair returned. Was the present always going to be lost to a split second on a mountain? Meaning lay in a moment that had slipped through her fingers. If she had only... what? Had faster reflexes? Loved better? There were endless questions for each mile, interspersed with the singing which kept her functioning.

She was keenly aware of what she was returning to. It's back to the boys. And makeup. And people who want me to be paying attention all the time. Close the door when I go to the bathroom. Close up all the buttons and zippers. Open a few for effect. She liked how her pits smelled after a set, the animal in her that could not be covered over. It made her feel real. It blotted out the odor of cigarettes and alcohol that accompanied the band and the audiences—Cade never needed deodorant. After making love—the thought had just drifted in. One moment of carelessness and the pain of memory pressed in. Her body would always hold their intimacy. If she practiced meditation more could she quiet her mind or would she ask questions like these forever? She screamed into the emptiness of the Painted Desert.

SIX

The history of the mesas is told in the rocks, the volcanic tuff, the caves, the petroglyphs. A history most of us cannot read today. Everything on the Pajarito Plateau speaks of the intangible bonds that once existed between the human and the natural world. Eons ago the natural attraction that connected everything, each to each, was felt as a binding force. The intimate connection that existed between this land and the Ancestral Tewa Pueblo people to whom it was home, was an essential relationship that is nearly lost to us in this century.

Tsankawi Saekewikwaje Onwikege—the "village between two canyons at the clump of sharp round cacti," is on the Pajarito Plateau, in the Jemez Mountains in New Mexico. Here the Rio Grande River flows through the Rio Grande Rift. Repetitive cycles of volcanoes throughout its geologic history have created an instability in the earth's crust. A pair of explosive eruptions from the Valles Caldera had coated the surrounding landscape in thick layers of volcanic ash called tuff. The resulting tableland is called the Pajarito, or little bird. To the east are the Sangre de Cristo (Blood of Christ) Mountains. To the northeast, the Española Valley. It is north and west of Santa Fe. 70 miles south are the Sandia Mountains, east of present day Albuquerque.

From the twelfth to the mid-sixteenth century, the first people came from Mesa Verde in Colorado and Chaco Canyon in New Mexico. Later, Tsankawi became home to the Ancestral Tewa people. They lived here among the cream-and-tan cliffs and piñon-juniper-forested mesas of the Jemez Mountains. Their descendents live today in nearby Santa Clara and San Ildefonso Pueblos.

Its history and ours are intrinsically linked. If one were to learn the language of the natural world—the trees, the stones and scat— our place in the world would be more rooted. If one is willing to engage with it, some of ourselves will be found.

SEVEN

Monday came before Alethea was ready to put aside what had happened on the mountain and be fully present for the children. She opened the door to the bright yellow and green walls of La Escuela Escalante classroom and Mauricio Allende threw himself into her arms.

"Good morning, Mauricio, you're back." Mauricio's words sputtered out, "Cold all gone." The part of the cold that was left was running from his nose. Alethea was the first person outside his immediate family that he'd been able to initiate contact with in his five short years. He fondled her chest absent mindedly as if her large breasts were part of the lapel of her jacket.

Alethea relaxed. With the children everything was straight forward. Honest. One by one she greeted them as they returned from the weekend, gathering Sofia beside her and sitting with both her and Mauricio on the floor.

"Why are you on the floor?" asked Timothy, coming over and joining them.

"I hurt my knee and I want to keep it stretched out, not bent." Alethea pulled up her skirt just far enough for them to see the red cuts that had scabbed over.

"Ouch. How'd you do that?" asked Timothy."

"Hiking. But it's not as serious as your arm. I just have to be as brave as you are." He forced a smile. Alethea didn't pursue it, knowing full well it may have been his father who'd broken his arm. Timothy had run away from home and had come back to her class before going to his own home.

"I don't want to go to Miss Ada's room," Sofia interjected. They all chimed in, "She's too picky. You're scuffing your feet. Don't slam the door."

Alethea was used to a class room of children all talking at once, but this morning she felt like she was in front of stereo speakers, with the children in one ear and the sounds of the weekend in the other. She took the children to Nadja's room, the arts and crafts teacher. Her work spaced was organized with scraps of wood and little hammers, and a tiny saw suited to their size. They were going to learn how to make a simple box.

Alethea was struck by Josefina who used the hammer as if the tool were second nature to her. When she was finished, she showed her box proudly to Alethea. "For you," said Josefina.

She had made a perfectly flush box, but when Alethea tried to open it, there was no lid. The top was hammered down; the box didn't open. Nadja looked at Alethea and said, "Sometimes I feel I'm in a box like that one."

The day ended with a staff meeting. A woman from Social Services told Alethea, "You've built a bridge between Timothy's family and our agency. It's made a substantial difference."

Alethea acknowledged her with an embarrassed thank you. She gave stone silence to the rest of the meeting, but her ears perked up when Maria Elena, the Principal, said, "I want to remind you of the budget crunch we're facing. We'll have to cut one position unless the staff can offer some ideas about reducing the budget in other ways."

After the meeting, Maria Elena caught up with her. "You were awfully quiet at the meeting. Social Services thanked you, and you barely acknowledged what you've done for Timothy."

"Just got a lot on my mind."

"Anything you want to talk about?"

"To be honest, I'm thinking of taking some time off. That would solve the budget problem."

"It would be a bigger problem to replace you."

"For now, I'll start with a request for personal leave this Thursday and Friday."

Maria Elena nodded. "I'll arrange for a sub." Alethea took herself and the box with no lid home. She placed one on a shelf and the other in the back yard. The warm late autumn sun was matched in stillness with the Sangre de Cristo Mountains that looked down on Santa Fe. Inside she was a form unsettled even as her outer shape sat motionless.

The door opened and Laurel glided out, bouncy and at odds with the space that Alethea was in. Laurel liked that insubstantial breeziness about herself and her body. She and Alethea never talked about weight, but Laurel's attitude about the weightless quality she exuded was clear. It was not an issue between them because they never dealt with substantive issues. Their relationship was a convenient sharing of a house. Laurel dated and frequently left for the weekend, much to Alethea's liking, for then she had the house to herself. She'd opted out of the social scene long ago, except for a few close friends. None of them dated; they seldom hugged or touched. The wave of sexual freedom had bypassed them, and they were invisible in a world which propelled women towards men and marriage. It wasn't the sanctions against large women that kept Alethea outside the social arena. It was a group of unspoken needs she couldn't express. An intuitive sense that there was more to life, but no sense of how to make change happen. Laurel was not someone she'd usually turn to.

"You were still up when I got home last night. Anything exciting happening?"

There was condescension in Laurel's words, but the foment and unrest caused by the two women on the mesa tempted her to talk to Laurel. She got the New Mexican delivered every day and might have read about the incident.

"Maybe. Something."

"That's your best description?"

"Okay," Alethea responded, "Try this name: Bejay Storm. Do you know who she is?"

"Of course I know who she is, don't you?"

"I know who she is, Laurel." Alethea's green eyes glowered. "A singer."

"*The* singer. The one with the beard in that indie noir group with their outrageous jokes about men. And she has a marvelous voice."

"I might see her in LA." The remark flew out.

"When did you get turned on? You know, there's rumors that she's a lesbian, Alethea."

"So?" The tenor of her remarks cut off any further dialogue. Laurel wheeled around and went back in the house. She would have known if the incident on the mesa was in the paper and if the connection to Bejay Storm had been made. It occurred to her that possibly she was the only one who really knew that Bejay had been on that cliff.

Over the next few days Alethea wandered in and out of a fog. She read the obituaries in the New Mexican. No one named Cade was listed. She reread parts of the journal, particularly the last entry about Bejay appearing in LA. How could Bejay perform with her lover dead less than a week? On Wednesday she picked up a copy of the LA Times at the local newsstand. In the entertainment section in bold black and white was an ad for the band's show. It was all the confirmation she needed. Resolutely she called Bass outlet in Albuquerque to buy a ticket.

The first day of travel was spent crossing New Mexico and Arizona, running endless questions through her mind. Something had interrupted the monotonous stream of her life. There was no way to share it with Laurel who'd sensationalize the incident—was that what Bejay feared? Alethea was still without clues about the incident or for herself Are you also running, Alethea? For reasons she could not fathom, she felt bound to Bejay and Cade, like a particle drawn irresistibly to a magnet.

The next day, once past the sparsely populated roads of New Mexico and Arizona, she ran headlong into the L A. freeways. She was relieved to have the speed brought to a halt by rush hour traffic. Waiting in the endless line of cars, Cade reappeared. It always came back to her the same way: the body floating in mid air, arrested between the sky and the earth. A horn blast from the car behind her brought her mind back to the traffic which had started to move again. The two women on the ledge were as present as the people in the cars around her.

In the early evening, she walked the streets she had seen in movies. On one corner she saw a record store with bright lights and loud music roaring out of gigantic speakers.

"Bejay Storm? Sure. The CD's are in the bins on the left."

Alethea thumbed through the titles, scanning the albums of singers and rock groups. The overt sexuality put her off—why didn't Bejay repulse her. She hung out listening to a tape along with two teenagers who had come in. Belay's voice echoed off the walls as she sang and cracked jokes:

Death and Sex, Sex and death. Isn't that the end all be all, you be here for? Audience laughter could be heard on the CD. Bejay said the word sex suggestively. Then stretched out the word d-e-a-t-h giving it a suggestive meaning.

The young girls hung on every word. If they didn't know more about life than she did, they probably knew more about sex. Alethea left the store before the cut ended, then returned, red in the face, to ask directions. Do you know where Bejay is performing tonight?"

The neon marquee with the words ***SPIRAL SHELL*** caught her eye. She stood against the wall watching the audience enter. Many of them bore little resemblance to any cornerstone she could identify with including some whose gender she could not discern. When two women appeared, one with sparkles pasted on her face, the other wearing all black, she tagged behind them. The woman collecting money assumed she was with them. Alethea stood on the periphery, waiting for her eyes to adjust to the dim light, a lone figure amid the electric anticipation of the audience. The audience was mostly women, and when the band began setting up and doing sound checks, she saw that the stage crew was composed only of women.

At the next table the loud voices carried over to her. "The cuts on their album are 1 and 2 on the charts. It's going to be a hard act for her to repeat. The critics are waiting for her to stumble."

"Well, tough. I like women-only energy. There's even men here tonight." The women looked around. The media had come in full force, setting up cameras and testing their sound systems. One man standing in the aisle next to her was already broadcasting: "Bejay Storm of the trademark beard has become a minor cult figure. Last month she was the feature story in <u>Gathering Moss.</u> Tonight this packed crowd is anticipating a wild show complete with the 'white man' jokes that the band is noted for. As I wait here with the audience, it's clear that everyone is making up jokes that go along with the rage."

The audience drowned him out, clapping and stomping their feet for her to appear. Without warning, a spotlight moved down the center aisle carrying Bejay with it. Alethea sucked in her breath along with the rest of the audience. Outlined in the beam of light—it was her!

Bejay leaped on stage and grabbed the mike. She sang an opening phrase, and it seemed like everyone in the crowd but Alethea was singing along with her. People stood and clapped with the beat. Some were dancing in the aisles.

There was no mistaking the beard. Or the eyes. The rush of performing was reflected in them, and ignited the stage persona. Alethea was spell bound. There were no binoculars between them as she searched the intense eyes. They were red, even sad, if she isolated them from the rest of the face. Those eyes had watched a woman fall off the mountain. And here she was days later performing. Suddenly Bejay brought her arm down by her side. The band stopped. No one moved. She had caught them off guard. "I just wanted to see if you were alive or if you were clones spinning around on one of my discs."

She spun her head as if it were a record on a turntable. She was mocking them and they laughed at themselves.

"How many white men does it take to change a light bulb?" Bejay threw out the question. That was all that Alethea heard. The answer was swallowed up in a tumultuous response. Bejay sprang a series of white men jokes on them in rapid fire. Alethea couldn't remember blinking. By the fourth joke, she was laughing with the rest of them.

"How can you tell a white man in a crowd?"

"He's the one charging admission," called out one of the faithful who knew the line by heart.

A male heckler screamed: "How many girls does it take to...."

The audience drowned him out with catcalls. The unified force of the audience took care of the antagonistic presences. The band began the opening riff of their latest hit. Then Bejay sang all three minutes of "Space Breakup," a crowd favorite. The band had a winning formula: Do an oldie. Do a number that someone in the band wrote. Mix it up, then give them Bejay again. She'd written most of the songs. The band had molded around her voice and style. Three straight hits in ten months. In their insatiable urge to consume, audiences couldn't get enough of her. Alethea was caught in the web between performer and fans. What had been distilling all week solidified. Like the seeker who goes in search of a prey, she was fatally linked, the hunter to the hunted. The incident on the mountain formed a cluster image, like planets orbiting around a sun. During intermission Alethea went back stage to come face to face with the sun.

From a vantage point left of the stage, she saw the band hanging out in a lounge, sprawled out on cushions and couches laid out against the walls. Bejay was not with them. Their rapid chatter parodied their stage roles, as if they were maintaining an intensity equal to the performance. To her surprise she saw no drugs or alcohol. They were passing around ice water. When they offered some to the security guards, they left their posts. Alethea grabbed a tray of dirty glasses and went behind the curtains, walking like someone who had a job. Down the dark corridor, until she saw a light in a dressing room, sending out a round beacon of light into the hall. Tentatively she stepped up to the doorway. Bejay was looking in a mirror. Alethea froze, watching a still picture of the face: the facial hair, the high cheekbones. The fullness to the mouth.

Bejay sensed her presence and turned around. They faced each other, one in shadow, the other in light framed with bushy hair and the black whiskers on her chin. Bejay could discern little of the shape in the dark hallway, except that it appeared to be a woman. The watcher peered out of large transfixed eyes. One second stretched into two. The prey sensed imminent danger, instinctively knowing whose eyes were watching her, terrified of coming face to face with the hunter. The moments on the cliff emptied out in front of her as surely as if words of accusation had been spoken. The eyes belonging to the woman who had been on the cliff gripped Alethea, but now she saw a person, not a caricature of fright. She saw green eyes set on a broad face. An eyebrow split from a scar, the full bottom lip trembling in an uneasy spotlight. A wave of sensuality swept over her. The particle flew away from the attraction.

EIGHT

Bejay ran to the doorway, shaken by the unspoken accusations and watched the fleeing figure of a woman disappear down the hall. From the back, she looked like the woman who had come by the house. Was she the one who saw? Would someone keep reappearing at unexpected moments? Panic rose up in her—it was just a matter of time. Once there had been many choices. Now there was only one.

She ran back into the dressing room. They were gunning for the good humor lady. It was just a matter of time. There'd be a trial, a "who dunnit" for America who wanted to know what lesbians did when they weren't in bed. "I ain't waiting for America to cash in on me. She threw things in a bag. Time to skip on out of here—she had skipped out already—on Cade.

"Time's up, Bejay." Someone in the band called to her. She was terrified to leave the dressing room. Her throat constricted.

"Get your ass out here. They're calling for you."

Cade flew off the cliff.

Calypso was at the door. "Damn it. We can't keep them waiting anymore." She pushed Bejay out. She put one foot in front of the other. Moved down the hall. Up to the stage. Everything was a blur. The rhythmic clapping. The audience chanting, "Bejay! Bejay!"

She grabbed the mike. "Are you there?"

The audience roared back. "Yes!"

In the pause came a voice from the darkness outside the spotlight, filling Bejay with dread. In the space of a breath, the words came out of Alethea involuntarily, "Yes, I'm here."

Bejay dropped the microphone and fled from the stage. At first, the audience thought the woman was a plant, another Bejay stunt. They waited. When Bejay didn't come back on stage, the band was at a loss. They tried to calm the audience by playing a favorite from their first album. The audience would not be mollified. They began yelling, "Bejay! Bejay!" By the time anyone thought to go back stage and look for her, she was gone, leaving sequins from her shiny black outfit scattered on the floor.

Teri and Calypso ran to the parking lot to see her getting in her car. "What the hell are you doing?"

"Don't try and stop me."

"What's going on?"

Not even they would believe her story. "Say whatever you want to people. I just can't do this."

"You're crazy. We're in the middle of a show. Besides, who are we if you leave?"

"I guess you're gonna find that out. Look, I didn't want it to happen like this. I just wrote three new songs." Then she remembered the songs were in the journal that she left on the mesa. Cade flew by. Her stomach clenched.

"You flipping out or something?"

Bejay looked from one to the other. Her tongue was bunched between her lips. Teri ran towards the font of the car to block it, but Calypso saw the hysteria mounting in Bejay. She pulled Teri away from the moving car.

"Hey, I ain't just disappearing—I'm telling you to your face. I don't want to be leaving like this," she screamed. She burned rubber out of the lot. Flight was the only door, and she turned to it as if it were a small opening between two massive mountains overlooking a mesa.

Once on the highway, she realized she was not fit to drive. The boulders on the mountain appeared on the freeway. Headlights came at her like spotlights. She dreaded any circle of light. Out of self-preservation, she stayed in the slow lane and tried to navigate between the white lines. The windshield blurred. She reached out her hand to wipe away the fog only to find it was her tears blurring her vision. A car honked at her from behind. She looked down at the speedometer. She was going 35 miles per hour. On the LA freeway that was tantamount to suicide. The word stunned her—was the death urge going around? That's what had happened. Cade had fallen into the clutches of death-going-around.

"Not me you son of a bitch. I don't want to die—I do."

She turned off at the next ramp and aimed the car toward the first motel she saw. At the desk she was met by a clerk who stared up and down at her. "Do you have a room for the night?"

He brought out the registration form. It asked for her name. She couldn't remember whether the top part should read Brenda. She always signed the bottom either Borrasca or Bejay. As the clerk glared at her, she felt for her wallet. Was he getting suspicious?

"You know how it is. I even forget what my checks say." She groped for her license and thrust it in front of him. She knew if she got through the fumbling tonight, she'd have to get her act together. Borrasca and Bejay were not going on this trip.

The clerk assumed she was another drunk off the strip. People checking in late had one weird story or another to tell. He handed back her license, staring at her chin hairs. It's another weird one, all right, he muttered under his breath. To Borrasca he said, "Room 119. Around the back and to the right."

Borrasca managed to park her car in front of the correct door and bolted inside. She fell into hysterical sobbing, her efforts at control falling away. She lowered her head into the pillow. In one week her life had unraveled into a bewildering conundrum she couldn't sort out. Her windpipe tightened into a knot. She coughed, choking for air. Is this what it felt like to go crazy, through a wild sequence of tumbling events, and then there was no way to find the road back? She fought her way to the bathroom and drank greedily from the faucet. "I'm the daughter of survivors," she reminded herself. "I can do this."

She went over to the full-length mirror on the closet door and saw her swollen eyes. She stepped back, put her hands on her hips and pointed into the mirror. "What could the person who called in have seen? What was there to see?"

"Ah ha, Borrasca." It was a voice with a foreign intonation suggesting a German accent. Her voice rubbed like sand against her voice box: "You and Cade were standing on the edge of the mesa." The German was right. It had really happened.

For the first time she was able to replay the scene before the fall. We had been arguing. No, that was the day before. Cade had backed away from me. And then...this was the point beyond which Borrasca couldn't go. Her stomach knotted. Someone else also saw Cade fall. Maybe the sun obscured things. All she saw was a hazy figure in bright light. She can't identify me. The German inquisition persisted.

"She saw everything. Being on the cliff was like being in the spotlight."

It could have been the same woman who came to her dressing room. She was standing in the dark hall, and I was in a lighted dressing room. Spotlighted again.

"No more. They can throw a search beam as far as they want, and they won't find me."

Singer Disappears. The headline sent her to the opposite end of the room where she had dropped the suitcase. She rifled through it, sending clothes all over the ugly green motel rug. Inside her cosmetic bag, now wet from a leaky vial of musk oil, she found her small mending scissors. She returned to the mirror and pushed her face against the glass. "You sure you want to do this?" She wasn't sure whose voice was talking. She backed up two steps and put her thumbs into her belt.

"No one will know you anymore without your beard. And you know what they do to strangers in these parts."

The humor backfired. The banter ended. She'd dug herself into a one way tunnel to hell. She stared at the green eyes holding the scissors high above her head, a creature uttering incoherent sounds. She reached for the paper bag lying in the disheveled suitcase and drank whiskey from the bottle until the burning in her throat forced her to stop. "Now wait," she answered continuing the dialogue. "We don't want to get absolutely plowed, do we? Hell yes. We want out of this scene."

She turned back to the mirror to see whom she was having this conversation with. These dialogues had begun in her grandmother's attic 28 years ago during a lonely time in her childhood. Her father was working 12 hours a day. Her mother worked and took care of the house. By then, her sister had been born, but she was still too young to play with. A memory over a quarter of a century old had revived itself in a wave of scents and pictures. Little Brenda would whirl and spin in front of the oak-trimmed, floor to ceiling mirror in her Bubble's big attic. She'd dress up in high heels and put on Bubble's old dresses. Even as a child, Brenda had never been thin, but the dresses had been many sizes too big, with room for imaginary breasts.

Next to that mirror was a photograph of Bubble's mother that was old even when she was a child. It had been taken in Vienna many decades previous. She was wearing a black lamb's wool coat and was standing next to her own grandmother, Brenda's great, great grandmother who knew nothing of Hitler or the camps or the Gestapo, because she had died in 1928 before the horror. Her look had an air of innocence. She and Borrasca stood on opposite sides of the holocaust, a thin gauze of history separating them.

Had Cade become one of the dead? The reality of what happened floated between denial and guilt. Borrasca screamed at the mirror, "You're the only one alive, Borrasca." She pointed an accusing finger in the mirror. "You're the one alive." She screamed it again engulfed in rage. Did someone knock on the wall?

Borrasca stepped back. The people next door could call the desk and complain. They'd contact the police who'd see her red eyes and ask questions. Someday someone was going to come to the door and ask questions.

It was 4:00 A.M. She stood still until she was sure no one was stirring. The silence of a sleeping world surrounded her. Only people who worked late shifts or had bad consciences were awake now. Even though the face in the mirror appeared with red eyes, she slid back into nine year old Brenda. Borrasca rearranged her posture and altered the facial image in the mirror. "Hey, sweetheart," she snarled, Bogie on her tongue, "have we got a script for you."

The best scripts had come from Bubble's attic. In one, straight out of children's storybooks, she would fall in love with a magical hero who had returned from a quest on a lathered horse. She'd enter an enchanted place far from her lonely world. None of the heroines had been Jewish or lesbians. No tale ever explained how in one week the heroine suddenly became an outcast from the world. Who'd listen to me? And what if they did? It won't bring Cade back. Cade, how do I do this without you. Where could she go?

Pictures of far away Shangri-la's appeared in the mirror, mountains and high lonely peaks in Tibet that she had envisioned when she practiced meditation. Who could follow her there? Bejay Storm was easy to find, but who could find her if her name was...No way! I can't take one more name. Besides, it wasn't the name that mattered. She stroked the hairs on her chin. This is what gets their attention.

This time the mirror told of a young woman who had the nerve to defy convention and stop electrolysis. Who learned a positive regard for the hairs on her chin and had the courage to say natural was good. She had taken odious female hair and made it a famous trademark. It had been liberating to let it grow, to flaunt it. To say fuck you to the view of what a woman should look like. But she couldn't escape if she didn't get rid of the hair that branded her. A woman with a beard can't hide. She took up the scissors and began clipping off the chin hairs. In a sudden flash, she decided to shoot for the works. She ran her hand through her wild hair one last time, and then attacked her large fro, her emotional state growing more frenetic until she stood in a pile of dark curls. She surveyed herself in the mirror. In the pit of her stomach she felt the drastic effect of cutting away her moorings.

By now the first light of the sun was beginning to show through the curtains. The toll of the night had brought her to the point of exhaustion, but she had to get moving before they spotted her car. The woman might have left her dressing room and gone straight to the police. If she got a decent price at a car lot for her old Volvo, it could get her a long way from here. This time it will be just Brenda. Brenda had not been on the mountain, she reassured herself, and someone named Brenda did not stand out in a crowd. The surety of the name would keep her from stuttering as she had done at the front desk last night. She packed quickly and stepped into daylight. In California to go to the Far East you headed west. You went west to go east; it made as much sense as the rest of her life.

The swiftness of the arrangements was startling. There was a seat on a plane leaving late that afternoon. By noon, she had sold her car to a dealership which seemed to think the Volvo would still sell. In their lot, she emptied out the car, flinging away the accessories of her life into a dumpster, all but a condensed pack of traveling clothes. Several times she paused to look around as if someone would come out of a whirlwind and seize her.

At the airport she filled the time until take off by standing in front of a phone risking an act which could trap her. Something tugged at her, a necessity that grounded her in essential relationship.

"Hello, Mommy? It's Brenda."

"Brenda, honey, are you okay?"

"I'm fine. Mom, and how's dad?"

"He's fine. Where are you, Brenda?"

"Mom, I can't talk long. Could you listen and not interrupt for a minute?"

"So I'm listening."

"Mom. Cade is... dead."

"Your girl friend Cade? Honey, I'm so sorry. What happened?"

"I can't talk about it now. It's too painful. I need to go away for a while."

"What do you mean away?"

"I need to sort things out by myself. I don't want anyone to know where I am. I don't want anyone should know from Borrasca or Bejay, you know what I mean?"

"Brenda, what happened?"

Her voice cracked. "Please, don't ask me any questions now." She struggled to maintain her composure, to keep up a good front for her mother. "I called because I didn't want to just disappear on you and Daddy. Or Mimi. Please don't worry."

"So now you think we won't worry?"

"You'll worry. But I wanted you to hear it from me. Don't believe everything you might read or hear. Listen, I'll write. I promise. I'll try and call again, but it may not be for some time. Please understand that I have to leave."

She cried into the phone: "Say you understand."

Her mother began crying. "I understand nothing."

"Don't cry."

"Don't tell me not to cry. I liked Cade. I feel terrible. Brenda, please come home."

"I can't, Mom. Trust me. Tell Daddy and Mimi I love them. Mommy, I love you. I got to go."

"So go."

"Don't say good-bye like that." I just wanted to hear your voice."

"You'll write?"

"I'll try."

"Do you need anything?"

When no response came: "Brenda, I love you. Please let me help. Promise to call me if I can help."

"I promise. Try not to worry. I love you Mommy." She hung up, looking around her as she ran from the phone booth, her lips trembling.

She tensed at the security checkpoint when they checked for guns and concealed weapons. Held her breath when she walked through the x-ray screening. As she put on her shoes, it occurred to her that she hadn't seen a paper. Would the national news wires carry the story of the death of a woman in New Mexico? They might. Cade's research was important. They'd for sure want a story if they knew Bejay Storm had been with her. If they suspected foul play. It was just a matter of time before the connection was made. Pictures of her and Cade would be in the National Inquirer. Her absence would be presumed as guilt. So much for their love of the good humor lady. She put her hand to her chin, feeing the smoothness, and then pulled it away, paranoid that someone might see her stroking her chin. There was no room for idle fantasy now. She could not afford to go slack in her watchfulness.

NINE

IN THE NEXT SECOND
Cade could not see
strands of her hair
whipped by the force of the wind
covered her eyes as she fell
into the sensate world beyond sight
the wind rushing had a feathery quality
giving the effect of wings growing out of her body
swirling in the whim of the currents
she sensed the magnitude of the situation
the wind became clammy cold against her skin
the strands of wings and hair
covered her mouth nearly gagging her
she who now moved without benefit of feet
had no sense of direction
though of course she was going down
down was the only possibility
her body slammed into a thick branch
both broke upon contact
her rib cage was on fire
she was a rag doll struggling to breathe
she who had tried to direct her life and its currents
went limp and followed another will.

TEN

Outside the nightclub, Alethea's feet moved automatically, her mind spinning at the tumultuous turn of events. *That was dumb. It just flew out of my mouth. Who'd guess she'd leave right in the middle of a show? Now I've got her scared and running. What did I think would happen?* Alethea retrieved her car and late as it was began the long ride back home. *She never saw me before tonight—unless she was home when I went to her house. She could have recognized me. She thinks I'm following her...I am following her.*

When Alethea tried to see the event from Borrasca's perspective, a sickening feeling washed over her. *Her lover is dead. She's grief stricken and has had no time to grieve. I suspect there's something else going on to trigger such alarm. Could be guilt. Maybe something I missed in the binoculars—Borrasca must have also panicked because of the journal. It places her at the scene.*

The morning light emerged, reddening the brown and red colored bands that characterized the painted desert of Arizona. At the next pit stop she got gas and coffee. The dry wind coming off the desert whipped her hair as she pumped the gas. A short exchange with the clerk made her see how she was more absorbed with the woman of three names and the woman who flew off the world than with people in her every day reality.

Two women have challenged all my beliefs about life. I keep stepping off the world with Cade. I thought my seeing and going for help would save her. I can't even save myself. Someone once told Alethea that she suffered from flat affect. According to her cousin Yvonne, who had traveled with her missionary parents to Fiji and was filled with the aura of foreign, exotic cultures, all Americans were bland. Boring as apple pie. Yvonne never understood how other cultures were not more romantic because they had unique customs. The point is...she was home before the point was clear.

She walked in from the clear desert air into a situation that affronted her. Laurel's latest boyfriend had moved in. His shoes and socks were by the couch; his shaving cream and underwear were in the bathroom. She stayed in her room for days at a time, avoiding them both, coming out only to go to work. She kept that up until the walls started to cave in. Until the low adobe ceiling with its cracked vigas weighed on her. The fall evening temperatures slipped into the freezing range. The cold of the high desert shaped her experience. It drew her out of herself and roused her from lethargy. One morning after a light snow dusted the ground, she was inspired to get the wood pile in shape.

The plum ax felt just right in her hands. She attacked the pile of felled trees that she and several neighbors had cut during August and chopped them into manageable pieces of firewood. She stopped to catch her breath, watching her breath steam in a trail outside her, feeling the strength in her shoulders, the value of expending oneself physically. The sun was hitting the peaks of the Sangre de Cristo range with that transparent quality of light unique to Santa Fe. Laurel came out and watched Alethea as she raised the ax and lowered it, splitting the pine.

"That's the most life you've shown in a while." Laurel said. She persisted. "You haven't functioned for weeks, Alethea."

Alethea shrugged her shoulders.

"Alethea, don't blank me out. What happened in California?"

The tone prompted Alethea to look over and see the anxiety written on Laurel's face. She wasn't being sarcastic; she was genuinely concerned.

"I don't know how to explain." Alethea climbed on the woodpile. Laurel sat on the stack of cut wood facing her with the good sense to be quiet. As she wiped away the sweat from her forehead, Alethea puzzled whether it would help to talk to Laurel. If she didn't talk to someone soon, she'd sink with the weight of the unspoken words.

She related what she had seen that day on the mesa, carefully sorting out the details about the two women. Cade fell again. Alethea mentioned the journal, without referring to Bejay by name. She wanted to know what Laurel might have read about Bejay Storm's disappearance, but she held her tongue.

Laurel didn't connect Bejay with the incident on the mountain. "A woman falling off the mesa. That's horrific. "

"I'm obsessed by it," said Alethea.

Laurel's usual flippancy was gone. "It's mind-boggling, but what I don't understand is why it's turned you into a zombie."

"I'm connected to them in some way I have to understand. They say if you save someone's life you are ever after connected to them. But I didn't save her. I can't even save myself. All my life I've wanted to break out of this—this passivity. One moment these women and the experience energize me. The next moment I'm as lethargic as ever. Same problem as always--how to translate thought into action."

"What thoughts?"

"My thoughts about these women."

"Say exactly what thoughts are running through your mind."

"Take the woman left on the cliff. She's the opposite of me. She lives in an exciting world. Has a glamorous life. Am I going too fast?"

"No, that was good. This as much as I've heard you speak at once in a long time."

"I've been running these thoughts over and over in my head. My life pales in comparison to them. I watch other people live. Even with this event on the mesa. I was just a watcher, not a participant."

"Hell you weren't."

"How's that?"

"What I see is a triangle of participants. You were not a mere witness. Your seeing gives the incident another dimension of meaning. Don't you see, it's like saying you can observe an experiment and not affect the outcome. In my opinion, there are no casual bystanders. You don't know the full impact of your presence."

"The fall sent one woman flying through the air and the other running, terrified, God knows where, said Alethea. "I'm still sitting on my duff."

"So follow her."

"Wrong, Laurel. It'd be just a wild goose chase."

Laurel's eyes lit up; she'd gotten a reaction. "There's something to be said for action for its own sake, Alethea. Things can't have just a mental existence. They have to take a physical form. Find out what else there is to know about her and why this incident has such a hold on you. Even if the trail doesn't lead to her, it will lead somewhere."

Alethea stared at her. She almost sounded wise.

"Don't you see, this event could be a catalyst for you. In its way, it already is. Go after her. Were there any addresses in that journal?"

"There's an address that might belong to her family in New York."

"Maybe they know where she is."

"Right, Laurel. It's a knock, knock joke. I go to their front door—if I can find it—and knock. They say, 'Who's there?' Then what?"

"I don't know, Alethea. But if you did it, you wouldn't be the same person. I expect you'll find a negative response to counter with, Alethea, and maybe that's something to think about, too." Laurel turned and went inside, leaving Alethea on the woodpile.

She breathed out puffs of cold air until the dropping temperature forced her inside. Laurel's words hung in the air: *even if the trail doesn't lead to her, it will lead somewhere*. She could leave. If she did, with the funding cuts pending, some one else could keep their job at the school.

With a huge effort of will, Alethea began the process of setting herself in motion. Plans took shape, many of them while Alethea sat for long hours in front of a map imagining New York. Saying good-bye to people at the school was the hardest part.

At the staff farewell party, Maria Elena was confounded. "I confess I thought you'd be here as long as me."

"The truth is I can't energize my personal life through my work. I want to become more myself, but I don't know how to do it here."

"Searching outside for yourself may only frustrate you. Everything you need you already possess."

"Perhaps I have to leave to find that out. It's not the worst reason for leaving. When I told Timothy I was going, his first question was are you coming back?"

Maria Elena hugged her. "Are you coming back?"

"I can't answer that, can I?"

At home she reread the card Maria Elena had given her, and the one from Ms. Ada with a quote from T.S. Eliot: *"The end of all our journeys will be to return to the place and know it for the first time."* She'd perceived Miss Ada all wrong—what else had been a function of her misperceptions?

And then she was air born. She marveled that it was Laurel who'd given her the final push. She even drove her to the airport. Alethea landed before she knew what to say after 'knock, knock.'

A cab took her from the crowded airport to a quiet street in Mamaroneck where it stopped in front of a two storied Tudor style house with dark brown wood trim. She peered out while she searched for a tip, fumbled for her luggage. The driver all but forced her out of the cab. She stood on the sidewalk, facing a house set back on a lot, the only house on the block without a fence. Its aspect was somber in contrast to the pink adobe homes of the southwest. She stood shivering in the cold air of early evening long after the taxi had gone, watching streetlights and the house lights come on, one by one. In the enveloping gray dusk, she peered at the sky through the dense trees and rooftops. Little patches of twilight became the blue black of evening, her favorite time of day.

It was now dark enough to see people inside the well-lit house as they walked from room to room. An old man with a paunchy stomach paced between the kitchen and living room. That must be her father. He had on a long, white scarf and for a moment she thought he might be preparing to leave the house. Then she watched him put on one of the round headpieces Jewish men wear. She couldn't remember the name, but she knew it had a religious significance. The woman who must have been Borrasca's mother walked up to him in the living room. Unheard words came out of their lips and died before the glass pane windows.

It was becoming impossible to ignore the cold. Alethea tried imagining herself in the house and the ruse worked. She walked up to the door. Her mother probably called her Brenda. She would ask for Brenda. With that intent fully implanted, she pressed the doorknocker.

"Who is it?"

"My name is Alethea. I am a friend—I know your daughter."

That response opened the door immediately. The woman was so short she gave the impression of standing in a hole. That was how Alethea was to remember her years later. Over the woman's head she could see candles burning in a holder. Had she interrupted something?

"I'm sorry if I'm disturbing you." The woman did not immediately reply. Did she speak English?

"No. It's all right. It's Friday night. Shabbos." She looked quizzically at Alethea. Each thought the other was unable to understand. "Come in. Don't stand in the cold."

Alethea walked into a bright white rug, prompting her to wipe her feet on the door mat. The old man padded into the room wearing black slippers. The woman was also wearing slippers. "Sorry, should I take off my shoes?" she said even before greeting him.

"Oh, no. It's not necessary. Please, say who you are again?"

"My name is Alethea--should she offer him her hand--I know your daughter."

"You know Brenda?" He didn't pronounce the 'r' the way she expected.

"Yes. I also live in New Mexico."

"You came all that way?"

"I happened to be out here, so I came by. I hope it's all right."

"Of course." They began to press her with questions.

"Is she all right?" he asked, brows furrowed.

"When did you last see her?" the mother asked, her hands wringing a dish towel.

Before she could answer there were more questions, turning her mind in circles. She saw the table with hot steaming plates. "Are you hungry? We were just sitting down to dinner. Will you stay? When did you say you last saw her?" Before the answers came to her mouth, another voice called attention to itself.

"Hey, Mom and Dad. Slow down. Give her a chance to think."

Alethea turned and saw a woman who was a younger, clean cut version of Borrasca. The same mold to the chin, square, with a sharp indentation. The same large, bright eyes. They held her gaze but did not draw her in the way Borrasca's had. She relied on something other than sheer power of will to engage with another person.

"Hello, I'm Miriam, Brenda's sister. You can call me Mimi."

"I'm Alethea." She offered her hand this time, and with that gesture, all of them connected.

"Nu, when did you get here?" the father

"I just pulled in. I came through the garage with my luggage. Hi, Mama." She hugged and kissed her mother and then began talking excitedly. "I know where Brenda is," she declared.

"Where?" All three responded in unison. She fished in the pocket of her jeans and pulled out a folded letter.

ELEVEN

When the plane lifted off, Borrasca felt a brief, weightless ease. There was freedom in action. In anonymity. No one had questioned her about her passport. It was all in order thanks to the tour the band had made to Germany and England last summer. Why hadn't the police thought to trace her that way? She had half expected them to be at the airport.

The glee passed when Borrasca realized she herself was now flying through the air. The image cramped in her stomach. She watched Cade fly away from her, and the safety of the plane was traded for a deep sadness that washed over her.

She fought for control, keeping her face between the covers of the monthly airline magazine. She let grief envelope her in the unreality of it, the disbelief and lingering shock. She leaned back in her seat and closed her eyes as the feelings washed over her. Cade continued to fall. "I can do this," she whispered to herself. The endless flight landed abruptly on a rough section of tarmac. The other passengers hurriedly prepared to deplane. She was the last one to leave the deserted cabin, the attendants all waiting for her at the exit. She was not prepared for the jammed, noisy terminal.

People were speaking in other tongues. She became confused and momentarily forgot where she had landed. She checked her ticket, but her red blurred eyes couldn't read the information. The billboards were in... Japanese. She was in Tokyo. People looked at her strangely—she, who had spent so much time divesting herself of strangeness by cutting her hair. What a dumb idea to come here. They're wearing western clothes. It's like being at home, except nobody can understand me. An

American in Japan is not enough out of this world. "I want out of this world," she screamed.

Her cry was louder than she realized. People milled around her. An American couple came over extending their concern. They backed off when she repeated, "I want out of this world."

She ran from them, unable to be near other Americans who reminded her of herself. No memory--is that what she wanted? She felt other eyes on her as her world threatened to collapse from the inside out. Not here. Not in an airport. Here people had only half their souls present—wasn't that what she had heard? The other part of the spirit goes on ahead, preparing the way. She grabbed her bags and ran outside. It was a mistake. There were hundreds of cars and more people. A taxi cab driver ran up. "You need a ride, Miss?"

The voice speaking in English with a foreign face confused her even further. "Yes. I mean no." She floundered. He moved closer. In desperation she retreated back inside to the ticket counter.

"May I help you?" The woman's insipid voice was irritating. Were people being solicitous because she looked crazed? Could they tell she was a step away from a breakdown? Was she?

"I want a ticket to..."

The thinking machinery went blank. People waiting in line behind her pressed closer, impatient. She struggled for logic. I am in Tokyo. From here I go to... Had she flown too far? That was it. You could fly too far.

"Do you want to look at a map, Miss?" The agent pointed to a map crisscrossed with lines. "This is a schedule of our routes. From Tokyo, you can fly either to China or India."

"Tokyo is the Far East. If I keep heading west, I end up in... "Tibet," Borrasca shouted.

"We don't fly into Tibet. You can go to New Delhi and from there go to Ladakh or Kathmandu."

"Kathmandu."

"Traveling there is not advisable in winter."

"Fine. Fine. I'll take a ticket to New Delhi."

"Are you sure?"

"I just forgot where I was going for a minute. Don't you ever forget?"

The reservations person spoke in a decidedly calm voice, reflecting her training to never argue with a customer. She explained that there would be a stopover requiring a transfer to another plane. Borrasca struggled to take in all the information.

"When does the flight leave?"

"In three hours."

Borrasca broke into gibberish before the agent's amazed eyes, "That's more time than angels need to change direction." She caught herself. "You're a very patient lady," Borrasca said. She grabbed the ticket and headed for the bar.

"That woman just had no sense of humor. More time than angels need—Mimi would have appreciated that one."

She ordered a drink. It's not more time than I can handle. She was Borrasca fleeing, Bejay answering herself with droll humor, and Brenda making the reservations. That was stranger than anyone would ever understand. She swallowed most of the drink, continuing her dialogue, sometimes out loud, sometimes as a conversation running in her head. She looked in the mirror behind the bar tender who had bent over to wash glasses and asked, "Where are all the friendly voices? Joan of Arc had someone to talk to—right? They teach you about Joan of Arc in your country?" she asked him when he made the mistake of standing up from the sink. "They burned her at the stake." He bent over the sink again, trying to keep busy.

Borrasca knew she couldn't keep it together much longer. Would she have the luxury of picking the time and place to fall apart—had she already? "Oh, God, please don't let it happen in this bar."

The third drink came right after the second drink which was served on the plane. She was the first one on board. Slowly other passengers drifted in. The attendant in the gold and red outfit strapped a seat belt around her, and the plane took off into the clouds. There are those who fly out and higher before they come down, Borrasca observed. Cade had gone straight out. And then down. There had been no clouds that day. Borrasca leaned her head back against the seat.

Time became a date coursing through her. She had left New Mexico in...September. Wasn't the Spiral Shell in October? She had missed Yom Kippur. She was always disappointing her parents. Never even sent them a card this year. The other passengers on the plane were drinking, too. It looked like they were celebrating New Years. What had happened to November and December? The man in the seat across the aisle from her stood and started a countdown... 10, 9, 8...

High above her on a screen, a space ship was being launched. The passengers were watching a clock inch towards count down. Everyone seemed to be focused on that event. And then the time machine went off. The space capsule broke free of the ground and flew straight up, sending the crowd at Cape Kennedy into a frenzy matched by the excitement on the plane. People were kissing and hugging as if they were trying too hard to have a good time. No, there were still some people in their seats, alone, immersed in their own lives. Did others hold their lives together tenuously?

She stared out the window, sitting, yet moving left to right. Cade flew by. She was going down. The spacecraft hurtled through space. Borrasca sat motionless while time and place shifted, waiting for any one of the flights to end. By the time the plane touched down and rolled across the ground to a secure landing, the ebullience on the plane had diminished.

With the stewardess' help, Borrasca gathered up her belongings and deplaned with seven other departing passengers. They went through a narrow, dim passageway which crossed the air strip, leading them to a small, fragile looking prop plane. It seemed incapable of carrying people, but none of the other passengers balked, and she forced herself on board. She was tempting fate to fly away again. This time there were no drinks. No announcements in English. They had hardly settled into their seats when the plane began its descent. The plane taxied into a tiny airport surrounded by mammoth snow covered crystalline peaks. All the passengers disembarked into a vast valley of stillness. They stood motionless before the whiteness encircling them. The immensity of the mountains dwarfed the passengers, flanking them in a mystical silence like guardians of the universe. The quality of light coming off the white peaks momentarily silenced the crazed thoughts flooding her mind.

The bitter cold soon forced the passengers back inside the plane. Only two others besides her were staying. As the plane took off, the three of them watched, frail silhouettes in front of the mountains. Then the other two walked off.

Borrasca stood there alone.

The bitter cold jarred the brain and the body. She was shivering, but had the odd sensation of being in a desert. The white silica sand of the desert, she had heard, throws back your own projections to you. It was what drove people who were lost in the desert to desperation. Yet, in this valley of white Borrasca also felt the grace of silence and a kinship with the snow. She watched one peak to see if someone would fall. She did.

Borrasca must have done something on that other mountain to cause the shadow of death to reappear here. She had fled from the mesa, from the funeral. From people's questions. A scream registered off the face of the mountains and came back at her. She who ran in the face of time had to decide what to do with the body. The luggage lay on the ground next to her, everything awaiting transport. Only a thin layer of flesh stood between her and the numbing cold. Her toes had already lost feeling. She searched in her shoulder bag to find the name she had: 'Boudhanath.'

The late afternoon light turned the snow to rouge. Her shadow became visible. From behind her appeared another shadow. An old woman came through the doors of the small airport. She walked slowly past Borrasca, head down. In desperation, Borrasca, threw the name at her, with a question mark in her voice:

"Boudhanath?"

The woman and turned and stared at her. Borrasca tried enunciating the sound carefully. This time the woman nodded. She held out a single, long, bony, finger and slowly pointed up the white embankment toward the high peaks.

"Up there?" Was it one mile or a hundred? Was she going to have to go up a mountain again?

The woman turned and continued walking. Borrasca paced in a circle. The old woman turned and watched her circling the same area over and over before she disappeared around a corner, leaving Borrasca alone near the runway. Several minutes later she reappeared. The wind blew the snow between them as she came forward in measured steps. Borrasca knew the woman was going to speak to her. Perhaps the thoughts went from one brain, up the white face of the mountains and back to the other brain. The wind swirled at the snow between their feet as they faced each other. The woman spoke to Borrasca's shoes.

"I can't understand what you are saying. I don't speak your language."

The woman motioned in a universal gesture for Borrasca to follow her. They walked into a mist of blowing snow, their feet crunching on the cold surface. Borrasca ducked inside her hood, keeping one eye facing out until they stopped in front of a building which was lighted up inside. She tried to peer in the window, but the thick ice frozen on the window panes made it impossible to see more than an orange cast of light reflected.

The woman motioned for her to go inside. Borrasca opened the stiff wooden door and poked her head in the quiet entrance where no wind blew. To her surprise it was an inn. When she turned to say thank you, the woman was already walking off. Borrasca ran outside after her and as she disappeared through a passageway yelled, "Thank you, thank you." Perhaps she was accustomed to disoriented people straggling off the planes. She had been kind.

Keep your thoughts out of other people's brains, Borrasca. You're having a hard enough time figuring yourself out. When she went back inside, a man was standing behind the desk.

"You speak English?"

"Yes. May I be of help?"

"How much for a night?" That may be a moot question at this point. Where else could I go, she thought to herself.

"To tell you the truth"—she had started to speak in her affected stage manner, but it was out of place here. "Can someone like me go to the monastery?"

"People do it all the time except most people don't try to go during winter. It is a long way. It takes the better part of three days hiking to get there."

"Are you the stop on the way?" The sarcasm of L.A. persisted, but he smiled good-naturedly. To herself she wondered: do you get people like me, crazy on arrival, calm on the way back from the monastery? As he bent over the form, she saw his collar was western in style, but maybe not made in America. He raised his head, his intense eyes set on his round face and looked at her affably.

"It's a way station. If you would like to attach symbolic meaning to it, please do." He swept the air in a lighthearted gesture.

"Sorry to sound so cynical."

He didn't respond to the last comment. The pen scratched across the paper. "I will make this an accommodation for one night."

She gave him the money indicated in American denominations on the form, pleased that she was acting coherently. She could function. She could make light conversation. Go to her room. Walk through the snow. Over the mountain. Down inside herself. The clerk had the narrowest of mustaches. Men wore mustaches and beards for social appearances. Some women also had beards, and for that there's electrolysis. Women are to have hair only on their heads. Not on their underarms or legs. No hair on chins. Why had no one taken a razor to her years ago? The mustache was staring at her as the internal dialogue continued.

"Room 402." He gave her the key.

Borrasca did not leave the next day. She slept. She slept the day after that and the day after that one. The high mountains stretched towards the sky outside her room, but she lay behind curtained windows that closed off the daylight. Nothing beckoned but sleep, a state of oblivion demanding nothing but submission. The retreat from reality that Borrasca longed for could not be facilitated by drugs. Pills opened channels in her when she sang and then took days to leave her body. Liquor wore off. Marijuana aroused sensuality and heightened awareness. She wanted no desire. She wanted the fullest amnesia possible where she had no name and no story. On the fourth day, a heavy knock kept repeating at her door, slowly forcing her back to consciousness.

"Wake up, Miss. Can you hear me? Are you all right, Miss?"

Borrasca mumbled, "Go away."

The knocking persisted. She stumbled to her feet and threw on a robe hanging on the door. In the dark she felt around for her slippers. No, there were no slippers here. Slippers were in California.

She opened the door, keeping it between her and the day clerk. The sunlight radiating off the snow glared her vision, haloing the clerk, and nearly blinding Borrasca. She shielded her eyes grown accustomed to the dark curtained room.

The halo spoke: "I have come to see if you are all right. This was just an overnight accommodation, but you have been here four days now. No one has seen you come out. We were worried."

"I'll pay, please don't get upset." She felt her knees shaking. I'm good for the money," Borrasca called out to her.

"Please, Miss, we are not worried about money. You haven't left your room in days. Do you need help?" she offered.

"I need..." Borrasca's voice hung between a scream and a plea. The woman's outstretched hand enticed her to reach for help. A voice inside warned that if she caused trouble, it would draw attention to her. The pull of survival competed with the drowning voices. She couldn't ask for help. Her trembling hand couldn't close the door on the clerk. Borrasca spun around and saw the condition of the room as the clerk saw it. Clothes were strewn everywhere. The bed was in shambles. The room visually portrayed the soulless existence inhabiting it. She herself must have looked like a ghost of a person torn away from the earth. Borrasca turned back to the clerk and saw the concern in her eyes. "I'm sorry. I've been ill. I don't want to be a problem." Her voice was contrite. She knew she needed help. She reached for the outstretched hand. Being on her feet after days of lying horizontal without eating made her feel faint.

As her legs give way, she heard the clerk's reassurance: "It's all right, I have you."

In her stupor, Borrasca became aware of hot soup and tea being spooned down her mouth. She heard conversations going on around her that seemed to be coming from an underwater cave. One day the curtains were pulled back. A white wall of mountain faced her, silencing her mind into reverence. So steep were the lower slopes of the sheer incline that they seemed to rise perpendicular.

The mountains began to call to her. If the mountains were calling, it meant that the earth had not exiled her forever. She must leave as soon as her strength returned. She talked to the closest mountain, to the day clerk who visited her frequently. Everyone was extremely polite, and the kindness had a mellowing effect on her. She was still disoriented at times, but also hungry for connection.

"This is such a remote area. How is it that you speak English?"

The clerk nodded. "We have many westerners come through because of the airport and the monastery. More English people than Americans. My husband and I took classes along with the Sherpas and others, some of whom you will meet at the monastery."

"May I impose on your kindness one more time. How does one hire a Sherpa?"

"Best to wait for spring. It's a strenuous climb. Takes several days, but it maybe impossible now."

Borrasca couldn't wait for spring. For several days she walked around the Inn. She packed. When the Sherpa knocked at the door, he was polite: Yes, it is best to wait for spring. Yes, he responded, with good weather and luck they might be able to make it in winter. Each took account of the other. Borrasca pressed money into his hands. He gathered up her packs.

She followed his steady pace, sure that her lungs would burst in the thin air. He slowed down, and the two of them trudged steadily upward. The sun disappeared behind a mass of clouds which rolled swiftly across the sky. Snow fell. The Sherpa looked at her with doubts lining his grave face. She urged him on. He shook his head in disbelief.

A white curtain of snow encompassed them, hanging like twisted sheets. She felt encapsulated in a glass snow globe like the ones her neighbors had on their coffee table. The swirling snow left her without a frame of reference. With no way to differentiate up from down. The wind blew at her in sharp stings, piercing through her jacket. Her gloves stuck to her hands. Snow froze on her face. She kept touching herself to make sure feeling was still there.

She looked up and couldn't see the Sherpa anymore. For one crystallized second, she panicked. Her scream pierced through the snow, and he came rushing back to her, barely visible though he stood right in front of her. He screamed back.

"We must turn around." His nostrils were completely iced. She knew he was right. He pinpointed his opinion about her and the weather in a phrase: "It's mad to be out here."

She had no choice but to follow him back down the mountain, stumbling in the direction of gravity until they returned to the Inn. The Sherpa offered advice which she heard through her stubborn defenses.

"Not possible to get over these mountains this time of year. Maybe try going to New Delhi first."

She went back to the same room, the same bed. The blizzard entered her dreams, trapping her in a bleached world. She tried to peer over the edge of white, but there was no edge. No ledge.

Several days later she left. She wandered in a world where the connections came together even though she could not remember each separate strand. There was a train. A man in a uniform helped her with her luggage. He passed her on to a woman holding a child that cried unless she gave him her breast, but there was little milk to appease the infant. A man appeared. A trader. He avoided her eyes. Yes, they could travel together. She sat with the mother until the next station. The trader got her a seat on another train and disappeared. During the course of the long ride she saw him only once. His beard was sloppy. He was drunk.

She traveled through corridors of swirling snow, longing for the comfort of a night without perpetual storms. She fell into sleep, only to wake up screaming, the words of the dream accusing her.

"You left a woman to die. You left your lover. Didyoukillher? Didyoukillher? Didyoukillher?"

She sat up gasping for air and threw a pillow at the taunting words, but the swift moving demons ducked.

"Who leaves a human to die? Didyoupushher? Didyoupushher? Didyou?"

In the camps her parents said a Jew would never willingly leave another person to die. Who would leave any human to die?

"I did," she screamed. "I did."

TWELVE

Running along the sides of the mesa are numerous caves, each carved out of the soft tuff rock by erosion. The texture of the tuff resembles dusty pumice more than granite rock.

For a millennia, the earliest people lived in these cave dwellings. They wore away the trails, creating the hand and toe paths as they carried water and corn from the valley below to the caves above where the people lived. They prayed in their kivas. Centuries later, after a long cycle of drought parched the land, the people left.

To the tourists, the site offers an interesting glimpse into a distant way of life. For the people of the nearby pueblo, it is much more. It plays an intrinsic role in their spiritual lives, a timeless connection that guides their lives.

Today countless tourists follow the ancients' footsteps, climbing past the caves to the mesa above. Sometimes a trail is worn away several feet deep, sometimes as much as five feet, the height of a grown person, until the trail becomes a narrow opening between tall boulders. To walk the trail, a person must often go sideways through the opening, surrounded on each side by the high walls. They come out on to flat ledges that are cracked, worn away by the change in temperature, by footprints.

Over time, some of the trails are worn down and disappear. The crack in the ledges spread. The mesa erodes and falls away.

THIRTEEN

Dear Folks and Mimi,

Hello. I'm writing because I don't want you to worry. Please understand that I'm sending the letter care of Mimi cause I don't want anyone to know where I am and cause Mimi, you have a post office box. Privacy is important for me right now. Of course the letter is for all three of you. I'm counting on you to honor my request and keep this on the q-t. Does it feel I've gone to the ends of the earth and deserted you? I'm afraid you'll be worried sick. Let's just call this a necessary trip. I'm far away, but I hold you in my thoughts and want to reassure you.

I've been in the Himalayas, you could say I'm on retreat. Soon I'll be heading for New Delhi. You can send letters to the consulate in New Delhi addressed to me as Brenda Firestone, yes, my original name, and with the return address from Mimi's PO box. There's no phone, no way for us to talk.

Mimi, I need a solid, middle of the road perspective. We've always argued because I was so extreme and you so square. Right now that appeals to me. Can you write me a letter of middle vision, good hobbit that you are so I'll know mom and dad and you aren't freaking out?

Please, it's important that no one else know where I am. I don't want the folks or you to have to lie if people come asking where I am. I don't want anyone to know. Not the band, not anyone. You'll be the only connection, kid. I need to be lost right now and how can I be lost if my fans can find me. Then I'll probably need to be found.

Wish I could say more, but I don't know more. You have no idea how much I want to see the three of you and hug you. Hug yourselves for me. I love you Mommy and Daddy. Please, don't worry. I'm definitely safer here.

I love you all, Brenda

Mimi looked up from the letter. The family stood with Alethea in the privacy of their kitchen. No one spoke. The father had a vacant stare. The mother was off in her own thoughts, her eyes strained open to prevent tears from running. Alethea felt an unnamed presence course through the room. Borrasca had been evasive in the letter, and removed emotionally. She didn't share much of her self. There was no hint that she was running from more than just fans and publicity. Did they know about Cade? In the prolonged silence of the intimate family moment, Alethea's awkwardness increased.

"New Delhi. Half way around the world. I know something's wrong that she's not telling us." This from her mother.

"If I weren't in school, and she hadn't entrusted me, I'd be tempted to try and find her."

"Well, well," said the father, shaking his head.

"We have to take her at her word that she's all right," said Mimi

They stood for what felt like endless minutes. 'Friend' had been Alethea's only token of admittance into this tight family circle. She didn't know what words to offer.

"We could continue talking about this while we're eating. Dinner's getting cold," Borrasca's mother said. She turned to Alethea. "You'll stay for dinner, yes?"

"Oh no, I couldn't."

They looked at her puzzled. The mother jumped in with the obvious. "I'm Rose. This is Louis. And this is our daughter Miriam. We should have done that right away. It's a strange time to arrive, in the middle of a family matter. With this news of Brenda coming and you here, we should keep...."

"Together. Don't be shy," the father said. "Having you here is like..."

"...Like a part of Brenda is here," added Mimi. They finished each other's sentences.

"I'm sorry. Of course I'll stay."

She joined the movement towards the dining room, drawn along by the current and the odors. Rose brought another chair to the table. Mimi watched Rose count them and then look up at her. In an unconscious moment of wishful thinking she had bought a chair to the table for Brenda. Without a word, Mimi stood to take the fifth chair away and then thought the better of it.

Alethea tried to imagine Borrasca or Bejay in this house. Someone named Brenda could have pulled up a chair. She studied Rose as she brought plates to the table, seeing some of Borrasca in her. The women of the family all shared the same indented chin, the large and intense green eyes. Borrasca's hair was from her father. He had lost some of it and was balding in the center, but the hair showing through his round cap was thick and frizzy along his ears and sideburns.

Dinner turned out to be roast chicken swimming in gravy with vegetables. Alethea was conquered. After months of listlessness, she found her appetite whetted and fed by the very family whose daughter had whetted her appetite for life. They ate quickly with little talk until the first surges of hunger were abated. Then came the inevitable questions.

"Did you know where she was?"

"No, I didn't."

"Brenda didn't write you?"

"No, I haven't seen her for weeks," said Alethea watching truth string around the words.

"There must be something we can do besides worry. I don't like the idea of her wandering through strange countries all alone," the mother reflected. She stared out into space, following the line of thought that trailed those words. Alethea looked around the table. The father was also off in his own world. The silent presence hung in the air again, nearly taking a palpable shape. She looked across the table at Mimi whose mouth creased into a smile. Did she feel it, too?

"I know she's a grown woman," the father finally broke the silence. "She can take care of herself, but it would be different if we knew she was all right."

Mimi agreed. "I know she's wanting to have someone around if she wrote me." There was a good-natured sarcasm in her tone.

"I don't understand what's driving her away from us. I thought it was my generation that had all the tsurus—pain," the mother explained to Alethea. She looked at her husband. "I want that her life should be better than ours."

Hearing the troubled tenor of Rose's voice, Alethea saw again that this woman was nothing like her expectations. She had been seeing Rose and Louis as stock characters derived from Jewish stereotypes in her mind, but they didn't fit that conception. Nor did they resemble her own parents who seemed never to have anything caring to say. Rose, like her daughter, commanded Alethea's attention.

"Do you understand what's happening, Alethea?" Rose wanted a response that would shed light on the confusion. Alethea saw the worry lines around her eyes.

"There are no simple people with simple explanations. Surely you know some of the things that have been happening in her life?" Alethea was hoping they'd fill her in so she'd have clues on how to proceed.

"We know about Cade, is that what you mean? Such a tragic thing."

"A very nice girl. Brenda brought her to meet us once," said the father, making a clicking noise. "To die so young." There were questions hanging in the air and threads of conversation happening simultaneously. New questions were asked before Alethea could think of how to answer the previous ones. Sometimes, after the long lapses into silence, they all talked at once.

"I know Brenda's heart is broken and she's needing time to grieve," said Rose, "but why would that drive her to the other end of the earth? Why didn't she come to see her own mother?"

The father turned to Alethea. "It's all so hard for us to understand. You think heartbreak was enough to send her to the other end of the world? Just leave the country without seeing us?"

"I think losing someone to death could do that." Mimi's hand covered his.

Her mother's face turned deep red. "I get one phone call. One call." Her palm slapped the table in frustration.

"Oh, Mom," said Miriam, reaching her other hand across the table and taking hold of her mother's closed fist. "I'm sure she's trying to spare you in her usual, unpredictable way." She looked at Alethea. "Can you tell we run this dialogue over and over like an old record?"

Alethea blurted out a thought, unaware of its implications. "Something has to be happening deep in your soul for you to go far away from everyone you love." The family looked at her. She had offered something without being urged.

The mother regained her composure. "India. Nu." Who in our family ever thought about such a place? First she calls. Now a letter saying she'll write soon. She maybe doesn't need money. We know she sold her car—the insurance company sent us a form because we had originally signed on the loan. Otherwise, her life's a big mystery to us."

"Maybe it's a mystery to her as well as us," Alethea offered.

"You're a friend and don't know," said Louis."

"Not a close friend, you understand."

He went on. "Maybe it was that band, too much being on the road. Living such a... fast life. We don't know much about that side of her," he admitted.

"Brenda tried to protect us from the band scene," Mimi explained to Alethea. "She never talked publicly about us in interviews. That's why she used the name Bejay Storm."

Another uneasy silence followed.

"When she left home years ago, she looked so different," said Rose. "If any of the relatives ever saw Bejay Storm, they'd never guess it's our daughter."

"We've only lived in this house since my father retired," said Mimi, "so not even the neighbors know much about her or us. We're a tight knit family, but there was always this private side to Brenda. She shared Cade with us as much as she shared any part of herself."

"There are things maybe she couldn't say to us because we're her parents. It could be hard for her to talk to us about Cade's death. I understand that," said Rose.

The other three nodded.

"You think she'd talk to you?" the father asked. "Say your name again."

"Alethea."

"That's nice. Does it mean anything?"

Alethea blushed. "It means one who searches for truth."

"Well, Miss Alethea, I have a straight forward proposition for you. You see, I like you. Right away. And I think you as a friend could do what I as her father cannot. You go to India."

They all laughed simultaneously, so outrageous was the idea.

"So laugh at me. You maybe should listen before you keep laughing." He continued. "It's not so funny. Just say we got you the ticket and you went to New Delhi. Being with her could be a blessing. Maybe she'd want a companion, someone to talk to. Maybe not, but it would reassure us if you were to see her. You could tell us first hand that she's all right. It would mean everything to me. I'm not rich, but we're comfortable. What's money for a ticket compared to your own flesh and blood?"

Alethea tried to speak but he continued.

"I want to be able to do something. I'm not saying you should persuade her to come back. Just for her to know we're thinking of her. It's not parents she needs, but a woman her own age, or someone gay, not an old man like me."

Gay—of course they knew Borrasca was a lesbian. Did they think she was also a lesbian?

"I can't take money from you. Besides, she doesn't want anyone to know where she is."

"Alethea, hear me out. We don't know each other, right?" Rose began to talk in earnest, as if her husband's words were, indeed, not a laughing matter anymore. "My intuition is that something serious is happening. You can't tell from that letter, but that's Brenda. She's not the type to let on. She's too guarded. She gets it from us. Everything with her has always been a secret. Always trying to protect either herself or us. Louis is right. We can't go. I respect her wishes. The band and anyone else, they don't need to know. But someone should go."

Mimi jumped in. "To leave this family so abruptly, with our history. Leave her home and friends in Santa Fe. Leave the band with such a successful album. If I were you, I'd jump on it. What have you got to lose? I think you can help."

Rose took another tack, "It seems to me something more is going on than just Cade dying, and I want to know what. Think of it this way. Instead of me sending her a letter, I'm sending you. You'll be the family emissary. Unless you've got something else you have to do."

Alethea could not believe the turn of events unfolding. They were pleading with her to go to India. She would have walked over coals to see Borrasca, though they could not guess how monumental it must have seemed to her. They waited for answer. How could she say no? How could she say yes?

"Say yes."

"What if I miss her? India's a big place. I travel all the way there and she's already left. What if I find her and she refuses to see me or talk to me?"

"There's a lot of if's. Your plane could crash."

"Louis, don't say such a thing."

"Now you wait a minute. Death is the most constant companion we have in life. Without knowing you, Alethea, do you want to know what my guess is about you?" He went on before she had finished nodding. "You're timid. Not a coward," he emphasized, "but hesitant to do things. You know how I know. You apologize for yourself a lot. Well, you won't have to apologize if this doesn't work out. Don't worry if you can't find her. I'll worry so you don't have to."

She tried to speak, but Louis kept talking. "You won't owe us anything, not even an explanation. I only ask that you try and find her and make sure she's all right. See if she's—mentally okay. If she's needing landsmen—family. If there's an emergency, let us know."

The words flew by faster than she could reply.

Rose nodded. "And it's all right if you enjoy yourself, too. It would mean a lot to us. You think my husband's lost his senses? If you had led our lives, it wouldn't be such a gamble."

"You could go, Mrs. Firestone."

"What happened to Rose? You want we should get formal?"

"Rose, why don't you go?"

"I couldn't. That would be ignoring her wishes. There's some reason she can't be with me, her mother, right now. But for you it's different. Like Miriam says, it's like you would be going instead of her. You would be that solid contact she needs without the emotional baggage that mothers and daughters have. In respect of Brenda's privacy, I don't want you to interfere with her. I just want a weather report: fair, good. Turbulent. And I want it first hand from you."

The weather analogy made Alethea smile. She saw where Borrasca got her humor.

"You're the perfect one to go, Alethea. Here you are on our doorstep when her letter arrives, and the idea comes to me real strong. You know, men get intuitions, too."

"Do you have plans this will keep you from?" "Are you able to be away from Santa Fe for a while?" As long as she was quiet, they filled in the space with words.

"I'm tongue tied is all. There's nothing holding me back." She disliked her subterfuge about her relationship to Borrasca in the face of their acceptance of her. "I can't imagine going to India. It's such a fantastical leap for me. Can I think about it overnight?"

All three of them chimed in, "Of course." And repeated it several times: "Of course."

"You can stay here tonight in Brenda's room." "Oh, no, It would be an imposition on you."

They could not understand how their invitation left her confused about what to do. "You're apologizing again," Louis said good naturedly. "Say yes, you'll stay."

"Yes. I'll stay."

It took them another half hour to show her Brenda's room. The bathroom. The towels. Finally she was by herself in the bedroom. Not alone, for Borrasca's presence was everywhere.

Alethea stood in the middle of the room not moving, but going somewhere. Laurel was right. She could not have known what forces would be unleashed once she got outside her head and activated herself. It was more than she could have imagined. The two women on the mountain would come along, persisting in her mind's eye as they had been for weeks now. New Mexico. New York, and if she could believe it, India. If it was right to go.

As she got ready for bed, she saw a picture on top of the bureau. Rose, Miriam and Brenda were standing in the garden, arms locked around each other, smiling out at—it must have been Louis who had taken the picture. The three women shared a similarity of expression that the indented chins gave to their smiles. The eyes, the cheekbones, the way they held themselves. Borrasca's shape was a young version of her mother's.

On an impulse, she went over to Brenda's closet and sifted through the clothes. Alethea was much heavier than Borrasca, but Borrasca must have had larger breasts and a bigger butt. She held up a pair of pants and looked in the mirror hoping to see a different aspect of herself. The same old Alethea looked back.

The change in time zones left her exhausted, but she was too wired to sleep. Curiosity drove her to inspect every nook of the room, especially the bookshelves that lined two walls. The titles beguiled her mind, revealing a realm of experience that was foreign to her. There were books by lesbians which said the word right on the front cover. There was poetry, and a bent for the spiritual. There was nothing about music, nothing related to her stage persona. It was Brenda's room. And Borrasca's. Alethea wanted to read them all, but she satisfied herself with a few titles and dug in, knowing she wouldn't be able to sleep right away. Did people read their way into consciousness? They did if they were Alethea Tomlinson and experience was calling. A web of gossamer strands had been woven, enmeshing their lives.

What would Borrasca think, thousands of miles away, if she knew the one who'd seen her on the ledge was reading her books? Befriending her family. Sleeping in her bed.

FOURTEEN

Cade was going out of time.
She had been doing that for several years
and now history was falling along side her.
She would die
and it might not be like she had imagined
or how anyone else had said it would be
She was afraid of the pain
when the earth and her body collided.
Does the body crumble slowly from the explosion,
or is it a quick flash?
Cade found herself repeating a mantra:
Om Mani Padme Hum
she needed compassion for herself
all the while wondering if she'd lose consciousness
but there was no black out
no rainbows or mystical light.
I don't want to be alone—I'm scared—
gone from what I love here.
Cade—at the moment of truth
do you still think life is a spiral?
Do you believe from this ending
there will be a new beginning?
What becomes of belief in the final seconds
Is that when death comes
sneaks in like a trickster and takes over the body
I want to be more than nothingness

I want light color sound
Ah, God. Who is flying with me?
The boys want to be the altar boys who light the candles and
participate in the mystery
while the little girls get bored in the pews
We give our stuff away to the boys.
I gave my stuff away to you, Borrasca.
It happens with magnets—charismatic people. Heroes.
We give them our power
and they, being our projections,
send no energy back to us.
Borrasca is gone
It's just me.
Dear Cade, what of yourself is flying with you?
Other women split up and don't talk to each other.
Are we killing each other, killing love?
We don't have to do it this way
you left alone, grounded
while I'm flying alone
through space...
free falling...
...the immensity of it...

FIFTEEN

The next day, Alethea remained secluded from the family, her presence accepted like the family cat which prowled the house, but otherwise stayed independent. The fact that she liked Rose gave her the courage to be straightforward and take the time alone to sort out her mind. She stayed in her room except to take long walks around the neighborhood noticing the manicured lawns that contrasted sharply to the natural look of Santa Fe. To find the best course of action that would give rise to an active agent within her. By the end of the day, she looked forward to being with them at dinnertime, but it was strangely silent at the dinner table. Mimi was not there. The parents were taciturn, speaking just enough to be polite, quite unlike the evening before. She was wanting to talk to Rose, but Rose was in her own world, unreachable, hardly recognizable as the same woman of the previous day who had punned about the weather. Louis, too, was formally polite, but became more and more withdrawn during the meal. They sat at the table isolated in their three bodies.

Alethea was relieved when dinner was over. She went outside to escape the constraints of the house and walked headlong into the bright globe of the moon. It riveted her. Was it the only constant? No, it too had been changing, growing. In the light of the moon the garden exuded an air of serenity. Was Rose peaceful here? Alethea sat, absorbed by the moonbeams until the cool air brought her inside.

This family had a kindred quality she would have wished for in her own family, which was a blemish on her ideal notion of a family. She had yearned for a loving clan even when she lived with them. Her parents smoked constantly, and she hated smoke. Her father drank. She hated his foul breath and swearing, his outbursts of anger when he was on a binge looking for someone to slap around. He wasn't the only intemperate one. Everyone yelled at everyone else. There was always a high volume of noise. An incessant television blared and there were no books except for the TV Guide.

Alethea had one sister and one brother. He was seven years older and wanted nothing to do with a baby sister. When she was entering first grade, he was competing: marbles, stickball, attention. He could not let a relationship develop that was not part of his competitive style. By the time she was twelve and discovering the blood cycle in herself, he was off to college. Except for vacations and obligatory family affairs, their paths never crossed, not even in each other's minds. Her most dominant impression of him was his thinness, always an oblique family reference held before her.

Her sister, who was eleven years older, was trapped in an early marriage, though she defended marriage even after a painful divorce and remarriage. Like her brother, she was competitive, trying to make sure she got more of her parents' attention. Alethea's response was to withdraw, clenching inside when they screamed, passing the years at home as a burden to be endured. Even as she withdrew inside herself, into a quiet world, she felt the loss of the companionship that comes from a having a close sibling. She missed the private language that springs up between them, saying what they want with a look.

At school she was never intentionally excluded; she just never learned how to access the inner circle, and remained on the outer fringes. In gym class, she heard other girls whisper intoxicating words: breasts, hair. Dating. Sex. The self-consciousness she felt about her large body added to her isolation. She'd towel herself dry in a corner.

Her family teased her about her weight, forever comparing her to the other siblings. It did not help her self-image. She retained the imprint of those early memories, remaining guarded, adopting the stance of a loner. One indelible memory that always stayed with her was that both her parents had accompanied her on her first day of school.

Her mother dressed her up in a green and blue plaid dress. Her father had on his church clothes. What she understood that day, even at that young age, was how important it was for her parents to uphold their concept of themselves as a happy family. When they arrived at the small schoolhouse, the three of them appeared as a smiling unit. The other girls from that small Kansas town were also with their parents. They grouped together for a first day picture, everyone smiling at the camera. It was a conspiracy she recognized early: to maintain at all costs their image as a loving family.

Sitting up in Borrasca's bed, Alethea looked to extract the meaning from that painful time. Dormant things could co-exist with one another in a non-relationship. That description seemed to hold for her family. It also described some of her attempts to relate to anyone meaningfully. Alethea leaned back on the bed and followed a trail of thoughts that led out of the house in New York to a never distant past which needed only a nudge to be summoned. College was how she escaped Kansas. She left home to meet people like herself and found the only human who had significantly pierced her protected armor. Eddie tripped into her life by accident. He had fallen on the carpet leading into the Student Union one morning, red faced and embarrassed. That awkward entry eliminated any intimidation she might otherwise have felt.

"You want a coke or something?" She tried to ease his discomfort as she handed him his books which had scattered. He sat across from her, and they found out they were both enrolled in the same lecture class in microbiology. In the course of an hour, they became genuinely interested in each other. No one had shared such a private space with her, nor met her on the relaxed ground of conversation. They ended up cutting their next class and roaming the wide stretches of campus near the Ag Department. She liked that he could talk for hours. He liked her ideas. When it grew dark, they wandered back and found more reasons to keep hanging out together.

Finally in her life, it seemed the small talk would end. They talked about feelings. She was on new ground here. Years later, she treasured the remembrance of what it was like to open to another human being for the first time. "You're not close with your family?" Eddie asked. He took the time to listen to her describe the queerness of her relationship with her family. In the middle of the conversation, he would open and close his mouth without speaking. He would nervously play with his lips until the thought he searched for found words. She watched his mouth. "At least when your father ranted and raved, he was showing emotion."

"Emotions weren't allowed in my house, Alethea. No one ever got angry or lost their temper. Their feelings sat inside them for days. Their whole lives."

"My father wasn't being emotionally responsive. He was abusive. He dumped all his feelings on us, tenderness not among them. It was never how we are to each other now."

She began watching his mouth more. He noticed. There were long walks. Movies on the weekend. One night they cooked dinner together. Afterwards, they walked around his small apartment cleaning up from dinner and bumping into one another. Reaching to touch the hand that walked by. Standing back to back by the sink. Alethea could never remember how they got from the kitchen to the bedroom. They had fallen on the sofa with their clothes on until he unbuttoned her blouse. When he touched her nipples, the intensity of the feeling rivaled the act itself. As they lay entwined, she felt him pushing against her, rising in a fever pitch which rose and crested and she swam with the waves. He waited before entering her, and they called out to each other.

Every weekend that semester they saw each other. In June over summer break, he came to see her at her home and told her he was transferring to another college 500 miles away. They promised to write. They never did. Where are you now, Eddie? Do you have a family? Do you talk to your daughter?

Alethea pulled the quilt up to her neck against the weight of memories rushing by. Love was an electrical magnetic charge that drew you into someone's field. But if the energy was not exactly right, you could stand on a mountain and scream for someone to love you and no one would come. She had screamed to the sky. Why hadn't someone come?—She sat up. Someone had come. Two women. She had stood on a mountain and they had come. A line of Cade's from the journal came to her: *Each woman is connected to others through a bond which crosses time and birth.* Goose bumps sprang up along the back of her neck. A connection existed between them, a magnetism that had already carried Alethea a thousand miles across country. Two women had drawn her into their wake.

She cast her eyes about the room. They came to rest in a corner where there was a shelf with rocks and shells. It was an altar. Fabric and stones had been laid out to ring a protected space, resembling the circle of stones she had found that day on the mesa. The fabric was a deep purple velvet. Many of the stones were clear crystals. One in particular was large and central to the arrangement. Alethea sat in front of the altar, wondering what kind of rituals Borrasca did. If Borrasca did magic. No, she didn't do magic. She was out of magic if the woman had fallen through the sky.

A soft knock came at the door, stirring Alethea from her ruminations. "Alethea, it's Mimi. May I come in, if it's not too late?"

Alethea jumped up and looked around furtively to see if she had defiled the altar. If there was evidence she had been prying.

"Come in, Mimi."

"I saw your light was on." She closed the door behind her. "I tried not pressing you for space all day, but I have this insatiable need to talk to you about Brenda and my family."

"Please sit down."

"How are you doing?" Mimi whispered.

"Still weighing my decision. I'm...confused, maybe even scared if you want to know the truth."

"I found something you might be interested in. I haven't shown my folks, so don't say anything to them."

"Oh no, I wouldn't."

Mimi pulled out a newspaper and opened it to the front page. The banner read *Gathering Moss*. "Do you know what this is? "

"Sure. An alternative magazine. Punk music. Stuff like that."

Mimi turned the page and there was a close up picture of Bejay. The photograph highlighted her wild eyes. Her bearded chin. Her audaciousness. The headline read: ***BEJAY, BEJAY, WHERE DID YOU GO?***

Alethea took the paper from Mimi and scanned the story. The article raised questions about why she left the band in the middle of a performance. It was written from a perspective that may have been real to most of the audience, recounting how she had walked off stage. But it was not all that had happened. No reference to the exchange between her and Bejay. There were interviews with members of the band who were dumbfounded at what had happened and miffed not to have heard from her. Central to the story was speculation about her offbeat lesbian life style. There was no hint that Bejay was also known as Borrasca, no mention of Cade or the incident on the mountain. That she might be in mourning. Was Alethea the only one who knew the connection between point B and point C? Alethea stayed lost in thought so long that Mimi took it as a clue for her to leave. She turned to go, but Alethea grabbed her arm. "Mimi, don't go." She gestured for Mimi to sit. "Please, let's talk more." Mimi sat on the rug and leaned against the bookshelf.

Alethea ventured to ask what she could not say in front of Rose and Louis. "Are you comfortable knowing your sister is a lesbian?"

"When she first came out to me, I had the usual straight reaction. I couldn't put it in perspective with our family. I thought she was going over the edge. It's been years since then, and I've become a feminist myself. These last few years I hardly saw her, what with the band and all, but now I understand how two women might fall in love. Mostly I understand how Brenda fell in love with Cade."

"So you knew Cade."

"I met her in New Mexico and I really liked her." Mimi smiled at the memory. "We spent several days together. Went hiking. She's actually much easier to talk to than Brenda. She's... she was a very warm, genuine person. No smart ass lines. Down to earth." Her eyes watered.

"I really cared for her. We all did. My parents liked her as soon as they met her. You couldn't help but like Cade. They forgave her for not being Jewish, and began to accept Brenda for being queer. Actually they never had much trouble accepting it. Too much loyalty in their blood. I can't believe she's dead either," Mimi's voice cracked. "I think it flipped Brenda out when she died, don't you?"

Alethea shook her head. "I guess. I can't imagine what losing Cade might mean to her. "It's strange to hear you call her Brenda."

"She doesn't like me to, but the name Borrasca doesn't come spontaneously. Neither does Bejay. They're not Jewish, you know what I mean? You haven't been around Jews much have you? See, I think you're missing something in this picture, something I need to explain for you to fully appreciate the situation. You see a wild, infamous lesbian. I see something else. She—we, are the daughters of two survivors."

"What does that mean?"

Mimi knew there was no quick way to fully explain their history to Alethea. "Any Jew living in Europe who did not die at the time of Hitler is considered a survivor, whether they were in a concentration camp, which my parents were, or in hiding, or escaped. That makes Brenda and I the daughters of survivors. It absolutely defines us in an ultimate way. My folks survived being in a concentration camp for nearly seven months. That experience has never left them. That past is still very much alive in the present. It's also part of us, and it makes for a unique parent-child relationship. Let's just say that while every family is unique in their own way, Brenda and I react to much of life in ways that reflect being their children. There's a special bond between the four of us."

"Of course, I became the 'goody two shoes,' and Brenda became the disruptive kid who acted out, and then the alienated rebel. But she never cut the cord. She's never just split from us like this. Neither my parents nor I can quite fathom why Brenda would run off and choose to be alone now rather than with us. They feel abandoned. Her letter says to me that she's at the end of some tether but struggling to maintain contact with us. We might be her only connection to the rest of the world right now. If you go to the opposite ends of the earth from every one you know, something on a very grand scale must be happening."

Alethea spoke in almost a whisper. "Your parents must have been very young when they were in that camp. Tell me what you can. I want to be more sensitive and not say the wrong thing."

"History talks about the cremation ovens and the parts of the Holocaust that can be captured on the news and television. What people don't fully comprehend is the enormity of surviving daily life in those camps. They were subject to a degree of degradation hard for my mind to fathom. They were denied basic human needs. Suffered from dysentery and physical abuse. Cruelty. They witnessed death and more death constantly. All around them. My parents were lucky if I can even use that word. Neither of them got violently ill at the wrong time, say during a midnight count when they'd suddenly be dragged from bed and forced to stand in freezing rain. I'm sure it was their youth that kept them alive. And do you want to know why else they made it besides luck? They made it because of people who became like family to them. My mother was taken to the camp with neighbors, including several of her classmates. They were already close friends, and in the camp it became like a blood connection. My parents didn't know each other before they were sent to Auschwitz. When my father met my mother and experienced the caring that these women had for each other, he saw how it helped all of them to stay alive."

"What matters is the loyalty that bonds survivors and their children. So of course my parents wonder why Brenda is off alone at such a time. Why, they wonder, has she gone off to be with strangers in a foreign culture? She's reacting in a way that is unfathomable to their basic instincts. I know for me being a Jew with this history is in my genes, part of my most basic reactions to life. Even before my parents explained what happened to them, it was part of our family dynamic. My parents didn't give up; I want to believe she'll be a survivor, too."

"Mimi, I don't know how to describe this, but there was a strange sense of silence when I was with them at dinner. Like all three of us were at the table, but I might just as well have been alone, like we each had dinner alone."

"Oh, I understand. I've never known how to describe that feeling that permeates the house, but it's very real. They were quite personable with you that first day. But they're not always able to be that that way. They often go about the house caught in their own thoughts. For me, I think it's that survivors live in durational time; you know, the past inhabits the present."

"So you're saying that they're remembering it?"

"Maybe still re-experiencing it. My mother especially. She says it never goes away. Dad says he's left it behind, and maybe in his way he has. But it's not really gone for him. It's hard to conceive what it was like to be a Jew in the camps, even for me. And after the war, when they came to this country, there was so much prejudice. It was the McCarthy era. The Rosenbergs were executed. Paranoia was rampant. Jews like my parents kept a low profile. The camps weren't talked about, even among other Jews. When friends of theirs would come to the house with numbers branded on them, no one talked about it."

"This is all so new to me."

"Umm." Mimi had heard this before. "I thought that Brenda and I as their children would react in similar ways to life, but we never did."

"Borras—Brenda, seems more like a New Yorker to me than you do. I know that's a stereotype."

"That's how she appears, but I know what a warm person she can be. When we were little, she was the one who was more demonstrative and affectionate. Ready to hug anyone. That's who Cade fell in love with. With Cade a different side of her came out. From the outside we don't see the dynamic that makes a relationship work."

"And then there's the Bejay side of her."

"I think the Bejay persona grew out of her rebellious teenager phase. When she realized she had a talent for singing, the name became the image she allowed the public to see. Bejay is her cover. It also protected my folks from public scrutiny."

"And you? Who is Mimi?"

"I'm initially friendlier, easier to know on some levels, but intimacy doesn't come easy to me. Socially I'm easier to relate to, but I can be guarded, and reticent about affection sometimes. I know that. I've spent a lot of time trying to understand myself emotionally and to integrate all this, but it's not easy. Maybe it's never finished. I don't know how much of our history Brenda's let herself fully come to terms with."

"This is why I wanted to talk to you tonight, Alethea. I'm convinced that what happened with Cade is triggering some of this for her. What else would make her retreat from her known world and go so far away from us? She can't run from it any more than my parents or I can. My folks don't talk about it, but I believe it's all coming back to them now with Brenda's disappearance, and they feel helpless to do anything about it. The past doesn't go away."

She touched Alethea's arm. "Do you see now why it's so important to them that you go to be with her? It's why I'm encouraging you to go. I don't think it breeches trust with Brenda. You'll be like an extension of me. Please consider it, if only for my parents' sake."

"Sometimes I feel as if I have no choice," Alethea said.

"If you go, will you email me, aside from whatever you write my parents? Tell me honestly what you think is happening. I'm afraid you'll gloss things over for them."

"You think I'll be gone long enough to write?"

"I guess we don't know, but I think that writing will ground you." Mimi wrinkled her eyes in thought and went to the bookshelf. "Have you've read Cade's book?"

When Mimi handed it to her, she was puzzled. It was written by a woman called Stella Maris and entitled *An Unsingular Universe*. Mimi saw her confusion. "You didn't know Cade's real name?"

"I think you and I are the only ones using our given names anymore."

"Well, my name is actually Miriam." Mimi laughed, the upward creases of her face throwing off the earnestness they had been immersed in. She placed the book in Alethea's hands. "Promise me you'll read this."

"It's that good?"

"It's that important."

Mimi went to the door and then looked back at Alethea." I've bombarded you with enough information for one night. We'll talk more before you go."

"If I go," Alethea reminded her. "Good night."

She held the book against her chest. This must be the Cade book that had been mentioned in the journal. She was too overwhelmed to begin reading it now. She'd bring it along to read on the long flight— was she going then? Mimi's brief description of the camps knotted up inside her. World War II had been a remote history to her. She knew about D-Day and Hiroshima, but she had little recollection of Jews in concentration camps. It was not mentioned by her family, and hardly by her teachers. The horror of six million people's annihilation was glossed over. It was not until college that she became aware of what had happened to Jews or to the Japanese held in internment camps. These oversights were compounded by the dulling effect of her family life. How expansive was her numbness, and what else in life had gone passed her unrealized?

Although she was still living in her head, she saw a subtle change. Process was going on, not repetition of thoughts like a rat in a cage. The search for Borrasca was leading her to essential questions about her own life and her place in a whole generation.

Alethea wrapped a robe around herself and went out into the garden. How far the moon had moved across the sky, the same moon that was shining on the Sangre de Cristo range in Santa Fe.

"I don't want to startle you."

Alethea turned towards the voice. Rose. Her profile was so like Borrasca's.

"Hello, Rose."

"I'm surprised you're not sleeping, Alethea."

"Must be the moon is keeping us from sleep."

"Maybe, but I don't think that's it," offered Rose who slid down the bench and patted the empty space beside her, motioning for Alethea to sit. They watched the top of the moon appear behind a cloud. Across from the bench several rows of bonsai trees stood out in the moonlight.

"You think it's crazy to go chasing my daughter across the world?" Rose invited an answer and then gave her own before Alethea could speak. "I came outside tonight because I was remembering being in this garden with Brenda just before she moved to Santa Fe. We had argued that day because I didn't want her to go 2,000 miles away from home."

"Why did she want to go?"

"To this day I don't understand. She was going to Columbia at the time, a fine school right here in New York. She said she had reasons for dropping out and going to school in New Mexico. She's always leaving for somewhere."

More than the profile, more than her frizzy hair, there was something familiar in Rose that reminded her of Borrasca. "It's a lovely garden. Are you the one that planted these bonsai trees?"

"Yes. My hobby. They respond to care so well, and I can manage their size. Nice, eh. I like working with my hands. It's a way to relax, and for all I know tending this yard is what keeps me on earth. Brenda hated these bonsai trees. Said they were unnatural and were too manipulative of nature."

Rose looked directly in Alethea's eyes, "Here I am, hoping you'll say yes and go look for her, and at the same time, I'm saying it's good to stay close to home." Her bottom lip curled over the top lip. "People are always leaving, but that's another story. I'm going to be true to my promise and not say another word to convince you." She touched

Alethea's shoulder and went toward the back door, still hearing Borrasca say good-bye that last night.

Rose had invited her to sit and then left so abruptly. The longer she sat there, the more Alethea became unseated from her resistance. The moon floated free of the clouds. She studied the bonsai tree closest to her. A family could no more escape their history than this tree could escape its own particular heritage. It had thrived the crossing from Japan, this one in a garden plot, and allowed to grow in a more natural way. Rose had fashioned it with loving care all the while carrying the shape of its history and hers within her. It wouldn't be a foolhardy adventure if she could be of help to Rose and Louis. She could do it for them if not for herself.

She returned to the bedroom and tried to sleep, her mind imagining what she'd actually say to Borrasca if they came face to face.

Hello, I am the woman who watched across the mesa. Who stood outside your dressing room. Tracked down your parents. Sat in their garden. Slept in your bedroom. Wore your clothes. Borrasca, compared to you, I'm a hollow shell of a person. I appear to be whole, but I have everyone fooled, being as much an actress as you. Inside me is a formlessness seeking a shape, needing tending as much as a bonsai. Borrasca, I don't think you'll complete me, but there's something you're going to teach me, and I guess I'll have to cross the globe to find out what it is. Borrasca and the woman who fell through the sky were compelling her forward.

She fell into a fitful sleep, only to be awakened by Borrasca standing at the foot of the bed, furious with her: "What are you doing here? Sleeping in my bed, being with my family. What gives you the right to pose as a friend? What gives you the right?"

Alethea had no words to explain. The two of them stood on opposite shores of being, opposite cliffs. But the three people in this house were counting on her. She could be of use. Even Borrasca might need her help though it remained to be seen if she could find her. How

101

the two of them might react if they were to meet up with each other was anyone's guess.

The next morning Alethea answered the question in Rose and Louis' eyes. She said yes and leaped into the world.

SIXTEEN

Someone else saw, said Brenda, running the dialogue in her sleep. I can't go back. I can't put my parents through any shame. Cade was there and then—she was gone.

And then? A demon in the seat across from her questioned her.

I ran for help, but someone saw. She told everyone what happened. Everyone knows but me.

God knows.

Borrasca sat up to see what God knew. Running from a lover is a cardinal sin. Lesbians do not abandon their lovers. We're sisters; we don't do that. I'm a woman who has broken one of the worst codes.

People think that you killed her.

Borrasca threw a pack at the voice. I tried to grab Cade and missed. By a hair. In that millisecond life and death changed hands.

The train moved across a stark terrain winding through the mountainous landscape that bordered northern India. When she dozed off, the nightmares returned, until she could not tell the difference between her mountain and the landscape of the real world. At other moments the panorama pulled her outside herself. In the face of the exquisite beauty, the mind machine slowed.

Suddenly the brakes were applied and the train screeched to a stop. The doors opened, and the passengers went outside to see that the storm of the night before had sent a volley of snow down from the mountain. The crew set to the task of shoveling the snow from the tracks. Except for the scuff of shovels there was only silence. The mountains stretched higher than she could see in this narrow gap between ranges. Half way across the field she saw a lone yak covered under a layer of fresh snow, looking out from large eyes, placid, as if the snow might actually be insulating him from the harsh weather. The thin air forced Borrasca to catch her breath, and she was relieved when the train whistle called her back on board.

She crossed borders and languages, snow white villages with only the dark trim of the houses appearing. Several hours later, after a climb up a very steep ridge, the monastery appeared, straight up from the village. Could she make it by nightfall? When they stopped at the station, the trader reappeared. The trek would continue. He helped her mount a yak like animal, a dzo he called it. The bones of the animal pierced through the blanket, and she found there was no comfortable way to stradde it.

What followed blurred in a landscape of white that penetrated to her core. The chalk-white bone substance of her life tumbled outside of her, and she wandered in a blizzard with her insides hanging out. The figure of the trader kept disappearing in the sheets of white ahead of her. The animal under her seemed to float on the hard crust of snow, and she could not feel it because of the numbness that had set in.

The trader reappeared out of the snow. "We're going to spend the night in the next town." He mumbled on, "it would kill the animals to cross the pass in this severe a storm. You can do what you want, but I'm not going any further."

She resolutely went on foot, shivering from the cold, stumbling in a world devoid of color or human landscape. Once, the lights of the monastery loomed in front of her, and she trudged hopefully on only to have them disappear. When night came the continual barrage of white snow on a field of black left her disoriented. Her footprints disappeared.

In desperation she dug a cave tunneling into the layers of snow, warmed by the sheer force of energy it took to dig. She didn't know how far down to go, but in her desperation she was able to build a snow cave large enough for her to sit upright, being careful to leave an air hole. She burrowed in, grateful she could hold herself together. The wind howled. She piled all her clothes around her, and there were moments when she felt warm. Resolutely she stayed awake, fearful that if she slept, she'd never wake up. Life and death. In a second one can become the other. It was a long night, but no demons came. No courier of death. In amazement she watched light appear in the world.

When she crawled out of her cave, her vision was blurry. Her eyes began playing tricks on her, for the snow had blood red spots and looked for all the world like watermelon. She even imagined the aroma of a fresh watermelon. It was either a mysterious phenomenon unique to the Himalayas or she was losing her marbles. She found herself babbling in nonsensical syllables and knew the watermelon snow and thin air were affecting her fragile hold on rationality. She plodded on in the direction of up until she wandered into a tiny village. The only person who could understand her said it was the way the Dalai Lama had escaped to freedom.

"Borrasca," she said to herself, "you are the Dalai Lama in reverse." She was able to keep to a winding road in what seemed a never ending journey through white, until the monastery appeared ahead, roof first. Borrasca caught her breath in the thin air.

She found a door. Hello. Yes, it was a difficult trip. Yes, I am cold. Yes, a hot bath. I won't be any trouble. The next thing she recalled was steeping in a bathtub. She could feel her toes tingling. The hot water and steam quieted the voices. In place of the harsh snow, a subdued light permeated the room. There were bamboo curtains. She heard tinkling bells. Everything seemed to be happening in the background.

A woman came in and sponged her back gently. The water warmed her and awakened her senses. Borrasca leaned forward in the bath and saw her face reflected in the water. Looking back at her was a red watermelon face with short hair sticking out. The woman helped Borrasca out of the tub and draped her with a towel. She led her to a chair and began to massage her head. The touch was comforting.

"Would you shave off all my hair?"

"Are you sure?" the woman asked. She herself was wearing long hair wound in a bun.

Borrasca nodded, pleased she had thought of it. The woman smiled: "Here one feels acceptance to cut their hair. But when you return to the world, it might distinguish you in an uncomfortable way."

"I'll go back to the world?"

"Yes."

"The dreams will go away?"

"Yes, indeed they will."

"I'm absolutely sure it's the correct thing to do. It'll grow out soon enough."

The woman lathered her head. Borrasca bristled momentarily at being covered in a white towel with the white lather covering her head, but the steady scratch of the razor was soothing. The last bit of hair fell to the floor. The woman brushed the hair from her shoulders and rubbed Borrasca's head with oil.

"You are second born, the woman offered."

"What does that mean?" Borrasca asked.

"The sages say the first birth is into the world of matter. The second birth is into the world of spirit." The woman handed Borrasca a mirror and stood back.

She was bald as the day she was born. But something was wrong. The woman saw her anxiety and graciously left to allow her to adjust. Borrasca was afraid of the bald headed woman. She ran into the bathroom, transfixed before the mirror. It was not the face of a newborn. It was...a shaved Jewish woman's head, sitting atop a concentration camp uniform. Borrasca let out a shriek and ran to the door. It was locked—was she a prisoner here? Where was the nice woman who had cut her hair? The mirror taunted her, repeating, "Death and sex."

The woman ran back in, but Borrasca could not be comforted. The woman left and returned with tea. "Please drink this. It will calm you."

Borrasca lashed out and sent the cup of tea flying. Hot liquid spilled over both of them. "Oh, forgive me."

"Forgive me," she called out again in her sleep. The camp image pierced her to her very roots. The terror from a time previous to her own birth became as strong as her torment over Cade. Cutting her hair was supposed to free her. Instead it bound her to a prior time. She was regressing.

In the night a familiar childhood dream recurred. Her body was being stretched like a rubber band as she was pulled between two worlds, one the present, the other of a previous birth. The rubber band reverberated, a frightful, buzzing sound. The dream terrain led her to a stadium lit up with bright klieg lights. A massive crowd was chanting.

Borrasca sat up in a sweat. Germany. It was just a dream she reminded herself. Triggered by the image of my shaved head. She was bound to a personal and collective history that hammered her with painful reminders.

Death and sex, ladies and gentlemen. Aren't they the end all, be all? The audience laughed, chanting: Bejay, Bejay, Bejay. They chanted louder and louder until she feared other people in their meditation spaces would be disturbed. Then she woke.

Death and sex. In old English poetry love making was compared to death. Sex defined her life and relationships. Kindled her stage act. Drove her, clitbound and restless. But life didn't come down to sex. It was the fear of death that set the boundaries. The time machine sent reality hurtling backward and down, but never forward. Death was Cade flying off the mountain. And Cade never landed.

She went back to the mirror. Swollen eyes and a bald pate stared back. The mirror distorted into a large egg with arms hanging at the side. A creature peered out from behind the egg, which divided into four smaller eggs. The images had the texture of objects that creep along the back streets of nightmares. There was a rent in the fabric of her mind. She had lost the ability to regulate tension and anxiety inside herself. She fell into bed.

In the morning she heard something outside the room. She threw open the door. There was no one. On the ground was a tray of food, tea, a folded black robe, a belt, slippers, and a prayer hat which bore an uncanny resemblance to a yarmulke. The slippers were something an inmate at a hospital might wear. She dressed and went to the window. It was the first time since she had arrived that she thought to look at her surroundings. Below was a serene winter garden. Low trees and benches were covered in snow. The limbs of one tree hung nearly to the ground covered with its weight. A few feet away was a statue of the Buddha. The mere sight of the statue changed her breathing. A hint of the sun shone through the clouds. She felt cut off from the peace of the natural world. Perhaps tomorrow she'd leave the room and go up to the tree. Tomorrow. Today she would try and meditate; that's why she had come.

Borrasca sat on the zafu meditation pillow and crossed her legs in lotus position, her eyes closed. The dark was nice. When her legs started to fall asleep, she shifted them. When the sun went down, she stopped meditating. She covered the mirror on the bathroom door. For the next few days, she sought out the dark. Yes, the dark was nice, but the past could insinuate itself into the present.

Each day the harping voices became more muted. One morning she opened the door and stooped to get the tray of food. She put the tray back down and stepped outside the room, gingerly placing her slippers on ground that was covered with new snow. She walked over to the tree whose limbs were bent nearly to the ground and threw her arms around it. She stayed in that embrace for several minutes. When she opened her eyes, she saw behind the tree a large meditation hall where people were sitting, each in their silent black-robed cocoons. No one moved; they hardly seemed to breathe. The cold forced her back inside.

The next day she resolutely brought a mat and blanket and tried meditating with the group in the hall. The quiet was unnerving. She reconsidered her intentions. I only have to deal with one thing at a time. Moment by moment we find our way. She was pleased she remembered that quote. The peacefulness behind her closed eyelids was inevitably disturbed when the dialogue returned. Agitated, she got up and went into a small alcove where one person sat meditating.

"You can't reduce life to the measure of one thing," she called out, her voice louder than she expected, reverberating through the room. She bent near the person. "That's the trouble with you men. You want to force all of life into a simple meditation. Simple, simple, simple. Well, it ain't that way."

The monk behind the robe did not turn around. His posture was impeccable. She became infuriated at his refusal to pay attention to her. The nerve of him to ignore her. She grabbed him by the shoulder and wheeled him around.

It was a woman.

Borrasca jumped back, There was no alarm or anger in the woman's eyes, although she regarded Borrasca with puzzlement.

"I'm sorry. Please, I apologize. I lost my head." The woman bowed her head.

To Borrasca she said, "And would you have apologized had I been a man as you thought?" Borrasca froze at the sound of English.

The woman continued: "Are you saying it makes a difference whether a man or a woman wears this robe? Will you not show the same side of yourself to me as to a man?" The calm aspect of her words had an unsettling effect on Borrasca.

Sarcasm dribbled out of Borrasca's mouth before she could stop it. "You check out of the world, find a safe refuge and then act like a saint."

The woman held her gaze. "You think I'm running away from reality? I'm dealing with the same thing as you, the only thing that matters—she suspended the word between them—death." Borrasca had crossed the world to hear this woman say in a detached, absolute way what she already knew.

"It doesn't matter how different our lives are. We all deal with death even though we may fight it."

Borrasca modulated her voice. "Forgive me."

"Most people come here goaded by pain. Everyone has a long, difficult journey." She turned back to the wall and her meditation.

Borrasca stared at her back, unable to walk away. She spoke to the back. "Why is death the only thing?"

"Death tells us who we are. All other things pass and fall away. Death is the constant. At every moment it threatens who we think we are. It says we cannot last. Life happens as impersonally as death—that's the part of the lesson that's been the most difficult for me." At that last admission, the woman's voice broke into a whisper.

There was no blinding snow throwing back projections at Borrasca. The woman's calm voice, the blankness of the walls, the emptiness of the space channeled the essentials right to her heart.

"It's not my death; it's someone else's," said Borrasca.

"The other death is also the point of the matter for you."

How was she to understand the impersonal nature of life when grief had left its personal signature on her? Death was very personal. And how did guilt fit into that impersonal concept?

In a sudden flash, Borrasca realized these reflections were coming before an outpouring of emotion. Her first reflex had been reason, not sarcasm or anger. A subtle shift had happened: an intention before hysteria. The woman sensed something, and respecting the necessity of the moment, bowed and left. Borrasca did not move for many minutes. Then she bowed.

She bowed for several days after that. A feeling of grace settled over her, a respite from the need to run and defend. She started to follow the schedule most people maintained, even attending sessions where one could receive meditation instructions: to follow the breath. To return to the breath when the mind gets distracted. Watch the monkey mind until calm returned. She rose to the morning bells and sat through chants and silence. No one questioned her right to be there. Soon she accepted herself. Each day she left her room for longer periods. Time ceased to gnaw at her, and she noted it only by the changing light. One afternoon as she was sitting on a bench by the tree, the woman she had confronted came up to her.

"Dorje will see you." When Borrasca did not understand, she explained. "He is the head of the monastery."

She followed the woman, her eyes fastened on the black robe in front of her. She was admitted into a large study lined with books and a floor covered by a brightly colored geometric-patterned rug. On the walls were silk paintings depicting the Buddha and fierce demons. The curtains and furnishings were mostly in burgundy and yellows. Incense permeated the air. In the center of the room was a cluttered desk, and as she walked in, a man rose from behind it and bowed. His robe was also burgundy and yellow. He gestured for her to sit, and they quietly surveyed one another.

"How is your time here being?" he inquired. Borrasca nodded her head affirmatively. "We don't often have people drop in on us while a blizzard is raging."

"I'm not usual, I guess." The sarcasm came rushing out before she could check it.

"Nor humble," he observed.

"But I am sincere, isn't that a prerequisite?"

"Yes. Indeed. Humbleness would also help."

"I have been humbled. Before immense mountains in two countries. Before winds and blowing snow in bitter cold. I have escaped with all my fingers and toes."

He waited before responding, sensing the desperation within her that poured out when the world of words consumed her. His face softened with acceptance. His gentle dark eyes set in a round, hairless face looked at her with compassion. He bent his large frame slightly forward towards her. "Yes, indeed you have. And would you stop running here?"

Borrasca didn't know how to respond except to nod. She didn't know how to ask to stay, but the question informed the atmosphere around them, and she nodded again. Neither of them spoke into the silence. He sensed there was something to be gained by her staying.

"Very well. You may stay." His mouth curled at the corners in an approving gesture.

Borrasca's mouth turned in a smile, but her glee was momentary.

"For a limited time. You have other things in this life that call to you. I hope you'll respect our needs in this community, and when the time comes to leave, you will honor those needs. I think the time will be apparent to us all. Is the meditation instruction being helpful?"

"Yes."

"Suffering does not go away. Not even here. But as you continue to sit in silence and listen to the dharma talks, you'll gain more compassion for yourself and the impermanent nature of life."

"I hope that will happen soon."

"You have already begun."

Borrasca bowed and left. Her place was assured, and that awareness sat peacefully inside her. Questions about time and the future desisted. She awakened at dawn with the rest of the community and joined in the group meditation while it was still dark outside. She squirmed, but remained in her position, mindful that others around her barely seemed to be breathing. She ate alone, then meditated again at noon and dusk and bedtime. Each day she walked around the expansive courtyard opening herself to the sky and exterior world. She estimated that she was probably on the opposite side of the earth from New Mexico. The sky here seemed kin to that sky across the world, a sharp, clear blue in rarefied air. She was not afraid of the sky anymore.

She read the words of a teacher who said the meditating body is like a jar of salad dressing which sits unmoving after it has been shaken. The jar is still, but inside the oil and vinegar and spices still churn. Allowed to sit, the contents settle, agitation ceases. Such a settling was gradually happening within her. The turmoil inside noticeably ebbed.

Then the initial grace passed. Prolonged periods of silent meditative states alternated with a recurring sense of dislocation. If she let her guard down, if she was not fully present in each moment, her emotions threatened to spill over. She watched the moods arise and pass away, just as the practice said it would, but only by maintaining a strict control over her mind could she function. In sleep, there was no control. The dreams left her ragged. A gate opened that she had shut down. Memories particular to her as a Jewish woman rushed in. Dreams of the Holocaust. The past was insisting itself into the present.

One day Dorje called for her again. She was not ready and dreaded the meeting. "I was hoping we could talk more. Perhaps we can use our dialogue to deepen your stay here."

He wasn't asking her to leave.

"I am still quite amazed at your arrival. Few foreigners come to this particular monastery, and no one wanders in once winter has set in. It's flirting with death."

"You think I flirt with death, well..." She caught herself before a sarcastic remark jumped out of the speech gate from force of habit. She digested the lines whole. They both sat silently. She tried again. "I'm still never sure which one of me will answer. It's reassuring to know change is the nature of reality. As for how I got here, I think I have been traveling with death."

"Death tells us who we are. How exactly did you get here, Miss..."

"No miss, please. First names only. Does that make you Lama?"

A smile crossed his face in response to the verbal forays that marked this woman's style. "My name is Tenzin Dorje, not to be confused with dorje, That is an object held in the right hand during some of our ceremonies. It's a representation of a thunderbolt, a symbol of enlightenment twirled in order to bring in truth. We have our own puns as you can see."

They both laughed and it set her at ease. "I am Borrasca, the sudden storm that comes up. Appropriate for me, eh?"

"I should say. How did this storm sitting in front of me roll in?" His eyebrows went up. "Surely not alone?"

"They told me there would be no way to go through the passes until spring. I tried waiting. That lasted two days. In my mental state there was no way I could have waited for spring. In the market place I was trying to find a native Sherpa, when I happened to overhear an Aussie trader telling someone he was going this way. I threw my lot in with him. He was cantankerous and mostly drunk, but he helped me for part of the trek. We took a train, which was easy enough. It was so crowded that the body heat kept me warm. At a stop he traded for these animals—dzo, is that the name? I never heard that before. Do you say two dzos?" she asked in a singsong rhyme.

Dorje laughed.

"There were actually four of the creatures. We rode on the backs of two of them and the others carried our packs. I was falling apart. I began to think he, too, had lost it or felt he had to be drunk in order to cross the pass in winter. I can't begin to describe the terror I felt as the snow turned into a blizzard. My face froze but that wasn't the worst thing. My butt also froze, and I couldn't feel the saddle underneath me and didn't know if I could hold on and keep from falling. The sheets of snow were falling into almost horizontal bands, and I couldn't see him ahead of me or anything behind me."

"When we got to a small village, he refused to go any further, and straight-a-ways found a bar. Said he was going to spend the winter there. I wanted to die rather than stay in the middle of nowhere. It was my stubbornness or desperation that made me think I could do it alone. I waited until the storm seemed to subside. I had no sooner set out than another storm came up. The wind pushed me two steps forward and one to the side. The blowing snow blinded me till I was sure death was going to be a white out."

"It's miraculous that you're here to tell the tale. How did you survive?"

"When night came, I dug into a snow bank to keep from freezing."

"A long dark night of the soul," Dorje said.

"One of many. When I wandered into a small village just below here, I was told it was the way the Dalai Lama escaped to freedom. "Borrasca," I told myself, "you are the Dalai Lama in reverse." Only he was greeted with asylum at the end of his journey, and I was in danger of being put in an asylum—you will want me out soon, won't you?"

"It's true you cannot stay here forever, but I'm happy for you to remain until spring or until you are recovered in any way you define that. We feared for your sight when you first arrived. And we feared..."

"...for my sanity?"

"It happens to people stranded in the elements."

She wondered at his impeccable English. She changed the subject away from her mental condition. "You speak excellent English."

"The University of Michigan. B.A. degree."

"In my pompous, perhaps racist American mind, I didn't expect you to have such an education."

"And what degree did you hope to attain here, Miss Borrasca?"

"You're still calling me miss."

"I forgot. Politeness is a fault sometimes."

"So is insolence. I apologize for my attitude. Do you know why I was desperate to be here? I didn't want to be Ms. Lama, or to be one with the one, which I think is the goal for some of the people here. I'd heard that in Buddhist meditation, one can silence the mind. I wanted to silence my mind or die."

"For many people life becomes one attempt after another to run away from pain and suffering. Some people become numb; others zip around, always moving like characters running at the speed of an old Charlie Chaplin film."

Borrasca laughed. "The description fits me. The events of the last few weeks feel like a bad movie."

"Ego needs activity in order to exist. For most people, not just you, the more desire and aversion we have, the more alive we feel. Watch your restless mind. Notice when ego arises."

"Do you mean like the Freudian ego."

"Ego in the Buddhist sense is quite different. Your ego gives you a false feeling of being a separate self, churning the thoughts and emotions around and around. This makes ego feel solid and real. But if you're not careful, you start to identify with the ego and confusion."

"I was driven by my demons, desperate to be here, not knowing if the monastery would even let me in."

"Many come here to escape their demons—I've met a few myself." He smiled. "We have a lineage called the "mishap lineage" because some teachers, like Tilopa and Milarepa, had what might be called 'mad yogi' ways. They even killed. Therefore, try to see your obstacles as gifts. That will help transform your present confusion into sanity, perhaps even wisdom."

He waited as she absorbed what he had said. "Use your time well while you're here. Even if it feels awkward, recite the mantra *Om mani padre hum* with the others. And by yourself. It is the essence of the entire teaching. We believe it invokes the benevolent attention and blessings of Chenrezig, the embodiment of compassion. Repeat it as often as you can. Compassion and waking up are the motivations for the practice. To be fully awake, you have to face your demons. But if you go rushing off into the snow again through these passes, I'll think you irretrievable."

"I will say the mantra, and I'll wait until the thaw has begun before I leave."

"There is a wonderful spring that happens here, though sometimes in the midst of the ferocious snows of winter it is hard to believe that spring will come. Judge the time to leave by your internal season. You have a personal winter to live through." He stood to leave and then turned back to her. "I may know some people who can help when you depart." He bowed and left the room.

Borrasca found herself saying *Om mani padre hum* throughout the day. How would she know when to leave? Last week she had lost her hold again. At any time a sudden storm could come up and wipe out weeks of meditation and calm. She walked outside and sat on a bench. She had at least one friend. When she was ready to leave, his offer of help along the way might be necessary.

She'd re-enter a world where Cade's presence was still being acknowledged, When she pulled back from the personal and perceived it through a wider lens, she could appreciate that Cade would be missed by other people, personally and for her research and her book. She had touched upon others' lives as a pivotal point of energy, drawing people to her as much as Borrasca ever did on stage. Didn't her death mean there was a rent in the fabric of the world?

She put her face up to the light snow that was falling, giving herself over to its feathery touch. She had thought of Cade's death without falling through a black hole. It had drawn her into her own flight down, but it was now being a gift in another way, drawing her into the grounding of her true self, the place she'd most resisted. Decades after the war and four decades into her own life, she was, with intention, looking at herself honestly, accepting herself as the daughter of survivors. To be fully awake in Buddhism meant being fully open to the present and the past. She could no longer ignore the currents of personal or cultural history.

Over the next few weeks, she was able to take full refuge in the practice. In Om mani padme hum. She became more mindful of the natural world around her, seeing how the late afternoon sun created fingers of light coming at a slant through the courtyard, as evanescent as in New Mexico. Radiant shafts of light came off the snow covered rocks and found her crying: "Soul where are you? Leave bread crumbs for me to find you."

The snows became less frequent. The daylight hours lengthened, and the stillness within her became more of a comfortable home. The practice brought her out of grief, if she let herself feel it instead of doing an end run around it. Emotions were again free to enter the being who had wandered in, ready to fly off a mountain of her own making.

After the morning meditations, she took to reading in the library, the warmest building in the compound. On the bottom shelf below the discourses of the Buddha and works by Tibetans such as Lama Yeshe and Dilgo Khyentse Rinpoche, there was a copy of *The Tibetan Book of the Dead.* She tucked that under her arm to read later. She knelt down sifting through the worn books left by previous retreatants, until her eyes hit on the spine of a tattered copy of a poetry book, *The Darkness Around Us Is Deep* by a man named William Stafford. She opened up to a page and her eyes fell on these words:

It is people at the edge who say things at the edge: winter is toward knowing.

She wept into the book. Two robed monks passed her in quiet walking meditation. Their slippers made soft padding noises in the stillness. It was the sound of the transformation occurring in her heart. This was her winter toward knowing.

"Dorje," she asked, at their next interview, "I've started reading *The Tibetan Book of the Dead.*"

"Are you getting into Buddhist theology?"

"Do Buddhists believe in life after death? Someone I know died recently, and I wonder if that means she's in bardo?"

"We interpret bardo to mean an intermediate existence after death and before one's next birth."

"Does that mean she could come back?"

It is not quite like that. Reincarnation does not have the sense of an irreducible self passing from body to body. There is no eternal soul or self that's returning. One's essence passes on, like a dying candle lighting a new one."

"How, then, do Tibetans pick their successors? If he's reincarnated as a young boy somewhere in Tibet, how can a very young child identify prayer beads or relics that belonged to his predecessor?"

It's complex to translate across languages and cultures, but I know you've heard of the collective unconscious." When she nodded, he went on. "Think of it this way, Borrasca, there's a stream of consciousness that links life with life. In some individuals there's only a very porous membrane that separates the personal from the collective unconscious. Especially in an encouraging culture like ours, some individuals have the ability to tap into it more easily. It requires a deep intuitive connection to this consciousness to recognize the signs and identify the successor."

"You see, the present Dalai Lama is not the same Dalai Lama that preceded him, but the essence, the repository of a spirit that resided in his predecessor and all the Dalai Lamas before that."

Back in her room, Borrasca reflected on his words. Dorje and the Dalai Lama represented an ocean of compassion that resonated in her, piercing her right through her skin. She wanted share it with Mimi.

Dear Mimi,

My dear sister, at last I'm able to write. I'm at a Buddhist monastery, closer to clouds than to civilization. Quoting the teacher here, I've had a personal winter to live through. It's moved me towards knowing the shadow side of myself and believing in the inevitable return of light. Slowly but surely I'm feeling more grounded. The community of people here has been my saving grace. And the practice has allowed me to feel more at home in my body as Brenda than I've felt in years. The need for Bejay no longer exists, but I'm able to feel some compassion for myself for having needed her. Being here has been a necessary refuge from the world of desire, but I really miss the three of you. I'm hungry to reconnect, but it'll be a while before I return. Be comforted knowing I've found a path that leads out of the wilderness and will lead me home to you. But first it goes through New Delhi and then west from there.

I wish I could say more. I spend my days in silence to keep words from running like monkeys through my brain, and it works. But it doesn't make for long letters. I promise more details later. Tell Mom when I think of home I see her in her rose garden. All my love to mom and dad. And to you. B.

She'd never wander the earth friendless as long as there was Mimi. She needed contact with her family, her biggest blessing. And women. A lesbian could go anywhere and not be alone. The eighth wonder of the world was that anywhere she traveled there'd be a community of women she could connect with. It was not something she needed to explain to Dorje when they talked again.

"When your spring comes, where will you go?"

"I'm not sure. West."

"Due west from here will not be easy."

"I'm no longer into tackling insurmountable mountains head on. I'll go south to India."

"When you go, I have friends who may be able to assist you on the way. You may remember that when the Chinese invaded our country the Dalai Lama and many Tibetans fled to India. A small community arose in Dharamsala. If you go there, ask for Ms. Dolma Phuntsok. Tell her that I send my blessings to her, and that you are my friend."

To be known as friend. She sat, tears falling on her robe. Her being had known days of grace no amount of guilt or sadness could wipe out.

SEVENTEEN

New Delhi, India. Alethea was landing in a country whose people and way of life she could not anticipate. The culture shock gradually hit her like the waves of heat which took her breath away as she walked out of the air conditioned plane. It was early morning and already the heat was oppressive. Several languages, one of which sounded like French, announced arrivals and departures. All around her was a sea of white clothing. Hundreds of cars were lined up, waiting for passengers. It was more crowded than Kennedy airport had been. She was about to hail a taxi when she caught the eye of one of the drivers in line who had friendliness emanating from his face. She gravitated toward him, not sure what to say.

He saw her confusion and came toward her with a light step. "Would you like a ride?"

She nodded in quick decision. He had fashioned a carrier with bungee cords which could hold her luggage securely. The ride would give her a sense of place. "Is it a long way to town?" she pronounced each word deliberately.

"Not far. 10 miles. But with some heavy traffic." He spoke far better English than she would have guessed, in a soft spoken voice laced with a British accent. As they headed toward New Delhi, the trip resembled the movement from the base of a pyramid to the narrowing apex, for the airport had been a wide, open space, and as they moved closer to the city, all the world seemed to converge there. Passage on the road became increasingly slow, dense with noisy motor scooters, carts, some top heavy with large bundles that looked like dung. Hundreds of questions came to her as they moved around people and vehicles. She leaned over to the driver, "What is that?"

"An auto rickshaw. I used to drive one, but now they're prohibited from the airport."

"Are all those styles of dresses called saris, even the men's?"

"The men over there," he nodded to his left, "are wearing dhotis." The driver appeared to know several drivers, even nodding to a man on a motor bike and murmuring "Namaskar."

The road narrowed, filling up with people as they approached the city. Their movement slowed to a crawl. Whistles began blowing, and traffic was halted for a funeral procession. Alethea saw a litter being carried shoulder high by men who were chanting. She could make out only the one word Jai...Jai. Another mile on there was another procession.

"Ah, a wedding," said the driver. The bride was resplendent in orange silk, and also heavily veiled, which made Alethea uncomfortable. Her tenseness increased when she realized her driver would soon want to know where to take her. She needed a cheap place. She had let the family give her only so much extra money in addition to the plane fare, insisting on using her own money. It was her search as well as theirs, though she was worried if she had enough. She would make do. Now, at the point of arrival, she wished she had thought to use the internet to book a hotel.

"Driver, do you know a cheap hotel you could recommend?"

"Do you want cheap or clean?"

"Both."

"Both may not be possible."

"How clean?"

"If you stay for a week, you keep the same sheets. You will have your own bath, but no one will come to clean the room. There will be some bugs, not the best air conditioning, and no guarantee that only Americans will be close by."

"Sounds all right to me." After all, she thought, at home I sleep on the same sheets for several days. "Will I have the only key to my room?"

"Perhaps. The employees of the hotel will have keys. You will be physically safe, but some employees do have access to the rooms."

"Do all taxi drivers speak such good English?"

"I don't really know. I'm not from here."

He turned around and looked at her. "Do you want me to play typical guide for the tourists, or can I be me?"

Alethea winced at his honest remarks, but then she saw his good natured grin, and they both laughed in relief. "Of course I want you to be you—My name is Alethea, and who are you?"

"My name is Chandi. I was born in the state of Tamil Nadu in the south, but I've lived in Srinagar most of my life. Do you know of that place?"

"Maybe not, she said."

"It's a very beautiful part of the Kashmir valley. I used to be a house boy to English people living there. That's how I learned English and was able to attend the university. I came here thinking to finish my studies, but my money ran out. So we—my sister is with me—are both working. I took this job because I speak English and can give information to visitors. What about you? Where are you from?"

They became enveloped in another traffic jam. Progress on the narrow street crawled by inches. Chandi wound his way to a modest hotel and began unloading her baggage. Suddenly she didn't want him to disappear.

"I still haven't answered your questions about me. I'd like to talk more with you. If I need to talk to someone, can I call you?" She didn't want him to misconstrue her intentions, but there was an easy camaraderie between them.

"By all means. Come and visit with us. My sister is very lonely here. We would both appreciate your company, she especially." He gave her a card which had the name of the taxi company. Below it was a hand written phone number. He put her bags in the hotel lobby. "This hotel is close to the Chandni Chowk bazaar in the heart of Old Delhi. An experience you don't want to miss. Everyone passes through there, but don't let the numbers of people frighten you, Miss America," he teased. "These are India's people."

He drove off, waving, as he left her to weigh his words. Alethea checked in and was led to a neat, though dimly lit room. It had a narrow bed with an airy thin blanket, a tiny closet, and one insubstantial towel. She turned on the fan, already drained by the heat. It did little to cool the room. The heat and her curiosity soon sent her outside. The hotel clerk pointed in the direction of the bazaar.

She quickly found herself on a narrow, twisting street hemmed in by people on all sides. At one point she was unable to proceed and stood looking into people's eyes as they passed by her. The veiled faces caught her off guard. Her heart was racing. She brushed away the claustrophobia, mindful of Chandi's words: These are India's people. She hadn't felt this way in New York, but here she was the only white person in sight. She recognized the fear of the other rising inside her. Determined, she moved with the crowd, letting herself be carried by the human river until the narrow street opened into a wide market area, giving her space to consider her reactions. She realized it was not only her personal store of stereotyped images, it was also the density of people. How, she wondered, could people here survive unless they maintained an essence of self within their bodies.

People rushed by occupied with their tasks, but she made eye contact with those whose gaze fell on her. Here where the unknowns abounded, the language foreign, curiosity dominated. She walked in the intense midday heat until she reached the heart of the market place. On all sides were mazes of little booths where people were selling exotic things. At each booth, she pointed and the merchants explained. Betel nuts, bidis, curry and beads, bright colored cloth. A variety of flatbreads: chapatis, dosas, akki and rotti. Naan was the only name she recognized. The scent of incense and cooking oil hung in the air. Children darted in and out. To her right were several old beggars; two were missing limbs.

Alethea wished she could see above the turbans to know just how expansive the bazaar was. She tried to stand on tiptoe but lost her balance. She teetered and backed into a stall in a little corner out of the path of the river of people. The woman in the stall was making chapattis filled with a mixture whose aroma flirted with Alethea's nose. The smell was alluring to her hungry stomach. She scrunched into a corner so as not to be in her way watching her work over live coals that surely must have been burning her squinting eyes. Her nimble hands deftly rolled out the chapattis and filled them. There were two pots on the hot coals. People came up to her and called out or another and she assembled the chapatti from the appropriate pot. Alethea caught her eye with one finger raised. The woman caught her off guard by speaking English.

"This one is karuma. Vegetarian. Very Spicy." The unexpected familiarity of language startled Alethea, but she paid attention as the woman pointed to the second pot. "Mutton."

"Vegetarian," called out Alethea. She wanted a dozen, but her stomach would have to be content with one trial chapati. The woman handed it to her while Alethea fished in her purse for money, hoping she was giving more rather than less. She looked into the woman's eyes and confronted another prejudice: she could take all the money and I wouldn't know how to determine how much change I should get. The woman held the bill tentatively. Both of them spent a moment of silence thinking about honesty. The woman reached inside her dress and pulled out a pouch. She gave Alethea three paper bills and some change from under her crossed feet.

"Thank you," murmured Alethea.

The woman replied, "dhanyavad" and turned to another customer while Alethea moved to the edge of the stall and ate. Karuma-- did it mean the name of the dish or vegetarian or spicy? It was delicious, but it intensified her thirst and finding a drink meant moving out of the stall. Huddled in the corner she realized she was feeling how large her body was among many smaller people. Old tensions reared, but she had been set loose in the world. She stepped out of the tent and joined the flow of people outside the stall.

Her forehead was beading from the heat. It intensified the smell of men whose armpits lingered behind them. Alethea spotted an opening in the crowd and darted out of the current. Curious: all the feelings about this dry hot place were expressed for her in water metaphors: seas of people, the flow and current. A merchant asked her a question, but his meaning was lost to her in the din of voices. A man to her right leaned into her ear: "He wants to know if you want vegetable or meat."

Being spoken to by a stranger speaking English still caught Alethea off guard. She looked up only to see a figure rush by, just a few feet away. Something in the gait, the way she held herself. Borrasca! It was a spectral figure of her cloaked in white. Surely it was Borrasca.

The sheer odds of being in the same place with her astounded her and rooted her in place. Finally her feet propelled her forward. She pushed her way through the dense mass of people, nearly all of them dressed in white, but it was to no avail. She had been so close, Alethea thought, I could have reached out and touched her, but now she was gone. There was no sight of her. Alethea spun around facing all four directions. Nothing but a sea of white turbans and dhotis. Were her eyes playing tricks? She was not mistaken. It had been Borrasca. A hand tugged at her sleeve. "Chapatti, Miss?"

She yanked his hand away all the while keeping her eyes moving, taking in as much of the crowd as she could. "Please, try this chapatti." She fished in her pocket for coins and dropped them in his hand before jumping back into the crowd, straining to catch sight of her. There! Several hundred feet ahead. Alethea shouted her name, a call that fell behind the wall of people. They pressed in on her, blocking her vision. Borrasca was swallowed up in the crowd.

A wind crept along her neck, an unforgettable sensation of cold waves rolling over her in the midst of the burning heat. Years later she would remember this moment, how the air was drawn away from her, caught in the force field of Borrasca's presence.

It's only my first day, I'll see her again, she consoled herself, weighed down with the hopes of the family coupled with her own.

She moved to the edge of the bazaar, her eyes still searching, registering her frustration. In her hand, the chapatti was crushed in her grip. She had been so close. Emotionally spent, she returned to her room and flung herself on the bed where she fell into sleep for several hours, waking in the cool of the night. She turned on the light and paced the room restlessly until the humidity forced her into stillness. The after image of the figure haunted her. It was her—but something was different. She was no longer the woman on the cliff, nor the energy whirlwind at the Spiral Shell. It was as if another life-force had taken over her body.

She searched in her bags for Borrasca's journal, by now a familiar world, and paged through it to a passage she had marked, a note which Borrasca had written unrelated to the band or Cade:

What is mine spiritually to claim as a Jew? For my generation it's defined as much by the Holocaust and defending against anti-Semitism as any spiritual philosophy or belief. Yes, it's my birthright but how can I know what true spirit is? Call it God, the Tao. An inner calling must be what guides me, or else I'll be driven by fad not principle, by image and not an inner calling.

Borrasca's journal offered a way to alternate between action in the world and immersion into herself as she defined the outlines of her own being. Alethea had been so caught up in herself, so intent on her own search, that she had not fully taken into account that Borrasca was not just running away; she had perhaps come here to find out on some deep level what was true for her. The loss of Cade would be enough to set her loose from her moorings. Borrasca's words revealed a hint of an inner life

Last night was strange. We were making love, but she was unable to let go. A circle of gloom was surrounding her. Sometimes she becomes attached to her depression and is unable to let me love her. Of course I felt guilty when she didn't come. I always do. She can always give to me, I always take. That sweet tongue. I would fly across the world for her tongue.

Alethea put the journal down. Two women, one of them perpetually flying through the sky, led her to see that all energy is electric and erotic. If someone had said to her at the beginning of this whole episode that it was Borrasca's sexual energy that was drawing her, she couldn't have accepted it. Yet, it was becoming clear to Alethea that the essence within her needed to connect with her sexual energy. That drive was directing her search as much as what had happened on the mesa, and all of it was inseparable from a spiritual quest.

Her inability to save the woman who fell through the sky had initially resulted in lethargy. Tonight she had come back from the bazaar and retreated into sleep first thing. The lethargy, she saw, was a cover for the emotions she was now allowing herself to feel. That the point of all the sojourns—hers as well as Borrasca's, the running up the mesa and down, going to New York, India—was the possibility of self-discovery. The keys were all around her.

From her suitcase she pulled out the book written by Stella Maris. The design on the front cover depicted shooting rays which exploded out of a central point. Off to the center in the lower right quadrant was a small dot, a particle of matter, appearing as if it were a body floating free in space. Eerie to think Cade might have intuited a body floating in space. The book's title, *An Unsingular Universe,* intimidated her. Science had never been her strong suit, but the book might shed light on what had transpired. And Mimi had insisted she read it. The inside sleeve quoted Cade:

"...The nebula and the points of the universe circle around one another, and like lodestars, we are drawn to the particles with the most magnetism. The currents of electricity contain the possibilities between us. And gravity holds it all together..."

The book's dedication said simply:

To B.

Alethea drew in her breath as she extended her hands, palms facing each other and saw the experience from a physics perspective. She was a needle leaping toward a magnet. When you hold a magnet in your hand and inch it slowly towards a needle—stopping just outside the magnetic field—the needle can sense the attraction, the impending movement of energy, even while it is still out of the immediate field. The needle is set in motion through intent and will before the pull of the magnet occurs.

She, point A, had watched points B and C on a mesa. Although her stance had been from a distance, she too created a charge; she had not been a neutral observer. The distance between them was constantly changing, as does the distance between magnet and needle. Still unknown was what effect she herself was having on the incident and on their lives. Her part in the interplay while not fully clear had impacted Borrasca's flight. Surely if she changed her part of the dynamic, the meaning of everything, her life and theirs, would change.

At this late hour, her energy was too depleted to read more, but the hook had been implanted. She was determined to find out the nature of the magnetic charge between her and the two women. The trail would be there in the morning.

EIGHTEEN

IN THE FOURTH SECOND

Cade started to go head first.
I am part of no world at this moment,
not of the earth, the living, or the dead
I'm free, and I'm petrified.
As she fell she found to her surprise
that she could feel her mother's arms.
She whose death had also come suddenly,
was already dead for many years,
Her mother had comforted her when she had
been alive and was still her strongest connection.
The period of time they shared flashed before her
complete in less than a millisecond:
I inherited her deep set eyes,
the long face that sat on a long neck on a long body.
A pleasing even attractive composition of the face.
That she couldn't have been in my longer.
After her death, I was more absorbed by ideas than people
but people were always attracted to me
Even when boys had sought me out,
though I didn't much return their attention.
I focused on school instead,
became the one the faculty remembered.
It was uncomfortable.
Years after I went away from home
people's memories of me became a trail spun after me

people made me a locus for their dreams.
I rebelled, didn't graduate college as expected
and dropped out six credits shy of a physics degree
Mom you didn't pressure me at all.
Dad worried about the family image.
I moved from the east coast
waitressing, writing
Others kept seeing me as a prime mover,
but it didn't compel me; it compelled them
which drove me further away.
I eventually completed my physics courses.
School fulfilled a very real need
I began reading again
brought books to work.
It cost me the waitressing job
I decided to go off for a few weeks camping.
Hitched rides until I got to Colorado
and stood high in the Rockies.
the most beautiful experience of my life
hiking through evergreens and blue spruces,
through stands of aspen shimmering in the light
delicate against the mammoth mountains
I wandered through a stand of lodge pole pines
into a meadow which opened like a story book,
every inch covered with wild flowers
I sat in the midst of the flowers
The colors laid out against the sky
and then I was the sky.
High as the clouds and peaks.
At night I was close to the stars,
close to small animals hovering outside my campsite
I never saw them, but I heard them
and felt them watching me

all of us breathing in the thin air
How did I ever breathe before then?
Nothing compared to those 2 weeks.
I moved to New Mexico thinking living there
would be like that time in Colorado
just one step away from the sky
living always in its intense quality of light
among the power points, the leylines,
but nothing ever took the place of that magical
point high in the Rockies.
I finished my advanced degree in physics
Los Alamos labs hired me, but it was the sky
the sky was the defining charge of my life.

NINETEEN

Alethea woke with a firm resolve. She'd give herself two weeks to look for Borrasca. If she didn't find her by that time, she would leave. The odds of finding one person amid the millions in Delhi with its winding irregular streets and cul-de-sac and alleys, much of it was accessible only to pedestrian traffic, were overwhelmingly against her. Still, she'd seen her the first day.

Mornings will be the coolest time to search. She could justify relaxing in the afternoon heat. Maybe try again in the evenings. Already the oppressive heat glared through her window, but she would make an honest effort. The US Express office was a mob scene overrun with Americans and other foreigners. There was even a line to ask what line to be in. After two hours of listening to rich Americans whine, Alethea became repulsed by their materialistic concerns and condescending attitude towards the Indian people. She was embarrassed to say that she was an American. Chandi had been kind to her; he could have assumed she'd be as narrow minded.

When her turn came, the clerk treated her brusquely, his thin, closely shaved drawn face exposing heat rash. A narrow tie divided his white shirt in half. He was acting the bureaucrat and clearly enjoying his impatient role. Alethea countered his rudeness with directness.

"If I were you, Madam,"

"Please don't madam me."

"Miss." He brought out a map. "I will circle the places where Americans are most likely to frequent. If I were you, I'd look here and...here."

"Are there any places off the beaten track, where people not so rich might go?"

He stared at her. "Many I suppose, but only if you are native and not a woman traveling alone."

"I'm trying to find someone who's missing."

"Have you filed a report with the police?"

"She's not missing quite that way."

He waited for a logical explanation, his fingers drumming the counter.

"Is there a hostel in this area where a westerner might stay?"

"Miss, there is a long line behind you, and you are obviously..."

"...on a wild goose chase? Perhaps it appears that way. But I'm an American in need of help. Don't you give information about hostels?

"We do routine transactions here. Cash checks. Help with legal identification papers. You should talk to the Consulate. We are a business, not a missing persons bureau."

With that, she gathered up the map and pushed past the curious onlookers still in line, her face reddening. The length of the line made her see how misguided had been her assertiveness. She'd been expecting them to ignore every one else to help her. The world didn't center around her. The journey was taking her out of her narrow limits, but her focus couldn't be too self-absorbed. She resolved to be more aware of her surroundings as she investigated the places the clerk had circled.

Over the next few days she went on a methodical search: restaurants, tourist spots, several hostels and hotels. Outside one hotel there was a beggar with an amputated leg juggling for the tourists. She watched the tourists toss small coins at him. He then had to crawl quickly along the sidewalk for the change before street urchins stole it from him. She placed some coins in his hand, knowing how it was for the homeless back home in Santa Fe who asked for spare change.

Everywhere she encountered a money class, not just Americans, but Europeans, Asians, other Indian people. They insulated themselves from the desperate poverty around them, fashioning a barrier with money, living in a separate world in the same city. Perhaps the rich thought that they were actually seeing the real India when they went from one Holiday Lodge to another.

It was with a different perspective that she returned the next day to the bazaar. She tried to pick out individuals and see distinct personalities aware that she was the oddity here: a single white woman able to travel freely in a country where women often walked behind husbands and fathers, aware she was watching scenes from the outside looking in.

The vendors cried out to her, but the food that had seemed exotic before, now sent a protest in her intestines. She circumnavigated the bazaar, walking the length of it before returning to her hotel. She spent days that way, going from one part of the city to another asking questions. Describing Borrasca. Looking intently at white robed women. Each day before dark she returned to the bazaar which had become her jumping off point. It contained a fascinating mix of people and kept her close to the pulse of the city. The range of artistry and craftsmanship exhibited in the modest stalls drew her admiration. Silk dresses and blouses made with intricate attention to detail, and there was the leatherwork of one family. Several times she watched a young boy hammer silver metal into small, fragile leaves.

One evening in her second week, there was a brilliant display of fireworks that brought Alethea out into the night to witness the festivities. People freed from the heat and from work were in a festive mood. She stood with a large crowd in a plaza that was enclosed with high stone walls on either side. The fireworks were elaborate, and she marveled at their vibrant bursts along with everyone else. Then a gold sunburst flare misfired, exploding only several feet above one of the high walls on which many people stood.

The out of control flare burst near a woman. It turned into a radiating star pattern of yellow, blue, and orange and shaped itself into the face of Borrasca. Alethea inhaled. As the flare fizzled and fell in a downward spiral, she was forced to run with the other spectators. The festive atmosphere dissolved into chaos even though the flare fell harmlessly, burning itself out. Alethea frantically pushed her way through people to the other side of the wall. Borrasca was gone. A cry caught in Alethea's throat. Perhaps she'd always be arriving after the fact, out of breath.

Alethea inched her way out of the crowd and went into a nearby hotel. She plopped herself down on a couch in the lobby, breathing hard, seeing Borrasca's face in technicolor. Something was different about her. The incident left her frustrated and wanting to talk to someone. She found Chandi's card and called him on the lobby phone.

"Hello, is this Chandi? This is Alethea, the American woman you brought from the airport a few days ago."

"Yes, I remember. Are you doing all right?"

"I'm doing well. Actually it would be nice to talk to someone. Are you busy? Would you care to meet me for some tea, or a drink?"

"One minute, please. She could hear him talking to someone. "My sister is with me. Do you mind if she joins us?"

"I'd love it." As they made arrangements, she realized how lonely she was for company.

Waiting for them on the couch in the hotel lobby, she couldn't help but overhear the conversation behind her. One man was speaking louder than he needed to.

"Well, to my mind the tradition of suttee is an example of a wife's devotion."

"That's not true," the woman replied.

"You wouldn't want to live after I die, would you, dear?"

"I don't want to jump into a burning funeral pyre. And I don't believe you'd offer yourself up if I were to go first," she snapped back.

"Oh come now you two," interjected a second man. "It's their custom. It's a time honored tradition, and we ought to respect such an expression of love." Alethea could not believe her ears.

Without thinking, she jumped up and turned to them, her emotions spilling over, "It was an oppressive tradition that is now against the law. Don't romanticize it."

One of the men was furious. He and Alethea glowered at each other, but his wife steered him away from the crowd that had gathered. The scene had caused a commotion. Alethea looked into the staring faces of those who had heard her outcry in the demure atmosphere. Were they upset that she had caused a scene in a fine hotel, or because she had expressed her views? What was her place here?

A few minutes later Chandi and his sister appeared out of the crowd. "What did we miss?" He saw her red face. "It seems there are lots of fireworks tonight, even in La Brittania Hotel. Were you in the middle of that?"

"Yes. Not the best way to meet someone," she said turning to the woman next to Chandi.

"This is my sister Lakshmi. Lakshmi meet Alethea."

Should they shake hands? Lakshmi took both her hands in hers and said, "Hello. I'm happy to meet you."

Chandi took them to a small cafe nearby, and over tea they talked about the heated conversation in the hotel lobby.

"What was it that angered you?" Lakshmi asked.

"They were talking about suttee—or I guess you could say immolation. What do women here feel about it?"

"I'm not from here."

"But is it still practiced?"

"As far as I know, not much by women of our generation, except in rural villages even though it is now illegal. Besides, what can one accomplish in the heat of a public argument with Western tourists?"

"But you're working with the health program and your woman's group to end female genital mutilation," Chandi said. "Aren't you making a political comment on the society in public places?"

Lakshmi wore glasses that were loosely fitted, and she had to keep pressing them against the bridge of her nose. The glasses did not hide her intense brown eyes when she countered, "But I'm working through the system, with people of the culture, not taking on opponents one by one. There's a difference." She turned to Alethea. "Do you know about female genital mutilation?"

"Some. I hesitate to comment because I know so little."

"I have no real certification yet, so I assist health officials. It's a practice we're helping to eradicate. It's more widespread than you might think, about 140 million worldwide and very dangerous."

"Still, it's not your tradition, Chandi argued.

"This gets complicated for me," said Alethea. Foot binding of women in China was also a tradition. But not all traditions are good for women."

"Precisely. Some of it is superstition, some of it is ignorance about women's bodies. And some of it is how men control women. This, dear brother is every woman's struggle."

"That part of it I understand," said Chandi.

"Much of the argument I hear is that western feminists are imposing their views on other cultures' practices," Alethea offered.

"Well, I'm not western, but I am a feminist. I know from experience that it's often done without anesthesia in unsterile conditions, and it causes severe pain at the time and all their lives. I can't accept anyone condoning that. And are you aware, Alethea, that it's practiced in your country?"

"Really?"

"Families who come from countries such as Nigeria, Somalia or Egypt, for example continue it in secret. You might read Nawal El Saadawi. She wrote a book on women and sex. Yes, I believe that genital mutilation is absolutely about sexual control of women."

Alethea nodded, thinking how little experience she'd had outside her narrow sphere in Santa Fe. "This is new for me, meeting people in a foreign country and talking about such matters."

"Well, I'm glad you let me go on about this."

"I appreciate your passion," said Alethea.

"Why are you here?" asked Chandi. "You don't seem like the typical tourist."

"I'm looking for someone, but I haven't been able to find her. Her family asked me to look for her, and I'm feeling the burden of wanting to be successful for their sake, as well as mine. I think I caught sight of her my first day here and just now, during the fireworks. I was standing near a wall where one of the rockets went out of control, and in its light I saw her on the wall."

"You did? What a stroke of luck."

"I tried to get through the crowd, but it was impossible."

"Are you a detective? Did she do something wrong?"

"No, no. I'm not a detective, and maybe it's me I need to find. But in the process, I'm meeting wonderful people like you." She shifted attention to them. "Who's the oldest, why are you here, and what do you do?"

They laughed at the rapid fire questions. "I'm three years older than Chandi," said Lakshmi. "I'm in a pre-medical program. I want to study immunology. However, I can study only if money can be found through a loan or scholarship."

"That's quite ambitious. And you, Chandi?"

"Juggling," he said with a mischievous grin. Alethea laughed.

"No, seriously I'm interested in the ways in which neurology affects our cognitive abilities. But like my sister, I end up juggling my studies with work in order to pay my way through school."

"I've been teaching at an elementary school until now. All I've seen of the world are Kansas and New Mexico. Those are two states in my country."

"Lakshmi's more worldly than me, said Chandi. She's traveled through Egypt, Indonesia...

"...Somalia. Places where populations practice genital mutilation." But I've not seen very much of India. What have you seen, Alethea?"

"Well, I've seen the bazaar, the consulate, and too many rich Americans."

"All work and no play," Lakshmi teased. "You'll be in no condition to find her if you don't take care of yourself and relax a bit."

"You and I have that in common," said Chandi. "We're both working hard, being too serious. Come to think of it, I have a few days of holiday coming to me. Let's go somewhere."

Alethea was surprised by his suggestion, but Lakshmi's eyes lit up. "The Taj Mahal. I've never seen the Taj Mahal. Let's go there. Who knows when any of us will return here," she said

"That's a wonderful idea. It's not far. It used to take four hours. Now I think only two or maybe more. If I arrange it as a private charter, we can go in one of the company's taxis and split the cost."

"It sounds very exciting, but I have to say that I'd feel a bit of guilt going on a personal excursion."

"You don't think the family would understand you needing a break? Doing something positive for yourself," Lakshmi said. "You can still be on the lookout for Borrasca. After all she might go there."

Alethea nodded. "That's true, and we really don't know when any of us will come back. I can be a tourist for at least a day."

"What about the day after tomorrow? Thursday. It's my day off," said Chandi.

To her great relief, something was being organized apart from the search for Borrasca. Alethea let her guard down for the first time since being in India. She had made two friends.

Back in her room her heart beat with excitement in anticipation of the excursion, and also for the cultural information coming at her. She couldn't believe how comfortable it was to be with Lakshmi and Chandi. She had come to a complex country---veils, suttee. Life here for many meant poverty. Why hadn't she or the Firestones considered how finding her in this densely populated city went against the laws of probability? That she may have seen her twice was a miracle.

Nevertheless she resolved to stay focused before the trip to Agra, and in the morning renewed her search. She tried hotels closer to the bazaar, once or twice having to walk through a line of alley dogs that tested her courage. By Wednesday, she was frustrated, feeling that she made a terrible Sherlock Holmes. The validity of the search and her values were all being brought into question. I've wandered in from the realm of the privileged, she thought. That argument with the British man was ineffectual, as Lakshmi so tactfully said. Problems wouldn't be solved that way, nor did arguing with tourists change the day-to-day wearing down most people face in the world.

If I leave without connecting to Borrasca, What will I say to you, Rose, that I may have glimpsed her my first day and then perhaps one night in the middle of a fireworks display? You want your daughter Brenda back, but something was different about her. I can't put my finger it. The old Borrasca may be gone.

She went over to the mirror hanging on the bathroom door and stared at her sun-darkened face. How had she changed? Who are you looking for? The old Alethea may be gone. Several times during the night the mirror entered her dreams. Crisp as a laser, Alethea stepped through the mirror and saw herself divide in four, then 100 parts. The one and the many. She drew back from the outer reflection. It had only the picture of Alethea with no inner being. Mirrors know only image. She had gone to the wrong oracle. In slow motion, the mirror began annealing itself into one piece again.

At 4:00 A.M. Alethea woke to see the woman falling through the sky. This time from Cade's eyes, watching the earth come towards her. She looked out the hotel window into a peaceful sky. The being that she herself hoped to fully create seemed more within reach. An interior sense of self was increasing with experience born from the interplay of thought and action. Having gone on a journey of unknowns, she was learning to create a new narrative. More than ever the questions she originally thought to ask Borrasca seemed irrelevant: I'm the woman who came to your dressing room. I was on the mesa. I saw everything. I saw nothing. Tell me what happened on your mesa? Over a sweet roll and tea she wrote letters:

Dear Laurel,

I'm in India. It's too involved to explain how I got here just now but I want to tell you how right you were. Setting off had unforeseen affects on me. I needed a way to begin the journey. I don't know who I am at this point, but I can't go back to who I was. Something else is coming for sure. I miss the sky and envy you that blue ceiling.

Alethea

The process of writing the letters came to have an effect on her much as journaling, opening up her subconscious thoughts. While writing to Mimi, it occurred to her why Borrasca had seemed different.

Dear Mimi,

I've thought of you many times. How are you? I have discouraging news. I may have seen Brenda twice, but it was always in large crowds. Once it was in a large bazaar, but I only saw a figure in white with Brenda's bearing rushing by. I tried pursuing her only to miss her. The next time it was at night during a fireworks display. I swear it was her, but she looked quite different amid the exploding lights. It was impossible to make my way through the crowd and get to her. It's frustrating to have been so close and yet so far from her. My gut feeling is that physically she's okay, but undergoing changes. Something is driving her besides grief. She might go from one place to another until she makes peace with herself.

The laws of probability strongly suggest I may not meet up with her again. That realization is very depressing. I'm trying to keep my hopes up, thinking she could be around the next corner. One day I hope I understand what the purpose of this all is. I wish you were here to talk to and to share the turn of events.

Love, Alethea

The two letters were cathartic; they finalized her decision to stay true to her mission. After the trip to the Taj Mahal, she'd look another week but then to return to the US. She went to the Hanuman Mandir temple and prowled an open-air shopping complex. She rested from the heat under shade trees in Lodhi gardens. She saw mosques and Baha'i temples, churches and Hindu temples. She made the days count for something, but was relieved when Thursday came.

They were a convivial threesome, despite the fact they knew so little about each other. Chandi was a few years younger than both women, but his wonderful sense of foolery complemented Lakshmi's serious bent of mind. Of the three, he was best suited for the role of guide, and as they motored to Agra, he answered what questions he could on the villages and sights they passed.

At the toll booths, she peered into the faces of the people. "This is quite a modern highway."

"This is the Yamuna Expressway, pretty new. They say the trip used to take much longer, but it went through more of the countryside."

"Do we cross the Ganges?"

"No, but we do see the River Yamuna."

Alethea opened the window and felt the heavy heat outside. As they moved along the stretches of the modern highway, she could see that the road removed the traffic from much of the countryside she would like to have seen. The expressway ran through Faridabad, Ballabgarh and Palwal, and so she got some sense of India as they wound their way to Agra. Many fields they went by were empty. She saw as many stray dogs as people.

She wasn't prepared for the awesome magnificence when the white marble edifice that was the Taj Mahal appeared No post card or history book had done it justice. Alethea couldn't help but be struck with the disparity of its grandeur with the poverty of Indian life she had seen.

Chandi was lit up with excitement and arranged for them to join in on a tour. The guide delivered his account in a sing song tone: "The mausoleum was built out of white marble in the 1600's by Mughal emperor Shah Johan as a memorial to his queen Mumtaz Mahal, one of his wives. This is an example of Mugnai architecture. It took 22 years to complete. Ustad Isa, a Persian Architect, is said to be the main designer and planner for this magnificent memorial. On full moon nights, the glory of the Taj Mahal is at its best."

Alethea marveled at the inlay work on the walls and the gem inlaid tomb. Splendor emanated from every room, but she agreed with Chandi who explained the cost of the lives to build the palace. Alethea looked over to Lakshmi who was intently studying a wall, her face giving no hint of her feelings.

After the tour they found a shady place to sit, and Lakshmi altered the post card perception. "It's the most beautiful thing I've ever seen, truly a monument of love. Tagore called it *a teardrop on the cheek of eternity,* but I can't help but be reminded that the palace was built on the backs of thousands of people."

"Many died during construction of the mosque," added Chandi.

"It's a marvel I've always wanted to see," said Lakshmi, "but of course, most remnants of history belonged to the rich."

""I appreciate being able to see this with you," said Alethea, "but I can't imagine how it must feel to the poor people who live near here." She looked around at the other tourists walking up to the palace, dwarfed by its immensity. They were mostly middle class. Many were American or European but there were also quite a few Indians as well. "Do you think most visitors have an awareness of the dual realities?" she asked Lakshmi.

"It's hard to generalize about people, but I think most tourists travel to see dead monuments." She pulled out a unique looking pineapple. "It's a giant Kew. Delicious. Taste it."

Between juicy bites, Alethea offered her observation of the 17th century in America. "The Puritans were settling the state of Massachusetts during the time this was being built. Maybe you've not heard of them, but they had strict moral codes and shunned almost all pleasures. There's nothing like this in my country."

"Maybe not anywhere, but I wish to add the United States to the list of places I visit. Hopefully to finish my medical studies."

Alethea nodded. "I admire your sense of purpose. I don't know what I'm doing with my life."

"You're traveling. It broadens the mind," said Chandi.

"Once," said Lakshmi, "I went to Peshewar. Do you know that place? It's near to the Khyber Pass. All Americans must know that from the movies, yes?"

"No," admitted Alethea.

"Well, it was my first holiday after being in school away from my family. I was walking alone through a section where perhaps I shouldn't have walked alone, when four beggars approached me. To them I looked wealthy. They got very mean, demanding my money. I panicked and began to make of them murderers, all manner of things. A passerby seeing my plight came and stepped in. I told him I had only my ticket home. He translated this to the men who backed off. As they left, he remarked: "Life makes beggars of some of us, but we are all victims.""

"It was then that I understood how money estranges us from each other. They needed to beg to survive, and I had assumed they would rape me or kill me. It got me to questioning the way money makes us perceive ourselves and others in the world."

"I would have succumbed to stereotypes if Chandi hadn't spoken honestly to me that first day," Alethea said. "Such a narrow view of the other we get. As it was, I had to fight my fear of being the only white woman in the bazaar. The throng of people closed in on me till I was sure I would be crushed."

"Racial biases seem to be part of nationalism," said Chandi. "We have the same problem in Srinagar. Constant struggles between Pakistan and India. Muslims and Hindus. We must make true connections to people. Certainly India is as much her people as it is this." He swept his hands over the scene.

"It's a shame to be so close and not see Itmad-ul-Daulah's Tomb, also in Agra. Smaller than this, but they say the white marble inlay work is even more exquisite. Yes, another tomb—we don't intend to bury you here," laughed Lakshmi. "It says here it was constructed by a woman Nur Johann in memory of her father Ghiasud-Din-Beg."

As they got in the car, the pale sun was lost in a haze above the monument. It looked like smoke. Chandi started to turn onto the highway only to be stopped by a man with medical emergency insignias. He looked at Alethea's American face and said, "Please exit the other way. There's been an explosion that has set off fires."

"Medical personnel," said Lakshmi. She pulled out an identification card. Alethea's first instinct was to go in the opposite direction. Lakshmi gave her no time to panic.

"There's very little water here to fight fires, and they'll need people to care for those burned or injured. You can wait here if you like."

"They might need my help, too," Alethea found herself saying.

As they turned into the village, they heard the sound of another explosion. A billowing wall of yellow flame churning with orange was rolling towards them at a speed which took her breath away. Hundreds of people, appearing like small stick figures against a mushroom cloud, were racing to stay in front of it. The car braked to a halt. Villagers ran by pressing against the car, making it impossible for Alethea to open the door. Chandi forcibly open the door and pulled her out.

They joined the swarm of people running to get out of the path of the fire which had turned the crowns of the trees into a conflagration. Alethea stumbled over the body of a man lying face down. She turned him over and saw that his face had been torn away. She froze, unable to move. Chandi saw her horror-struck face and grabbed her arm, and they continued running. A man carrying a singed mattress was in front of them followed by two little screaming girls. A piece of burning bark flew through the air and landed on one of the girls, igniting her dress in flames. She became hysterical, running, fueling the blaze.

"Stop," cried Althea. She pulled her down, rolling her on the ground until the flame was smothered. Then Alethea caught her up in her arms and ran till they were safely out of the path of the fire, comforting her until the frantic father came to get her. Alethea translated his unknown words as gratitude at finding his daughter alive. Lakshmi spoke to him in Hindi and reassured him.

Lakshmi took charge. To Alethea she yelled, "We'll make this a triage area." Alethea responded working side by side with Chandi in the intense heat, applying gauze and salve as Lakshmi directed. She looked up several times to see Lakshmi covering one body, applying cold compresses on another's eyes to soothe them from the smoke. On either side of them a long line of people were passing buckets of water. The sparse number of trees allowed them to contain the fire.

People came to express their appreciation, bringing water for the three of them. "Good work," said Lakshmi putting her arms around her brother and Alethea. "I'm proud of you, Alethea. You saved that little girl from being seriously burned."

"Back there, I saw the face of a dead man that I couldn't get out of my mind. I wasn't going to let death claim that little girl. It was your decisiveness, Lakshmi, that made me so determined." In her mind she remembered Kurt Demming's remarks about what people do for life.

In the car on the way back, the dark was welcome after the intense glare of the fire, Alethea contemplated how it hadn't been a mistake to come. If only because I could help here, she thought. If only because I've found two beings I otherwise would never have met. It's like blindfolds have been lifted. My perceptions of others and myself are changing. The search for Borrasca had not been in vain.

To them she simply said, "Truth has a way of presenting itself when you're least looking for it." Lakshmi nodded caught in her own thoughts. Perhaps all people were illusion makers. She would have to sort out again what had happened on the mesa to see what was real and what was the function of her limited perceptions.

The woman who has been shadowing you will leave, Borrasca. May your pain also go away.

TWENTY

It wasn't wrong to come to Dharamsala. This was as suitable a stopping place as any other. She hoisted herself up on a large rock and relaxed in the warm sun, awash in the heat radiating off the rock. It was exquisite relief after the cold of the monastery. The heat prickled on her skin producing a fragrance that reminded her of Santa Fe. At last—memory allowed for a range of images, and one remembrance did not overshadow all the others. She closed her eyes to meditate, but life tugged at her. From this vantage point, she could see the community as it went about its life.

The people in the village of McLeod Ganja in the upper reaches of the Kanga Valley were part of the Tibetan Diaspora. A people in exile had found a spiritual resting place among Himalayan Cedars that had become known as *Little Lhasa,* after the capital of the Tibetan Autonomous Region. It was a sanctuary where they could follow their customs and teachings, their religious observances, and be safe. Many still hoped one day to return to Tibet. Similar to the law of return, which was the right of Jews to return and take four steps in Israel. Similar to the Palestinians who vow to return to their original land.

She had originally planned to stay longer with Dorje's friends, but by the time she arrived she was already in different space than she had been when she had made the plans. It was time to move from the security of a protected community and make the transition into secular life. This was a safe haven for now, but she'd stay only until she was ready to be on her own.

Her rock was outside the clinic of a woman doctor known for her herbal healing treatments. A stream of people entered, many of them in traditional scarlet and gold robes. One woman came with her weight resting on the elbow of a younger man. An hour later she emerged, walking with just a cane, her body radiating strength. She shuffled by her rock and unexpectedly looked up into Borrasca's eyes. The exchange was silent. The silence expanded; the healing filtered into Borrasca who held her clear gaze until the woman walked off.

She wondered if the doctor had been born here or had fled from Tibet. Strange how some people remain in one geographic place their whole life and others are forced away from their point of origin. Dorje had left the monastery to go to school. Did he ever miss the United States or yearn to return to Tibet? He kept to the role he had been trained for since he was a young boy. Others have to change all their lives to survive. Her father had been an apprentice tailor in Europe prior to Hitler. Now he was a semi-retired accountant living in New York, buying fresh bagels every Sunday morning. What mattered? Dorje used the term "outside illusion," the idea that one appeared to change outer form, but something of the inner essence, certain tendencies, remained the same. For Jews, the world was a different place after the Holocaust and many of them were significantly changed. What of herself had fully changed?

A woman walked by carrying one child on her back and leading a second child by the hand while clutching a load of wood. Although the world was changing for women, the winds of change were slow coming to this mother. A cluster of values existed in women's communities not always parallel to the conventional world. Was that a transient illusion?

So while the internal dialogues had not gone away, today they had a rational flavor. Borrasca could follow a train of thought inside herself, yet still be attentive to the rest of life. She moved between worlds with a greater degree of ease and control, her mind able to analyze and not be overwhelmed by her emotions. Buddhists read *The Tibetan Book of the Dead* or The *Path to Bliss by* the Dalai Lama. New age folks read holographic physics and marveled at how it resembled Buddhist thought. Citing ancient records gave an aura of truth to beliefs. Few, she noted, referred to matriarchal records many of which had been destroyed. Women often had to survive on their own terms outside the saving illusions.

Failure to change results in frozen lives. Frozen vision. Death. Even as we speak one word we have changed. And when all the word are spoken, you will have become another aspect of your self.

The words from Cade filled her with hope. Singer, are you there? No voice came to her. No melody. The Bejay persona had faded. Borrasca is here, she reflected, and tomorrow I'll be somewhere else.

She stood on a platform the next day waiting as the train to New Delhi jerked its way to a stop in front of her. Only a handful of other people were boarding. There was flicker of genetic memory—she was getting on a train. Her parents had each ridden a train to the camps. Walking down a narrow aisle, she found a seat near a window as the train pitched her forward in her seat and then flung her back, as it moved out of the station into the light of an intense sun. The low talk among the passengers seemed different from public babble in America.

The temperature shot up. Heat trickled down her stomach which was covered by the shapeless clothes she had thrown on, the way she had draped herself at the retreat. She looked around at the other people, mostly Indian, some dressed in secular clothes, some in white in sharp contrast to the gold and burgundy robes at the monastery. She was aware of how disembodied she had been.

A welcome breeze came through either end of the cars. As they moved into the interior of India, the hot weather allowed her to focus on her body instead of her thoughts. At the end of the day, she took that body off the train at New Delhi and found it safe lodging, a small room set back in a narrow alley which the taxi driver had assured her would be safe. Her room was on the second floor with a bathroom shared by six other people. She fell into bed; the excursion back into the world had exhausted her.

The next morning, with renewed energy, she was eager to explore, setting out early from the hotel before the intense heat set in. It became quickly apparent that the heart of this section of the city was the Chadni Chowk bazaar. She spent the morning amid thousands of people streaming in and merchants calling out their wares. She loved how in the middle of the clamor, artisans sat quietly on mats absorbed in crafting things. Others moved through the bazaar begging. There were booths selling pungent curries containing asafetida and other exotic spices. She had heard that every section of India had its own curry. The first day the heat soon enfeebled her; she returned to the hotel, but it was only slightly cooler.

Over several days, she took to going to the bazaar in the early morning and again in the evening when it was cooler and found a place from which to observe the bustling activity. In one stall she observed a young boy painstakingly hammering a silver leaf until it was thin to the point of translucence. He hammered nearly a hundred blows without stopping. From a small portion of the pounded filigree, he fashioned a fragile ornament, which he carefully placed on display in front of him to sell. But most of the thin silver he wrapped and laid carefully in a box. He noticed her watching. Over the course of several days he began to look for her.

Trying to figure out what he did with the silver he put in the box was only part of the intrigue for Borrasca. There was this: to observe a being doing the same repetitive act day after day. What happened to a human who sat in the same spot in the bazaar, day in, day out? All his life. Did it make him a different being than she who was chameleon-like? What was the relationship between constancy and change and what was the essential that remained?

They developed a curious, silent relationship over the course of a few days. Perhaps he regarded his daily routine as a work meditation just as watching him served as her own meditation. She gestured at him: what do you do with the leaves of silver you put in the box?

He smiled at her, his stoic work expression gone. He tapped on the shoulder of a vendor sitting cross-legged near him and said a volley of words. The man nodded and spoke to Borrasca: "Medical," he said.

"For medical purposes?" inquired Borrasca hoping for more than a one word response.

"He sells it to hospitals."

"What is she doing," pointing to the elderly woman whose back seemed permanently bent, working an 8-inch brush over the floor of the stall. "Dust washer," he said. "She makes money collecting the silver dust and remnants."

She nodded, not understanding why hospitals needed silver. But it was enough to know that, and knowing, she was free to move.

One day as she prowled the bazaar she felt an odd sensation on the back of her neck. She turned, half expecting to see someone she knew. No one was recognizable in the crowd. Her gaze fell on a chapatti merchant dwarfed by two large pots resting on her hibachi like stove. Pots that were never empty.

The strange force came again, turning her in a circle several times thinking to see the presence of a particular person. The movement of her white robe was the only breeze in the incandescent heat. Her most vivid sensation was of wind propelling her forward. The movement made her feel faint. She stopped and grabbed on to a tent pole to keep from falling, the color draining from her face.

With that strange occurrence, something shifted. Borrasca's inclination to remain in New Delhi vanished. On the way back to her room, the small alley dogs, for whom she was by now a familiar scent, wagged their tails, too hot to move in the heat. She ran up the flight of stairs into her tiny room. There was a comfort in having a small, defined space with the curtain closed to keep out the heat.

She pulled out maps from her suitcase and sat down in the middle of the floor. Her restless fingers led her eyes across the maps, following the routes that led ever westward from the Bay of Bengal through Afghanistan and the Black Sea until her eyes came to rest on the furthest edge of the map. Was she really leaving? She threw open her pack and pulled out more maps, piling them around her, amused at the randomness of her life. She was tempted to close her eyes and pick a place by chance, but random did not mean chaos. Nor did she need to maintain a schedule, as it had been when she traveled from city to city touring with the band. One city had looked like another in those days. She might as well have gone nowhere; maybe that's exactly what she did.

Today the mental landscape did not overtake the physical landscape. She could bring order into her life and still be open to the random twists of fate. Change was in the wind, and she was not panicked. But if there was clarity today, she knew confusion might also return. Best to make a decision while direction was a choice. She scanned the maps, imagining herself crossing the continents. Take a train again? That would be all right, but where?

Her finger inched along moving in a westerly direction. The Baltic States, Yugoslavia, Austria. Germany—can this Jew go to Germany? What would Rose and Louis think? What were they doing right now? The thought rubbed against her bones. She had let them down. They deserved better.

During Kol Nidre services one year the Rabbi at the temple had said, "Families should strive to keep singing." There was much about organized religion that Borrasca had grown to distrust, but in her house, part of being Jewish was singing. It was from Rose that the singing came. She had sung with Borrasca throughout her childhood, teaching her the special prayers and songs for Friday night shabbos and the holidays. There had been no son to learn the traditions, so Borrasca had asked the four questions during the Seders. She had learned the Hatikvah before she learned the Star Spangled Banner. Luckily she hadn't needed to say the Kaddish prayer for her mother. Only for Cade.

A memory of Cade came into the room, the maps sprawled all around the floor. The train of free association led to Cade's mother. They'd had one of the most special mother daughter relationships. Why were mothers never portrayed as vital, creative beings like her or Rose. They were too often pictured as a generation with habits and ways of being which stood between them and their daughters. Cade had told her that she'd never known her mother as old. Marjory Kincaid Maris had left college while in her sophomore year, already three months pregnant to marry the man who was Cade's father. The child who was born in her 19th year was to share that youth. Cade came in the spring, and each spring her mother found herself revitalized. There were two other children, but it was Cade and Marjory who were the creatures of spring. Cade, who had been named Stella Kincaid Maris, hated the name Stella. Early on she took to referring to herself with her mother's maiden name: Kincaid. When that proved too long, it became Cade.

By the time Cade was starting school, her mother had come to her first quarter century. When she was 10, her mother crossed over to 30. She never, according to Cade, acted as if growing up was a decaying process. In fact, as her children grew older and left her house, there was a lightness of being about her. Whatever connection Marjory had to the other siblings, she and Cade remained the original twosome who could talk intimately to each other, Cade about school, and going from a girl to a woman. Cade's mother was hungry to talk.

When she was nearly 20, her mother was double her age and wondering what women do after motherhood. When Cade went to college, Marjory contemplated returning for her degree. She wondered what happened when sex and desire ebbed for married couples. Did it have to mean a drifting apart? Marjory knew whatever passed as passion with her husband had long since gone, and friendship was what she shared with Cade.

Cade had appeared her at house one morning wakening Borrasca with a violet, a very particular violet. She recounted a special memory of her mother sitting at the kitchen table with her, a violet plant sitting between them, a profusion of lavender buds. A dreaminess appeared in her mother's eyes. Cade wanted to tell her mother about a woman she was becoming attracted to, but she couldn't find her way to the words. The violet represented all the wonder she could ever hope to express. One day they'd talk, but it was still too new for Cade to articulate. One month later, Marjory was stricken with a sharp pain and within six weeks she died.

With a cringe, Borrasca realized that Cade had not even lived to be her mother's age. Cade was dead. They'd never again sit with a violet between them. I'll never see her again, never hold her. Borrasca sat on the floor, the maps forgotten, allowing herself to feel the part of her that had died with Cade, the heart break that she had run from as much as guilt. Borrasca let herself grieve in a way she hadn't been able to in Santa Fe or at the monastery. Time had worked as Dorje said it would, eroding the edge of terror. She had let memories of Cade enter and had not crumbled from the sadness even though the amnesia about what had really happened that day had yet to lift.

Somewhere on a back street in India, she stopped looking over her shoulder for someone who might be following her. If a crystal was the connector between spirals, maybe Cade had become a crystal. Cade would have appreciated that her life and death were intrinsic to the very pattern she had tried to describe in her life's work. But how did flesh alchemize to crystal? Cade was still flesh to her. Warm skin. Warm embrace.

TWENTY-ONE

IN THE FIFTH SECOND
O Western wind
when wilt thou blow
That the small rain down can rain
Christ that my love were in my arms
and I in my bed again.

She loved that old English ballad
and loved it when Borrasca would recite it to her
Borrasca, where are you?
Am I alone for good now?
It ought to be night
when suicides step off bridges
Ernestine, are you flying with me?
Where did you go?
I remember a morning at 3:00 A.M.
You had tried to go cold turkey
and were crouching over the toilet
the alcohol betraying you.
Saliva dripped from your lips
but you were too weak to wipe it away
I knelt down besides you
and washed your face with a cold towel
Even in your stupor, Ernestine
you felt my presence
Above us, the naked bathroom light bulb

dangled from a long cord
It swayed as we knelt by the toilet
a soft whoosh in the early morning silence
The shadows in the room danced with the cord
I felt meaning creep along the shadows with the light
a meaning that did not explain itself
The ceramic tile we sat on sent waves of
cold through my joints.
There was weariness in my stomach.
You leaned over to me:
"No one's showed me such compassion."
You slurred the word 'showed'
The liquor had left you vulnerable
but nothing detracted from your dignity
We sat holding each other on the cold floor.
It was when we stood to leave
and I saw the swinging light bulb,
that I gleaned the gist of what crept along
the shadows with the light.
I couldn't let myself be vulnerable with other people
I could handle admiration, but never pity
Unlike you, Ernestine, I'd never be so direct
My body had yet to fail me in front of others
What was it the doctor suggested
No, he didn't suggest, he declared
it was progressive ALS.
Slow developing. That was a year ago
No one was the slightest bit suspicious yet
Some days I could hardly tell
There was no signal from the body
that it might cease to function one day
That diagnosis helped my work fall into place
The world was atrophying

and I was going to live out the theorem
Others would watch as the disease gained control.
I would see myself unravel against time
And wind.
Oh... Western wind.
Oh...Borrasca

TWENTY-TWO

On the way back to New Delhi, Alethea considered how it had taken a trip half way around the world to see that she was the quarry as much as Borrasca. The journey had taken her out of the usual patterns and Lakshmi and Chandi's friendship clarified some of her perceptions. Lakshmi, quiet and soft spoken, had proven to be very wise, at variance with the narrow traditions Alethea had grown up in which did not confer wisdom on women, especially women from other countries.

When it came time to say good-bye, she stood before Chandi, their faces and arms smeared black from smoke. "We make quite a picture. One I won't forget," she said. She hugged Chandi several times, "I can't possibly express my appreciation."

Lakshmi's thin arms wrapped her in a warm embrace. Alethea was unprepared for such a display of affection. Her view of women was constantly being challenged, but her body understood instinctively. She threw both arms around Lakshmi and felt the warmth of their bodies running down the front of hers. Lakshmi finally pulled away saying, "You are a very special—and smoky woman, Alethea. You've changed my views of American women."

Alethea laughed. "This time has meant so much to me. I'll write if you will. I'll write even if you don't."

"I will," Lakshmi promised. "Our connection will embolden me to go to school in your country. I don't want to lose contact with you."

Their touch stayed with her long after they were gone. Alethea was lonely with a sense of self that was new to her. She went through the motions of packing and finalizing her return flight even while continuing to look for Borrasca. Tentative questions about what she would do with her life flitted in and out of her mind. She held up a shirt in front of the mirror, then stood with her hands on her hips. What the mirror told her today was that her body was pleasing in its roundness. It wasn't her weight as much as her attitude about her size that distanced her from others. Mimi and Lakshmi and Chandi accept me for who I am. I'm the one who bought into the Twiggy illusion. Cade and Borrasca represent what full women can be in the world as do Lakshmi and Mimi. The distance between where she was and who she wanted to be was a leap of consciousness she could make. She went out for her last dinner in India at a small restaurant on a quiet back street. A young boy came around to each table with sand paintings he had made, each of a different god. "This is Shiva," he said. The figure was intricately composed of minute sand particles. He also sold little cards with sayings from the Buddha, including one that interested her:

We are what we think
All that we are arises with our thoughts.
With our thoughts we make the world.

Alethea smiled as she handed him coins for the card. Back in her room, with several hours to go before her flight, she propped herself up on the bed and read more of Cade's book.

The arrangement of material invited the reader to jump around from one section to another, following a train of thought rather than chapters. Her eyes came to rest on a page: *There is a duality in the world. As soon as we have reflections on experience, we are separated from experience. Gravity is the most measurable means of demonstrating there cannot be a singularity in the world, for to have gravity, one thing must be inextricably drawn to another. Two things. A field. Not, as Stephen Hawking has tried to show: a singularity, a point that is fantastically, infinitely small, a theoretical edge to space and time. Hawking asserts that all matter races towards that point, sucked in through a black hole. It is necessary to see the social consequences of such thought. In a singular world, there is prime cause, first cause. A one which began and begat. Men have always assumed that all matter rushes to this point, and they call it God.*

She skipped to another section:

Women must take responsibility for describing the universe themselves and understanding it spiritually and scientifically. Creation has always been our function, and now we must create new descriptions of the universe. It does not have to be in opposition to the men, as in death to the loser. It only has to be. In one world, the black holes increase. In another description they disappear.

Alethea closed the book. Cade's dense style required concentration, making it impossible to read much of the thin volume in one sitting. She'd woven a combination of science, philosophy and controversial social thought. The book stretched her mind to understand and to synthesize, but foremost, it left her sad. The woman who had written these words was dead. If she lived she most certainly would have made other contributions to the world. Maybe Cade had fallen to a final understanding of the universe.

Months after her death, Alethea found herself grieving for her. She was a body of matter who had drawn sustenance from other stars, and now one of the stars was dead. Alethea felt the loss of Cade and was able to appreciate the deep despair Borrasca had succumbed to. She mourned for all three of them.

TWENTY-THREE

IN THE SIXTH SECOND
Cade fell away from her bond to Borrasca,
from the planet.
She was alone.
The earth was coming up to meet her
and terror struck.
She wanted to return as part of the natural spiral.
But what if death was an endless nothingness?

Never to see Borrasca again.
Or make love again.
The first time we made love—
Borrasca brought me to a plane no one ever had.
When our breasts touched,
the thinnest veil of skin separated us.
my whole body vibrated,
and like that I floated free.

Death, are you out there? Is it time?
Do you have a voice, and will you sing to me--
I used to think when Borrasca was singing,
it was the Goddess crooning in all her tongues.
Goddess, call to me now
May the voices be with me
I am grateful in this second not to be afraid.

TWENTY-FOUR

As the train crossed the border into Germany, the landscape was barely visible in the grey dawn. The train emitted a plaintive whistle as it entered the black mouth of the mountain, plunging Borrasca into the darkness of the tunnel. When they came out the other side, Borrasca became more aware of the two people across from her, a very old woman and a young boy. He could not have been her son; there were too many years between them. He showed her deference, even seemed a little too responsible for his young age. She noted his blond Aryan looks. The old woman's dark eyes set on a wrinkled face did not offer any hint of lineage. All of them looked out the windows into the grey morning light.

The continuous rain of the night before had let up, but the dampness settled on her shoulders and on a landscape lush and green with the moisture. The gloom did not herald spring. What prevailed was the heaviness of a morning at 6:00 AM when day and night have not their sharp divisions. The rain induced a lethargy in the passengers who preferred the warmth of their blankets to waking.

There were few towns on this stretch of track. Occasionally a farm appeared with square paneled fields spread across the land and brown cows grazing. No people were visible at this hour. Borrasca wondered whether this had been a route for the trains which had taken people to the death camps.

The woman bent over and asked the boy something in muted tones. He got up and left.. Borrasca and the old woman sat in their rumpled clothes with sleep still calling amid the train's cadence against the tracks.

Borrasca looked over and found the woman watching her. She held her gaze with a friendly countenance. Was there anything they could find to say in their various languages?

"Guten Morgan." The woman's voice echoed in the grey dawn. Schlafen? Did you sleep well?"

"Yes," answered Borrasca tentatively. "And you?" She bowed her head deferentially, out of force of habit acquired at the monastery.

"I don't sleep much anymore. The young need it. The old are afraid of it. And the wary."

"What are you wary of?"

"Germany. I am always guarded here." Before she could explain the young boy returned with a tray of coffee and three cups. Borrasca searched through her string ficelle bag and found the sweet rolls she had purchased at the border to share with them. The three sat drinking and eating in punctuated silence. Several times Borrasca tried to initiate conversation again, but the sentences led nowhere in the day of no sun.

An hour or so later, the boy and the woman spoke and once again he left the car. As soon as he had gone, the woman turned to her and began where she had left off.

"I was here in Germany over half a century ago. I did not ever intend to return." Her right hand trembled on the tray in front of her, but it did not minimize the regal bearing of her posture.

Borrasca sought for words to urge her on, afraid the boy would come back and the stony silence would return: "Why is that?"

"Would you return to a scene of death?"

The question held double entendres for Borrasca. There had been flowers, las flores de la quebrada, she remembered, and white clouds against a deep blue sky. Cade fell through that sky.

The boy opened the door to the compartment, rendering a tomb-like stillness again. Why could they not speak with him present? And what irony that the conversation halted with her remembering the scene of Cade's death and no way to move beyond it. Borrasca sat dumb as a stone on the mesa, the past stealing into the bleak morning. When the train reached Berlin, Borrasca collected her luggage. The woman extended her hand and Borrasca took it, half expecting to see concentration camp numbers branded on the woman, but the long black sleeves of her dress covered her arms down to her palms.

Once on the platform, she hesitated, not wanting to lug her things around until she decided which hotel to check into. She disposed of all but her shoulder pack in a locker, and free of their weight, walked into the grey mist which had become a steady rain. She walked the cobble stone streets resigned to being wet while all around her people scurried, heads bent against the sheeting rain. When she saw a public library, she darted in to find a restroom. In the stall there was graffiti on the back of the door. She tried using her limited German to get a hint of what had been scrawled there. There was no missing the intent. A swastika. When the band had toured here last year, she remembered there had been several incidents of violence involving skinheads. The hate on the walls pushed her out into the rain, but the weather prevailed on her to find a dry place.

At a bank she cashed in dollars for Euros. There was still a small source of money from the sale of her Volvo and royalties that would last another few months. She took out her address book and scanned it for the names of women that had come from concert connections. No, she wouldn't re-enter the world as Bejay Storm. On a hunch she went back to the library to use a phone book. When she saw the word *Gaia,* she wrote down the address.

On the outside, the bar reminded her of the Spiral Shell. Its neon sign was obscure, maybe intentionally. The neon no longer worked, adding to the invisibility of the bar. Perfect, thought Borrasca. The sign underlined her belief that there was a connection between lesbians being invisible in the world and the psychic phenomenon of the hidden, the occult.

She stood at the entrance until her eyes adjusted to the darkness. The walls and fixtures were painted in primary yellow and purple, giving off an inviting ambiance. She took a seat at one end of the bar, adjusting herself to a stool that was too far off the floor for her legs. The bartender had blond hair cropped short and busy hands that were washing glasses. She didn't look up until every glass was clean, but she came to Borrasca with a smile. After months of not drinking, Borrasca wasn't sure what her body could tolerate. A glass of white wine? She ordered a Perrier. The woman brought her the drink and left Borrasca to herself.

For a time, there were only four other women in the place: the woman behind the bar, two women who sat at a table in the corner, their arms wrapped around each other, and a fourth woman who sat at the other end of the bar, lost in her own thoughts. It stayed that way for nearly an hour until working women began coming in after their jobs. The atmosphere shifted with the evening scene. The ones near her at the bar were friendly but not imposing, leaving her to her corner. She was pleased at the anonymity, happy to be among women. No one recognized her though she had performed here the previous summer. She ran her fingers through her hair which was still cropped short, her chin hairs still plucked. The one who was usually in the spotlight liked the view from the sidelines.

When the jukebox got louder, and the empty spaces began to diminish, Borrasca knew it was time to leave. Soon she'd need to test herself among other women to know how she'd handle relationships. Today she needed only the solace of being on the periphery of a woman's space.

She found a gasthaus, with a small room and a shared bathroom, talking to no one but the bustling woman who ran the accommodation. Borrasca began a routine: she rose late, walking the city until afternoon, went to the bar, and then returned in the dark to her room. Recurring faces became familiar, especially those of the older Germans who would have been alive during Hitler's time. What she found was a seriousness that could be explained by a week of solid rain.

There was, however, no mistaking an undercurrent of hostility one morning as she stood at a flower stall a few blocks from the boarding

172

house. It was run by a gruff man who seemed out of place with flowers. On the other side of the street were four people of color, one of them a child, also selling flowers from a movable cart that they were wheeling through the streets. A woman who had been shopping in the flower stall crossed the street and headed for the flower cart. The proprietor began screaming at her. The woman stopped in the middle of the street and screamed back at him. A crowd gathered and immediately began siding with the man, raising their hands at her and the flower vendors on the other side of the street. One word kept repeating: Romani. Though she wasn't sure what the word meant, in her gut Borrasca knew the confrontation was about racism. The man in the flower stall was pointing at his license. The crowd continued yelling until the police came and forced the vendors to disperse.

She headed for the bar, feeling shaky. When she ordered a glass of white wine instead of mineral water, the woman tending bar noticed.

"Switching drinks, are you?"

Borrasca smiled. "How nice you can remember what your customers order."

"Many of my customers are friends. How is it for you, traveling in Germany alone?" she asked.

"Fine. Well, not really. Today I'm beginning to feel somewhat unsafe. Tell me what does word Romani mean?"

"Gypsy, but the people refer to themselves as Romani. You saw something?" Borrasca related the incident to her.

"I wish I could say it was only punks. It seems most of the neo-Nazis are young men, but in general there's more discrimination of every kind. There are violent incidences against Turks and North Africans who immigrating here, and still much anti-Semitism. They're defacing headstones in cemeteries. Sure, there's economic problems, but to me it's the old Aryan line. Veiled, you know, as if it were protectionism for jobs."

"I feel safe in here with women."

"You know, you'd have a more balanced view of Germany if you met lesbians as well as strangers, but you don't come at night when you could meet more women."

"It's true."

The bar tender studied her eyes, her fingers tapping the glass. "My name is Else." She offered her hand. "What did you say your name was?"

"Borrasca."

Else saw the tentativeness about her, something not quite steady. It could be cultural shock. She asked her as much.

"Certainly there's some of that. The truth is that emotionally I'm having a hard time right now."

"Happens to all of us at one time or another. It's not easy if you also happen to be in a new country. Have you liked anything here, besides the bar?"

"I spent some time at the Deutsches Technikmuseum. Quite wonderful."

There's also a memorial for the Holocaust not too far from here."

Borrasca looked directly at her. "That's partly why I am here, to discover what it means to be a Jewish woman in Germany today. But I feel a bit unsure about being a Jew here."

"I'd say you're right to be guarded about who you talk with. If you ask me, the older ones have a guilt they haven't resolved. You can't talk to some of them about it. They aren't any more candid with me than they'd be with you. Much of that whole generation seems unreal to me. Even some my age--I'm 52, and you?"

"41." Else's stream of words buoyed Borrasca's spirits even though her description of events was alarming. She was a German not afraid to be critical of her country.

"I like to think among lesbians you will find more willingness to discuss issues openly."

"Six millions Jews were killed in the war, which is unfathomable to me. I'm grateful my parents survived. But I'm curious to find out what

Germany is really like in the 21st century. Not in any accusing way, mind you. I'm drawn to find out what the truth is for me. It says something about me as much as Germany, and my connection to my own history."

"You know, my friend Gabriele can help you more than me. She's a Jewish woman with a wealth of history. I get off work in half an hour. Why don't we go see her?"

Borrasca found herself seated in an old Audi that wound its way through narrow streets. "Else, I didn't expect conversation to get so heavy right away."

"Don't apologize. It beats the shallow talk I often get in the bar."

The car headed out of the central part of the city towards an area where residential houses were mixed with small shops. Lining both sides of the street were buildings in close rows, with businesses on the first floor and living spaces above. Gabriele was two flights up. Borrasca caught her breath as they waited for her to answer their knock.

"Else."

A tall woman with streaks of grey in her hair came to the door. She gave Else a bear hug, and they immediately engaged with each other, speaking rapidly in German. Finally they turned to Borrasca, apologizing for keeping her waiting.

"Borrasca, this is Gabriele."

Gabriele had penetrating green eyes, and Borrasca could not hold their gaze. She took in the rest of her. The sharp swath of white that ran the length of her long hair on the right side. The slight scar above the left eyebrow, which twisted and forced the observer back to her eyes. Borrasca could think of nothing to say in front of those eyes. The three stood there until the silence became awkward. "You do speak English, don't you?" teased Gabriele.

Borrasca laughed. "Of course. Hello."

Their eyes continued to find each other, and Else felt the air drawn from the room. She recognized the source of the energy immediately. Gabriele ushered them into her modest apartment. Paintings in bright primary colors hung on the walls, with striking poses of women, many of them with round bodies. Their faces had been intentionally drawn with exaggerated cheekbones nearly forcing the viewer to peer over them to see the eyes. These portraitures hung in no particular order along with posters of marches and demonstrations. The room was a visual treat after the monastery. She wanted to keep staring at them.

Gabriele ushered them into the room, the desk strewn with papers and books, sets of pastel crayons and a pile of photographs. Gabriele quickly gathered up books from a chair and motioned for them to sit.

"No," said Else. I'd prefer to go home and recuperate from work. I'll let the two of you talk. The Gilde Strasse bus is a block from here and takes you right back to your guesthouse, if you feel safe doing that."

Borrasca nodded and Else said, "Ciao."

Borrasca was left alone with Gabriele, feeling vulnerable, realizing in that instant how she'd previously hidden behind her bushy head of hair. She self-consciously ran her hand through the short nappy. She of the glib tongue felt herself reddening in the silence.

"Feeling shy?" asked Gabriele.

"I haven't been with lesbians—anyone—in a social situation for several months. Guess I've lost the art of small talk. I'm assuming you're a lesbian."

"Of course. I'm Else's friend, aren't I? And you can see my posters and art work."

"A very distinctive style. I like that the women are not all thin and that you create. many different planes in a picture."

"How wonderful you can see a style. I'm just beginning to call myself as an artist. Else said that I might have information for you."

"I was nervous about coming to Germany as a Jewish woman. I'm curious about how Jewish women who live here feel about it?"

"For myself, I know what I think, but there's a wide range of response. No two people react the same. I have access to materials that might be of interest to you, but I don't know if I can put my finger on something right now."

"Well, let's meet again when you have a chance to look."

"You don't have to go so soon. You just got here." Borrasca was already standing, her anxiety at being in a room with this woman had propelled her to her feet. It might seem abrupt to Gabriele, but for Borrasca, engaging with two women in one day was progress.

"I can give you a ride."

"No. Thank you. I'll take the bus."

"Tomorrow I'll go through my files for you. Will you come for tea Saturday afternoon?"

Borrasca edged toward the door. "If I can find my way back here. Where am I?"

Gabriele grinned. "I'll draw a map so you can't lose your way."

"I couldn't possibly lose my way," repeated Borrasca to herself as she walked down the stairs.

Over the next few days, Borrasca went to the Jewish Museum. The interior architecture was intentionally disorientating and baffled her. There were dimly lit areas. Passage ways which zigged and zagged, recreating the stark physical sense of the Holocaust and the Jews' history in Germany. Aware of the potential for discomfort, she looked at historical displays from the time of Frederick the Great, Moses Mendelssohn and the period of Jewish Enlightenment. Even then Mendelssohn had to be granted the status of "Jew under extraordinary protection." There was much history that she had never learned, and she could take in only so much at a time.

On Saturday the bus took her to Gabriele's in 15 minutes. Next time, if it wasn't raining, she could walk. Next time. She had to get through today.

"Let me take your rain coat."

Borrasca was glad to remove the damp layer, but with it off, she felt guarded. Gabriele saw her tense. Maybe, she thought, the woman hasn't known many lesbians.

"Borrasca sat in the chair nearest the desk. Sitting felt easier.

"You're wound pretty tight. Are you not a lesbian or did you recently come out?"

Borrasca howled at her comment. "Oh no!"

"What's so funny?"

"I've been out longer than you'd ever imagine." They both laughed. Borrasca heard the sound of walls breaking around her and breathed easily into the open space of laughter. Gabriele had instinctively gotten them onto a topic which universally invited familiarity between women.

"How long?"

The impulse to hold back rose in her, only to be driven back by the brightness in Gabriele's eyes. "Well, it began when Sara McElvoy sat next to me in the third grade and we held hands during recess."

"Ah, that is early."

"Then her parents moved away. I was heart broken. But in Junior High School, I went to summer camp, and guess who showed up as one of my tent mates?"

"Sara McElvoy." Gabriele answered.

"It was a glorious summer. Swimming. Sneaking under the blankets at night. Hugging and kissing. Telling our deepest secrets. After that summer, we never saw each other again. But of course I've never forgotten her."

How quickly she had jumped in and talked about relationships. They were already on familiar ground. She wanted to back out and run for cover. Gabriele blocked the chance.

"You still don't say how you came to be with your first woman lover?" Gabriele noticed that Borrasca had paused and seemed to go far away. "You can't stop in the middle of the story."

Borrasca sucked in her breath. After all, telling your coming out story was a lesbian ritual, and Gabriele was enjoying it.

"Only if you promise to tell me yours." Gabriele raised her eyebrows in promise.

"In college," Borrasca continued, "I didn't have the nerve to do anything. You know, lack of information. But right after graduation, friends and I headed to LA—Los Angeles—to be in a rock and roll band. Borrasca wanted to take back the words. She could reveal too much.

"Yes? Gabriele prompted, seeing Borrasca again retreat. "You okay?"

"It's nothing."

"Look, perhaps it's too personal for having just met." She was letting her off the hook; Borrasca could change the subject. This is a safe place. Relax, she told herself.

"And miss the chance to hear your story? No way. Once I got to the West Coast, I went to the Women's Building in LA. and saw books and exhibits that turned my mind upside down. And I met a woman there. Glory Jacobs. Pardon the pun, but one glorious night we went to bed. That was it for me." Surely Gabriele wouldn't remember her offhand comment about a band.

Gabriele was intent on Borrasca's wide bottom lip and wished that glorious night had been hers. "Your turn," challenged Borrasca, eager to hear her story.

Gabriele threw her head back and laughed. "My mother was a lesbian."

"Really." How lucky, no family to explain yourself to."

"Berlin was the lesbian capital of the world at that time. There were at least twelve social clubs, and if you can believe it, as many as twenty bars according to my mother. Cabarets. She worked in the *Chat Noir* on *Friedrichstraße*—that's the black cat—with a friend of hers, Claire Waldoff. Claire was a very popular entertainer at the time, and she lived openly with her lover Olga von Roeder. Of course they flirted with the soldiers to keep away suspicion. Do you know these names?"

"No, I don't. And I didn't know the cabarets had lesbians as stars. It sounds like an old Marlene Dietrich movie to me."

"They didn't sleep with the soldiers," Gabriele emphasized. "Most never let on that they were lesbians, for they would have been sent to a camp themselves. But in that cabaret and others, information and people were passed on. Many like my mother were resisters. Like Rosa

Valetti. She starred in Berthold Brecht and Kurt Weill's Threepenny Opera. She regularly performed her most famous song 'Die Rote Melodies', that's The Red Melody, a powerful anti-war song.

"If she was a lesbian, how did you get born?"

"One night news came that the Gestapo was going to raid the cabaret. My mother and grandmother had planned for that and fled with the help of some man about whom I know nothing. They headed towards France hoping to cross the Channel to England. From there, they would try to get to Canada."

"As it was impossible to travel during the day, they went on foot at night. My grandmother became exhausted. By then, the man who had helped them initially was no longer with them. Towards the evening of the third day my mother and grandmother stopped and slept in a barn, only to be caught by a farmer. He started yelling and threatened to turn them in until his son came into the barn. It seems the threat was based on the man's own fear of detection. The family was Polish and they themselves were posing as Germans. The son, who was about my mother's age, convinced his father to let them stay."

"One night, shots rang out. There was mass confusion and they could not tell where the shooting was coming from. In the middle of the chaos, the son ran in yelling that they had to get out immediately— he was going with them. My mother said it was a terrifying night. The three of them squatted near the barn for nearly an hour, waiting for the right moment. My mother had to kneel in fresh cow dung which ran all over one leg. Then they made a run for it. My mother was 28, but my grandmother, who was courageous as hell, had badly swollen ankles and slowed them down."

"They started across the field, crouching low, the son leading the way. They were nearly to the other end of the field when German soldiers spotted them. There was a volley of shots. My mother ducked and threw herself face first on the ground. My grandmother could not react fast enough. She was hit in the back. The son picked up my grandmother and ran with her into the trees, my mother was right behind them. Not one soldier followed. Not one."

"The son helped bury my grandmother. All night he held my mother, comforting her. The next morning they were up at dawn, forced to travel in the light, but again no one followed. The two of them walked mile after mile, skirting fields, once finding milk at a farmer's dairy. It was days before they were able to find safe refuge in someone's attic. They must have felt they were all they had in the world. It drew them close, and they became lovers. And so it happened. She never told him she was pregnant. By the time she knew, he had left to go to Canada. He wanted her to come with him, but after the war she returned to Berlin. Her friends helped raised me."

"Did you ever want to know him?"

"How would I have found him? I don't think my mother even knew his last name. He would have been a farmer somewhere in Canada, if he was alive."

Borrasca was caught in the web of the dramatic story, but in her mind she saw the grandmother fall and die. Saw Cade fall. Gabriele watched her withdraw.

"What were you thinking a minute ago."

"I can't hide from your perceptive eye," she smiled. "I love hearing your story, but forgive me, I have to go. I'm sorry to leave so abruptly."

"I didn't give you the materials that I found at the Women's Resource Library."

"I'll come back tomorrow. Your story gave me things to think about. Can we continue tomorrow?" She was at the door and out of it before Gabriele could respond, "Tomorrow."

The next day, with no comment about her sudden departure, Borrasca returned and said, "Shall we go for a walk?"

Outside in the open air, Borrasca breathed in and out deeply. "Oxygen always helps the brain, don't you think?"

"It also eases tension." Gabriele guided Borrasca by the arm and led her to a scenic hill that overlooked the town. In the distance the old and new architecture stood out against the sky.

"What a view," said Borrasca. Just below them a man on a bicycle rode into an old cemetery. "Shall we?" said Gabriele. "After all, not everyone gets the cemetery as part of their personalized tour."

Once in the gate, thin spines of metal curved into crosses marked the graves, a contrast to the heavy granite headstones of Woodlawn Cemetery in New York. Borrasca found it more comfortable than she expected. Gabriele pointed toward a marker. Borrasca leaned closer and saw it was Marlene Dietrich's gravesite, with an inscription.

"What does it say?"

"Here I stand at the frontiers of my life." She wanted to be buried near her mother."

Afterward at an outdoor cafe Borrasca said, "I'm the daughter of survivors. I can't imagine how it is to live as a Jew in Germany."

"After I told you about my mother's escape, you left so abruptly..."

"That was rude."

"I'm not looking for an apology. What I want to know is did the story trigger some personal issues?"

"I wonder if it could happen again. Jews and witches have been persecuted here. I've called myself by both those names as well as lesbian. Perhaps witches and women threaten the psychological structure of patriarchy."

"I'm not comfortable defining evil in psychological language," said Gabriele. "To reduce the systematic German persecution and murder of approximately six million Jews—plus the Romani, the Slavic peoples, Russians, Jehovah's Witnesses, not to mention homosexuals—to the psychological is to flatten the complexity of what happened. Look, Germany had lost WW I and was in very bad economic straits. There was a mix of social and political factors in the culture, and sadly there was also a convergence of megalomaniac ideas, the theories of men like Nietzsche. Maybe you haven't heard of Fichte or Treitschke. Or Ernst

Haeckel, he was about the same time as Darwin. Some say he introduced ideas into German intellectual thought and maybe influenced Hitler's twisted thinking of a superior race. But it's too simplistic to point to Germany for the root causes of evil and say there—this is how we can explain it."

"Doesn't everyone ask why it happened here?"

"Of course, and I understand that. There is a male ethos of violence and Hitler exemplifies that to me. But when Primo Levi was in a camp, and he asked why, a guard replied: 'Hier ist kein warum—there's no why.'

"Maybe there is no answer. But what we can do is witness and survive, and create change."

After living in the interior regions for months, Borrasca listened to Gabriele evaluate experience in a different way.

"I don't know if I'll ever understand why millions of Jews died here in my mother's lifetime. There are Germans who do a denial number: it wasn't me; I wasn't responsible. But there are many who deeply regret it and feel a commitment not to repeat history."

Borrasca related the incident with the flower vendors. "Don't the incidences of racism happening now mean history could repeat itself? Neo Nazis instigate terror in America as well as here."

"Which you have to concern yourself with," Gabriele responded, "just as I feel responsible to respond to what happens in my country. Jewish cemeteries are being violated all over Europe—why are you standing?"

"Please, understand. I have to go now. I won't always be jumping up and I will explain this jitteriness. Can I come back soon?"

"When?"

"Day after tomorrow?"

"Come after 4:00. I'll be at work until then. Borrasca, will you always be running out?"

"No, I promise. Beginning is what's hard. Don't give up on me."

Gabriele sat after the American woman left, weighing the reasons she might have fled, thinking about her lips. When Borrasca returned to her flat, Gabriele vowed to stay in a light hearted mood, unwilling to scare Borrasca away with heavy discussion.

"Let's walk again. Actually, I insist we play." Borrasca stored her thoughts about Germany and let her attention move into the aura of Gabriele, so captivated was she with her energy and buoyancy. After several days of drizzle a blue sky had finally emerged though it was still chilly. They walked arm in arm, looking at a multitude of small stores until Gabriele stopped outside a gallery.

"I hope I'll be able to show my things here one day. They're doing a mixed media show which could include my work." They went into the gallery and several more after that. The accumulation of color and creative forms pulled Borrasca out of herself. By the time they re-entered the apartment, there was the familiarity born of hours of shared friendship. It had a telling effect on Borrasca who ventured to talk on a more immediate level. She had no sooner sat down than it burst out of her: "My parents were in a camp," Borrasca said directly.

"I wondered," said Gabriele.

"I'm not good at talking about it. But I need to assimilate what I know inside my own consciousness apart from what my parents have told me—its all in there, mixed together. See—she plunged into the opening—I have a more present concern with death. My lover died several months ago."

She said the words out loud and waited. Rearranged herself on the couch. Why wasn't Gabriele speaking? Fueled by the anxiety of having said the words, she kept talking before the source dried up. "Made me a bit crazy. I've tried to exorcize the pain. In the last few months, I've learned how much I identify with pain and death."

"Losing a lover. That is not easy. I'm sorry."

"Dealing with her death and my personal grief has me coming face to face with my family's past and mine. I get trapped inside my head between my their tragedy and losing Cade. There's also guilt about how my lover died. I was so desperate that I retreated to a Monastery to save me. That let me detach enough to survive. Now it's time to deal with her death and my history more directly if I'm going to have some perspective."

"Most of us, myself included," admitted Gabriele, "have a hard time integrating what went on here in Germany with our present lives. Me, I've had to remember to keep loving myself through out the process—and I have to keep learning it." She reached over and touched Borrasca on the shoulder.

At her touch, Borrasca reached up and touched her hand. "I've been missing this. Meditation gave me enough detachment to survive, but I'm lonely for touch. I hold myself in tight control so I won't fall apart. It would be such a comfort to be held."

Gabriele reached out and held Borrasca, sensing the depth of her anguish; yet, she was aware of her own uneasiness. She was feeling more than care and empathy. The story of Sara McElvoy and Borrasca's lips had aroused her, but she couldn't play on Borrasca's vulnerability. And being held wasn't all that Borrasca needed in order to resolve things.

The self-imposed period of isolation ended as Borrasca came inside the circle of Gabriele's arms. The flood gates opened, and washed over her. Just saying the words to another person—my lover is dead—was cathartic. Borrasca willed her mind to surrender to a day which still flew by her—her feet always in perpetual motion, always a second too late, the reach of her arms not long enough.

Gabriele felt the nappy quality of Borrasca's hair against her cheek, torn between two rivaling emotions. She whispered, "As a daughter of a survivor, I want to offer support. The offer is genuine, but I confess I'm liking an excuse to hold you. I don't want to betray your trust."

Borrasca felt a wave of guilt at Gabriele's touch. Was it a betrayal of Cade to feel close to another woman? She pulled away. "I love this, but I need more time."

That night back in her room, she reckoned the effort it had taken to maintain. The time had served her well as had the meditation practice. She who was basically a social creature had been alone and introspective for months. By staying in the moment, she could balance those two poles. It was good to be touched. The next evening she flew into Gabriele's arms. Her mind stopped trying to control everything, and she gave in to the grief. She felt the world slipping away. The next thing she knew Gabriele was leading her into her room. She helped her get in bed, shut the curtains, kissed her forehead and left.

Borrasca slept in the comforting dark. Several times she awoke to hear Gabriele moving about in the house. Why had Gabriele put her to bed—had she fallen asleep? Was it late? What would happen when it was time for Gabriele to sleep?

In the morning Borrasca woke up alone in Gabriele's bed. She went to the kitchen and found her having a cup of coffee. "Good morning."

"Good morning. How did you sleep?"

"What happened?"

"You cried, for a long time. I brought you into my room. I don't think you heard me come to bed."

How could she not know Gabriele was lying next to her? "I didn't come here expecting you to take care of me."

"One night is all right. You would do the same for me."

Borrasca had wanted to appear competent and strong. Instead she'd been a person in need. Never had she met someone under those conditions. Over the next few days, the two were inseparable, sharing intimate details of their lives, except that Borrasca never talked about Cade, never about that day, although Cade hovered in the background of her mind as the two of them opened to each other. One night Gabriele showed slides of she and her friends protesting at Greenham Commons Peace Camp in England many years earlier. "The women were fearless, facing down the potential violence from the police," Gabriele remembered.

"Was anyone killed?" Borrasca found herself blurting out: "Were you ever lovers with anyone who died?" She didn't wait for an answer; the question was for herself. "I feel like I'd be betraying her—she looked into Gabriele's eyes—if I were to enjoy life without her. I can't reconcile my loyalty to her with the attraction I'm feeling for you."

"You will be able to put it behind you—it's enough now to feel affection for someone."

Borrasca reached over and touched Gabriele's cheek. "Part of me is ready now. Would you kiss that part?"

Gabriele's lips came down on hers softly, her own fragility in the moment expressed in the soft imprint. Borrasca yielded to the passion which had been growing in both of them.

Cade, it's me. I'm back. Can I see you for lunch? How about dinner and dessert, and bedtime and dessert again, all night.

I can sneak out of the lab by 4.

At 4:30 Borrasca pulled up to the house which was obscured from view by a long adobe wall skirting the length of the property.

Did you miss me?

Hmm, oh yes.

No, you got involved with the tour and the adoring fans.

I did, but I missed you every night.

Cade straddled her lap. She rubbed her cheek against Borrasca's fuzzy 'do, anticipating the brush of hair sliding along her stomach. Borrasca's insides churned as the weight of Cade's body as it came down against hers.

Borrasca lay alone on Gabriele's bed, listening to her moving about in the kitchen. The erotic had returned. The morning light came through the window mottled by frozen rain and wind that blew objects across the face of the window with the fury of a spring ice storm. Gabriele opened the door and came in with a tray of tea and a plate covered with a towel. "How nice to see you in my bed. Are you doing all right?"

"Oh, yes, very, very fine."

"Do you want something healthy to eat, or something decadent?"

"Decadent." Borrasca pulled away the towel to find two croissants. They ate snuggled under warm covers while the wind rattled against the window. Borrasca held Gabriele against her. "Thank you for last night. I confess my thoughts sometimes flashed to Cade."

"You do seem to live several lives at once. There's Cade. Traveling to the Far East. Climbing mountains in snow to a monastery. Riding a train across the continent to Germany. Very intense."

"Like a restless haunt." Borrasca said.

"We all have times in our lives when the heads and tails of experience find us at the tail end. I don't judge you, but less self-pity would help. Try and see your life in the context of what many people in the world have been through. Germany and elsewhere. You're not the only one to have known pain."

Borrasca pushed aside the impulse to run. "Knowing more about what happened to Jews in the camps might give you a perspective larger than your small peep hole on tragedy. Do you know about the Auschwitz memorial? We could go there."

"The idea unnerves me, but I need to stop running and come to terms with it."

"It's also unfinished for me. May always be. I'm free on Friday."

While she waited the three days, Borrasca looked at how she had wallowed in a morass of ego. Ego was a trap and prevented her using pain as a way towards understanding herself and entering deeper into experience. There was no way to compare that day on the mountain to what her parents had experienced. But each event created a history that clustered inside her. She alone could appreciate how far she had come and how much more there was to do. But if she was to come to grace, it was to go through the fire of the memories of Germany that she'd experienced in her earliest childhood dreams, and then to reconcile it with what had happened with Cade. There might never be a neat conclusion.

Gabriele's Volkswagen bus flew by the villages along the way. Were they peaceful while Auschwitz had been operating? Borrasca remembered an aunt who had been in a concentration camp. After the war she had lived in a small miniscule apartment with a pink kitchen and a spotless stove. There was just one other room: a tiny living room area with a couch that opened at night into a bed. The sheets and blankets were stuffed into a small closet out of view during the day. Borrasca found it claustrophobic to visit her. The woman had lived to be free and was spending her life with her linens and her life crammed into a suffocating space. The old terror rose up in Borrasca.

Gabriele saw her tense. "Are you ready for this? Stay with your feelings, Borrasca."

At the entrance to Auschwitz, Borrasca saw the words 'Arbeit Mach Frei' above the gate. Gabriele translated: 'Work makes one free.' Arriving prisoners believed it was a work camp."

They walked by brick buildings whose pall was heightened by the dense cloud cover and cold air. As they crossed the walkway she saw the tall trees that grow beside the fences and the double rows of barbed wire. They passed an organized tour, and Borrasca heard the tour guide say, "If you want to see the Little Red House or Bunker..."

"What's that?"

"Gas chambers."

"I don't want to see them. I want to be where the people were living inside the barracks. And the Museum."

They began with the photography exhibit. None of the pictures in LIFE could have prepared Borrasca for what she saw. One photo was of a rally in *Nürnberg* in 1937. Borrasca gasped. As if no time had gone by, she began reliving her earliest remembered experience, being pulled like a rubber band was coursing through her body. She was pulled into a rally. Thousands of people were shouting. The glare of lights rising vertically into the night sky blinded her. The sound of Hitler's voice surrounded her. A sickening sensation in the pit of her stomach told her this photograph was of that place.

"What is it?" Gabriele saw the horror on Borrasca's face.

"I was here, this stadium!"

Strident voices blared through microphones chanting the same phrase again and again. The lights. The rubber band buzzed through her body. Behind her a documentary film shot by the Russians the day the camp was liberated was being shown. Emaciated images of the inmates appeared. Borrasca screamed.

The lights came on. People turned to look. The movie continued to run behind the backs of audience, the prisoners staring out from the screen. Cade fell. Borrasca screamed.

"It's all right, Borrasca; it's all right."

Gabriele and two other people helped her out of the auditorium and brought her into a lounge. A doctor bent over to give her a sedative. Borrasca saw the needle and terror struck.

TWENTY-FIVE

She was on the train again, expecting that the old woman and the young boy would reappear. The car began filling up with people carrying their possessions in odd suitcases and handbags. Brenda searched the faces for the old woman, but there were too many faces to take in. Soon she had only the smallest corner to stand up in.

The train lurched forward, throwing everyone into the center. Brenda grabbed on to the sides of the car. Surely they will move some of these people into other cars. But after several hours, it became clear this was how it was going to be.

Evening was fast approaching. Brenda, who had at first been upset by the density of people, became even more distressed when she had to go to the bathroom. In her innocence, she had hunched around notions of decency. Those notions began falling away. People found ways to relieve themselves in buckets set up in the middle of the car.

In the light of morning, Brenda saw more of the people around her. A family directly in front of her huddled together caring for each other's needs. The father was quite old judging by the deep furrows on his face. His wife seemed considerably younger. He helped care for the two small children. One of them was a young girl whose hair tangled easily despite the ribbons holding her long braids in place. At first they tried to keep her neat. The father would braid the girl's hair over her cries. Despite their efforts, it began to resemble a beehive.

Another couple held an infant who alternately slept and cried. At its loudest moments, the father would become mortified with embarrassment, especially late at night when people were trying to sleep standing up, jammed up against one another. A woman in front of

Brenda, who had come on the train heavily made up, tried to put on lipstick, but one lurch of the car had sent her headlong into the people in front of her. When she regained her upright position, the lipstick had smeared over her face and blouse. The woman vented her anger at everyone around her. No one accused her of vanity, everyone acutely aware of how these small acts helped maintain a semblance of order.

A man to her right kept taking out a gold watch fob from his pocket and looking at the time. Brenda watched him look at it one morning when it could have made no difference whether it was 6:00 or 7:00 AM. Brenda peered out of a small crack to see how many other cars snaked along the rails, but she couldn't see any. They had been going by farms yesterday. Today she saw a barren landscape. The sound of the train was a constant background. There was a screeching against the tracks when the train would stop for unexplained reasons. The train cars never opened. Occasionally there would be a whistle, voices outside yelling authoritatively. Brenda's body moved with the train even when it was stopped.

In the corner to her left was a young man with long peyes and a yarmulke davening while saying his morning prayers. "He's Jewish," thought Brenda. The woman carrying the crying infant had a Jewish star around her neck. Are we all Jewish? She saw Jewish stars sewn on people's clothes. Many wore yellow armbands with the star. Panic rose in her throat as she inspected everyone in the cold dawn. Hundreds of Jews crowded like cattle into this train car. How did they know I was Jewish, too?

Fear and the stench of piss and shit had forced passengers to withdraw into their skins. A heavy curtain of low clouds hung over the landscape. People woke hungry. They searched in their pockets, finding precious little packets that had been secreted away. Brenda had a small piece of bundt cake and some cheese in her bag, but how to eat with people staring and no way to share equally.

The woman standing closest to her, who disdained to talk to anyone, watched her intently. Brenda took a piece of the cake and passed it to the family with the crying baby. As they reached for it, Brenda gave one piece to the woman who smiled in gratitude before eating the piece in one bite. Brenda fingered the cheese wondering whether to leave any for later when she might need it, but the cheese was growing soft and warm; it had to be eaten or it would spoil. She took a hunk for herself and passed the rest to the davening boy. His father eyed the transaction. The boy bit off a section and passed it to his mother. The father ate his stubbornness. The crammed bodies raised the temperature in the car, and the terrible stench of excretion became overwhelming. Brenda buried her nose in her bag which smelled of cheese.

An old man dressed in the black clothes of the orthodox came into their car, reassuring everyone. "It will be all right. When we arrive there will be work for us and food."

"You don't know that." A passenger challenged him. "Don't build up people's hopes falsely."

"I was informed we were being taken to work camps. Many among us have not worked for months. Now we will be able to support our families."

The stubborn father came over and pulled on the man's arm. "Excuse me. Are you a Rabbi?"

"I am Samuel Weiss. Hasidic."

Above the clack of the train wheels the father responded, "I respect the Hassidim, but we aren't being transported for anything good. I don't want to frighten anyone, but don't play on people's faith."

Weiss turned red, his peyes nearly curled around his raised arm. "You are one with no faith."

"I have much faith in G-d, and few illusions about the Third Reich." They glowered at each other. The train lurched as they were propelled into the darkness of a tunnel. People lost their equilibrium and tumbled over one another. When they came out of the tunnel into the light, Brenda saw that the two men had fallen on one another.

The train went on relentlessly. People grew weary. The putrefying odor increased. At night they wept quietly to themselves. Some slept fitfully while the train careened into the darkness. The woman's baby cried less and less; the mother cried more. Brenda tried to comfort her, but she was becoming desperate.

"My milk has dried up. The baby has nothing to eat. She'll die if we don't do something soon." Brenda herself was weak and parched from thirst. One night as she nodded into sleep envisioning a turquoise lake, the abrupt screeching of the train woke her as it ground to a halt. They clawed their way to one of the two cracked openings, trying to see in the early light of dawn. From her angle, Brenda could see a smoke stack in the distance, emitting an odor fouler than the train car. The side doors were thrown open, and a man practiced in the ways of meanness began screaming at them. "Get out. Line up!"

Several soldiers stood behind him with rifles. People grabbed for their belongings, dropping some of their possessions in the confusion. Several hooked arms with one another, afraid of being separated. Brenda was behind a tall man and couldn't see where she was going. Behind her, a surge of people pressed in on her. When the man jumped off the car, she jumped, right into the arms of a soldier who jammed the butt of his rifle into her shoulder and flung her to the side. She fought for balance, knowing she must stay on her feet. Another uniform pushed her into a line.

They were being divided into two different lines. Her shoulder was on fire. Her insides screamed terror, but her lips remain closed. She scanned the lines and saw the boy who had been davening. His eyes were glazed with the dread of that moment when no prayer was possible. The other line had the woman with the baby. There were several guards separating the two lines. Brenda instinctively knew the call was to life or death. She determined to go with the young boy and grabbed his hand. People all around were yelling in the chaos. Herded by rifles the other line started to move away. They were not of the same world anymore. Brenda's line was turned around and headed toward the opposite direction. Then her line was separated into two lines, this time by gender. The boy went off with the men, and she was cast into a large room with women. Guards shouted, "Strip. Take off your clothes."

There was no time to think. Her shoulder seized up as she unbuttoned her blouse. The fingers functioned as if they weren't attached to the rest of her. A large woman with the thinnest upper lip she had ever seen stood in front of her, inches from her face. "Mach Schnell." Brenda willed the fingers to work, tearing off her clothes while the guard went off to prod someone else. She hesitated with just her underwear on, but the guard leered back at her. Her pants were stained with blood. Would having her period make her life worth less? She hid the pants under the pile of clothes.

Another woman came and inspected her body. She raised Brenda's arms so her fingers could sift through the underarm hair. She yanked the jammed shoulder. The shoulder popped at the joint. Brenda's frame shook with the effort to contain a scream of pain. The woman bent down and pushed Brenda's legs apart. She had to have noticed blood. Someone came behind Brenda and forced her into a chair and began shaving her head. She was immobilized by the two of them, fearful that if she moved the scissors would cut her. In that helpless state, she surrendered her body.

Towards afternoon she was lined up in a large courtyard filled with hundreds of other women. Each wore a shapeless work dress and an expression of shock. For hours they stood. No one was allowed to talk. At dusk replacement guards came. This time they were put in new lines. Registration. The term was being whispered around her. A number was tattooed on her arm. More than the invasive examination of her body, more than the shaving of her hair, the inscribing of numbers indelibly etched itself into her being. By the time they were marched into barracks for the evening, she was a shape falling into numbness on a pallet next to three other women. She was grateful to lie down for the first time in days, nearly oblivious to the pain in her shoulder. It only mattered that her body did not have to be upright. She prayed for sleep. When she awoke, she prayed for food. Bundt cake.

A woman sat down on the pallet near her and spoke. "I am Sima. Someone was speaking kindly. "My name is Brenda." She studied the face smiling at her. Pale, the skin tightly drawn against her cheekbones. But her eyes were sharp clear beads radiating intelligence. All of her seemed to be resting on her haunches.

"Where are we?"

"This is Auschwitz. You are forty-five minutes from Cracow and five minutes from the crematoria."

The smoke stacks. The odor. Brenda's mind fought against the conclusion. She brought the back of her hand up to her mouth to keep from screaming.

Sima pulled the hand down and held it. "You came on last night's train?"

Brenda nodded. "How long have you been here?"

"Six months."

"Why have you singled me out?"

"I haven't seen you before, but that's the key—don't let yourself be singled out for any reason, good or bad. Watch what I do for the first few days. We'll talk again."

She started to leave between the line of women who had gathered around the cot. "Wait." Brenda grabbed her arm. "How can this be happening?" she asked.

Sima looked into her eyes. "I can't answer that. The better question is how do we get out of here alive?" She hurried off.

Brenda woke hungry. She'd eaten nothing since the cheese. A woman came over and looked her up and down. "Come with me. You'll work in the laundry."

"I haven't eaten in so long, how can I work?" Should she have admitted that? Her fear of having erred subsided when the woman reached inside her dress and placed a piece of stale bread in her hands. Brenda gobbled it down while following her.

The laundry building felt warm to Brenda's chilly body. Along every wall there were women washing and sorting. The supervisor stopped in front of a huge mound of clothes. "Wash these." Brenda spent the day elbow deep in water standing by a large pile that never lessened. She searched through pockets for bread, sweets. Crumbs. Gum, she discovered, was a rare treasure that conferred the illusion of having something to eat for hours. Her only meal was a bowl of watery soup that evening.

In the middle of the second workday, there was a break and Brenda was allowed to go outside with the other women. She stretched her back which was bowed tight from bending over. She could see the camp stretched out in a long series of barracks. Between the rows of building the ground was a wash of mud from the rains. She slogged through the mud and peered over the fence at the closest barrack. A group of men was carrying heavy loads and piling them on wagons. A woman came beside her, whispering, "Don't let anyone see you staring. Those are graveyard workers. Each morning they collect the bodies of those who died the night before."

Brenda jumped away from the fence. "That many, every day?"

"Do you know how many prisoners are here? And more arriving every day."

"All Jewish?"

"Mostly. Not all. Romani, homosexuals. Some political resisters. You're still alive because you're young and strong. Like me. Some get sent there right away." She nodded to the chimneys. "Jewish people are being cremated there."

They saw her body freeze, her mind go elsewhere. "Look busy, the guards are watching." Someone poked her in the ribs.

Brenda turned her head, surveying the tower out of the corner of her eye. They were indeed watching her. As the women trooped back into work, the woman whispered, "Do not forget where you are. Don't stare. Make yourself indispensable. Don't get sick. And don't fall over."

Daily Brenda saw death in her barracks. The grave workers made their pickups. The reality of death in its gruesome aspect was in marked contrast to her job at the laundry where everything was clean except the prisoners themselves who increasingly resembled walking corpses.

Brenda learned from watching another woman that a pouch hidden between her legs went a long way to helping her survive. She contrived her first one from cloth scraps gathered at the laundry. Since she was unable to control the daily and endless dysentery, the pouch gave a semblance of hygiene and control. She made a second pouch which she hid near her stomach to keep bits of food. The hoarding of food obsessed her even when all other bodily functions failed. She searched pockets meticulously before washing clothes. Her period stopped. Her back and shoulder ached. Lice crawled over her body unless she nitpicked assiduously. Brenda had barely enough energy to do her job and find food.

One day a new group of workers came into the laundry. Brenda looked up and saw the old woman from the train. She ran to her. The woman held out her arms to embrace her. The long black gloves were gone, the camp numbers were visible for Brenda to see. The woman looked around cagily before speaking. "They took my nephew away. I think he was a spy." She went to a sink and began scrubbing. Every day she joined Brenda in the laundry, but they never spoke again.

At night the searchlights and dogs woke her. She was greedy for sleep to escape reality. She slept and swam in lakes. As she became weaker, the time from morning until she could sleep again became interminable. Her mind was unable to fathom the cruelty. It was death in process. They lived off death. They lived off the food left by the dead whose bodies they searched before the grave workers came.

She awakened one morning with her head still clinging to the night's fantasies. Outside the laundry she halted until a guard screamed at her. She turned towards her station, but he thought she was ignoring him. He raised his rifle to hit her. She instinctively reached to protect her shoulder, and he jammed his rifle butt into her stomach. Brenda started to double over when the woman's remark came to her--do not fall. She forced herself to stand even though the wind had been knocked out of her. "You have no work?" he screamed.

"Yes, Yes, I work in the laundry."

Did he understand? Why was he so enraged? Three women appeared. One went up to the guard and told him that Brenda had cleaned and ironed the starched white shirt he was wearing. Wasn't it a perfect job? Her coddling manner mollified him. The incongruity was absurd. One of the other women handed Brenda a pile of stinking clothes. The guard backed down. Absurdity took the place of logic. The women noticed the dislocation in her eyes, and they marched off with her, one on each side. She managed to work the entire shift, aware the other women in the laundry were scrutinizing her. Later they followed her back to the barracks and gathered around her bed.

"Brenda, can you keep it together? You drift off. This has happened before. It's important. You could have jeopardized all of us in the laundry angering Boris so. Unless we had come and helped, he'd have beaten you, and then vented his fury at the rest of us, all because you weren't paying attention. Stay alert."

"Wait." Sima came to where they stood in the dark, illuminated every few seconds by the searchlight that skimmed across the window. "Ganging up on her won't help. She turned to Brenda. "But they are right. The actions of any one woman could kill us. Keep a sense of the situation around you at all times. It will protect us all."

"You came alone here, yes? It makes a difference. We were captured together and already knew each other," said Sima. "We try to watch out for one other. That way they can't single us out and batter us down one by one. Today you threatened all of us as well as yourself. How can I help? You've been here only a month. Probably it's still the shock of being here that causes you to go off in your mind and forget where you are. Be present in each moment. Think of those around you, not just yourself."

"You think I'll get used to this?" challenged Brenda.

"No one ever gets used to being in this hell. The viciousness. Death everywhere. You don't get used to that. All I am saying is this. I think the war will end soon. Within the year, according to our sources. In any case, I must believe it will soon end. We must all believe we will survive. And we do it by being watchful moment by moment."

The searchlight hesitated at their window. The women fell on the bed, Brenda's face mashed against the maggot infested mattress. The putrefying smell gagged her, but she didn't move. Sima was right. In that moment while the search beams sought them out they had acted as one unit. The light beam passed. When they stood, Brenda felt a surge of renewal. "I will be more aware."

Throughout that winter of misery, Brenda felt buoyed by their combined strength. For months she was able to maintain. In February nothing seemed to help. The numbing cold and lack of nourishment began taking its toll on her. Brenda developed severe diarrhea and fever. For several days she answered roll call with shit running down her legs. Defecation was all over her pouch, her shoes.

One day, the guards stormed into the laundry, ordering them to line up outside in a snowstorm. For hours they stood whipped by blowing snow. People began falling in the bitter cold. Brenda felt faint, but just as her knees gave way, Sima was at her side. She grabbed Brenda by the elbows and kept her on her feet. Another woman came on the other side and the three of them propped themselves up in the snowy dusk. Evening turned to night. The searchlight moved silently across them. Infinitesimal snowflakes shimmered in its beam. They were white figurines entombed in a frieze with only the sound of wind blown snow except for those struggling to breathe, their coughs punctuating the white silence. To fall was to die. Brenda wiped snow on her face to stay alert. A woman several rows away looked just like her mother. Rose? Mommy? It couldn't be her mother. A prisoner shifted position, blocking her view. Soon she could not make out anyone, all of them covered with snow. Her frozen toes lost contact with the earth. To fall was to die.

It was nearly dawn when the guards dismissed them to their work stations. Brenda's fever sent her into a sweat. Sima finagled a way to get Brenda into the hospital. She slept on white sheets. She woke terrified of the color white. The snow. Her own skin. The fever induced a frightening sequence of white dreams:

Are you traveling alone? A snow shape with peyes questioned her.

No companion walks with me. I do not go alone though. Death is here with me. She keeps falling through the sky. I lie on my bed and she falls. When she lands everything is pristine white--how is death with you? The snow shape opened its mouth and Brenda fell through a maw.

She woke with a start. Where was the Hassidic man Mr. Weiss with his peyes? Did he have faith that there would be soup that night? Faith that someone would remember him and sneak him a piece of bread? The old woman had stopped coming to the laundry. Did they kill her? Brenda rubbed away the dream, sending Mr. Weiss and the old woman scurrying into a dark corner of her mind.

Death lived in the bed next to her three times that week. Attendants would bring in a patient who would die in the night. One came in, said hello to Brenda, and never woke up. Brenda stayed in the hospital as long as Sima could manage it. In her last dream there were two white skeletons walking a white road to the chimneys. Brenda sat by the side of the road and watched their bones go by. She woke, surprised to find herself still alive.

The next afternoon she left the hospital, and by 5:00 she was back at work as if nothing had happened. She fell into a routine which stretched through the long winter. One day she realized that one of the women working in the laundry was wearing a different triangle. She knew green ones were for criminals. A brown triangle meant Romani. Red was a political prisoner. Brenda's was yellow. This woman had a pink triangle. Brenda watched her pick up a large stack of uniforms.

When she had gone, Brenda went over to Sima and asked what the pink meant.

"Lesbian." She saw the quizzical look on Brenda's face. "That's just who she is. She's a very good worker."

Brenda had overheard gossip about the head kapo who was said to be a lesbian. But that woman was nasty. The woman in the laundry carried herself proudly. She didn't talk much with anyone. No one did; talk was draining. Several nights later the woman came into Brenda's dream, still wearing the pink triangle. They walked to a lake. When Brenda dove in, she saw the woman underneath the water, swimming towards her. Brenda quickly rose to the surface, taking in a large gasp of air. The woman floated away. Unsettling dreams kept reoccurring. Her nerves were jangled. Her work slackened.

She watched the others toiling away at the sinks, scrutinizing their skeletal faces. Brenda felt her cheekbones, The compulsion to look at herself persisted though the women said never to look in a mirror. When she took the laundry over to the hospital, she remembered a mirror there. She walked quickly through the side entrance and up the stairs carrying the laundry basket. On the third floor, she glanced around to make sure no one was in sight. She walked up to the mirror.

An emaciated, crazed looking woman with large balloon eyes looked back at her. The wide expanse of face had disappeared into her cheek bones. A corpse was looking back at her. Where was Brenda? She hammering the mirror, which began screaming back at her.

People came running. Brenda realized it was she who was screaming. She ran around a corner, eluding the chasers. Down the steps. Outside to the hospital grounds. Inside the laundry. The women looked up from their work as she ran in, her dress blood stained from hammering the mirror. Quickly she threw off the dress. They wouldn't know who it was if she could get into one of the grey dresses. They'd all look like death. Frantically she pulled on the zipper. It stuck. The lesbian ran to her side, pulled up the zipper and stuck the bloody dress under a pile of laundry.

When the hospital attendants entered flanked by guards, the women were working quietly. Brenda stuck her bloody hands inside a basin of clothes and scrubbed. The men peered into every face unable to single out one of the walking corpses. One guard went up to a woman who turned and smiled malevolently. She had no teeth and the empty spaces in her mouth emitted a vile odor. The guards left empty handed. Brenda slipped a piece of bread to the lesbian.

"You're forgetting what we talked about," Sima reminded her. We are still having to carry you, Brenda. This week we must all stay focused. We need you to be alert now more than ever." Sima was not angry. It was a cold statement of fact.

The next day in the laundry there was a low buzz of voices talking in whispers. A series of explosions rocked the building. Something was happening.

"What was that?" Alarms were going off. Brenda strained to see outside the laundry window. In the distance she heard a volley of shots. Word filtered down. Crematorium IV. There had been an uprising by the Sonderkommando, the men assigned to dispose of the corpses from the gas chamber.

That night the women huddled by a smuggled candle and pieced together how the Sonderkommando had learned that they themselves were due to be liquidated. Women smuggled gunpowder from the munitions factory to them. The men attacked the SS and Kapos with axes and knives. They used grenades made from the gunpowder to blew up the crematorium, killing several SS men. One was pushed alive into a crematorium oven. "The crematorium is ruined—it may never be used again. There was a muted cheer."

"Sadly," Sima's voice choked up, "most of the men who took part have been killed. At least three hundred men. Even those who had managed to run away were caught." The air went out of the room.

"But it was five young women who smuggled the powder into the camp. Five brave women. They were tortured, but none of them betrayed those who had plotted the uprising."

That night their names were intoned throughout the camp: Ala Gertner. Ester Wajcblum. Rojza Robota. Regina Safirsztajn. Fejga Segal.

Rojza's last message was a note scratched on a piece of paper smuggled from her cell: "Hazak V' Amatz." Be Strong & Brave.

At the beginning of January, the five women were hanged. Brenda stood in the evening shadows, and gathering her courage, began singing. Her voice rang out across the barracks. She had told no one she could sing, and the wonder of her beautiful voice lifted their spirits. She sang as one who had transcended the place of pain, and for a few moments, the women were united in the deepest part of themselves. Sima smiled at Brenda. In three weeks, the Soviets liberated the camp. When the Russian troops arrived, Brenda was still singing. She had moved out of her own mitzrayim, the narrow place that constricts the soul.

TWENTY-SIX

"I used to sing. I used to sing."

Gabriele shifted the cold washcloth on her forehead. Borrasca struggled to sit up and look around. The room with white walls was empty save for an empty cot and a doctor standing on the other side of the bed. Gabriele nudged her back down. "I'm all right. Please, can we go?"

The doctor nodded. Borrasca leaned on her shoulder to raise herself up, but it froze in pain. She fell back on the cot, the pain radiating down from her shoulder. She grimaced, but said nothing fearing they might keep her here. The antiseptic, unsettling white of the room had the effect of placing a white sheet on top of a victim of snow blindness. Gabriele took her arm and led her out.

On the road back to Berlin, Borrasca saw the tall poplars lining the road on both sides, all bent in the same direction, witnesses to history. She was grateful for the green countryside after the stark white. A late afternoon light filtered through the verdant leaves. It gave her a sense of momentary peace until the angle of the sunlight made her realize how many hours had elapsed. How long? Five, six hours? A lifetime?

"I know I caused a scene."

"The memorial stirs up deep sadness. Don't apologize. Everyone deals in their own way."

She was at a loss to explain her experience of the camp. Meaning lay somewhere in the interstices between morning and 60 years ago. Between herself and a woman falling who had opened her to death. "I want to talk about it, Gabriele, but I can't just drop this on you."

"Let me be the judge of that, Borrasca." Climbing back up the stairs to Gabriele's apartment, Borrasca wondered if she should call her parents and tell them about the camp memory. Later. Sleep now. Talk to Gabriele in the morning. In the middle of the night she sat up, pulling the covers off Gabriele who grumbled.

How to reckon the camp experience? She took two aspirin for the shoulder pain. Memories of the camp replayed. Cade fell.

There was still no illuminating perspective from which to see that day. How could she direct her life with intention if all the pieces of information from the two most important events of her past couldn't be integrated inside? She fell into a tentative sleep. She saw the chimneys and screamed: "I was there. I was."

A voice curled out of the chimney smoke: "And were you also on the cliff?

"I was. I'm the woman who was there."

TWENTY-SEVEN

IN THE SEVENTH SECOND,
her body slammed against a jutting rock.
She careened through the sky,
the momentum propelling her
through the air corridor.
She collided with the world,
and from the impact of the collision,
she flew upward, only to meet
the ever present force of gravity.
She hurtled through space in pain
her right arm and ribs burning
the skin raw and punctured,
bones piercing her.
The pain dispelled any illusions
of being carried by celestial whim.
Fear flew with her along the canyon walls—
she was falling alone towards death.
Who now stands with me?
Cade, who are you now?
Scientist? Borrasca's lover?
Meaning flew by.
I've been so obsessed with the search for meaning.
I don't know who I am apart from that search.
Is death going to be meaningful?
I am going to leave the body alive and electric
when we made love, all time was gone

all the past and was.
all the future and will be.
I am. . . alone.
I don't want to be gone from what I love here
we've had more pain than joy recently.
other women split up,
and don't talk to each other.
A year later and it's as if
they'd never been intimate with one another.
Do we have to split with one of us dying?
Is this the only way we know to end?
Do I still believe it's a spiral?
As I fall headlong, do I believe
from this ending will come a new beginning?
What becomes of belief in the final seconds?
Maybe when there's no belief,
Death sneaks in like a trickster
and takes over the body.
I want to believe
there's more than nothingness
I want light and color and sound.
I want to believe.

TWENTY-EIGHT

The flight to New York was interminable. When sleep didn't come, Alethea pulled out Cade's book which had become an island of sensibility. It demanded concentration while rewarding her with its power to illuminate:

The cosmic joke is the one we play on ourselves, thinking we understand time. We define history as a straight line running through time. It presumes the world runs in a linear pattern. But time moves in cycles and spirals. The journey of life is the passing of one another through the spirals. We move through these corridors on the way to the future. Other times we pass each other on the return loop. The present becomes the future which becomes the past, and then the present. That is why the past can feel so present. It is why we can talk of deja vu and why the past haunts us. The texture of time has the nubbiness of an old black and white movie. In dreams we move freely through all the loops of time and space which interchange. The future rolls by sooner than the present can leave the stage. What is the language to describe such a fluid universe where the visible and invisible alternate? With the universe and time moving this way, our language cannot be static, nor our perceptions.

Any time there is an event, there is the thing observed and the observer. The watcher changes the nature of reality and directly affects the results. Two scientists doing exactly the same experiment may have different results. If that is true, then we must enlarge our view of truth in line with the laws of probability and the findings of quantum physics.

Alethea knew that she had been a witness and there were other perceptions to consider. In the grand scheme of things more than one meaning was possible. The overhead seat belt light came on and the pilot announced they were in a holding pattern. It would be a half hour before they landed. She shut off the overhead light and tried to image the future beyond picking up luggage.

She was not prepared for the reverse culture shock that hit her at the airport. The mother on the plane with three children in tow returned to a husband who barked out orders as if she hadn't ever managed for herself. Alethea drifted around the airport waiting to claim her baggage. In that time she understood she needed to spend a day on her own before calling Borrasca's family. And after that? She wasn't ready to go home—she wasn't sure where home was anymore. She circled the baggage claim area a second time. She had been changed by her experiences, but old ways of being might resurface—no, it wasn't true. Something was unalterably different. She could figure out how to create the kind of life she wanted.

The trip into Manhattan was not unlike the inverted pyramid of India: going from the wide spacious airport runway into a crowded city. When she got out of the taxi, she stood at a cross light watching businessmen swinging briefcases. A young boy carrying a loud blaring radio against his ear brushed by her.

What to say to Rose and Louis? That she thought she saw Brenda in a crowd in the eerie light of fireworks? That there had been something different about her? Days after seeing Brenda, she realized she had no chin hairs. She had shorter hair. Even the eyes weren't the same. There had been a mad, frenetic quality in those eyes on the mesa. Everything might recede into a vague recollection.

She put down her bags and rested from their weight in front of a store. Inside the window display were nude mannequins who threw back perfect bodies at her. Her own reflection appeared to her. Quickly she turned away from it and walked ahead a few paces. Then she stopped and backtracked. She turned sideways and looked at herself again in the store window. The body size was the same, but clearly something had changed. Large woman had gone on an adventure, and she looked—different. Vivacious. It was her eyes, the doorway to the spirit. The image excited her. She smiled back at her reflection and watched the cheeks fill and her dimples broaden. She scrutinized the mannequins with rouged cheeks and unseeing eyes. The fake coloration in their skins and their anorexic bodies were a stark contrast to her own vitality.

She threw up her arms with joy to the puzzlement of those passing by. There was no flaw in her. The fault rested with other people's perceptions if they could not imagine a large woman going on adventures and having significant philosophical thoughts. She wanted to celebrate. Go to a show or museum, but it was late. Tomorrow she'd contact Rose and Louis. Tell them the little she'd learned of Brenda. Thank them for opening a door for her. It would be good to see them.

After securing a hotel, she took a taxi to China Town, remembering lines from Cade as she ate dinner and walked the streets:

...by the time the words are spoken, you shall have become a different aspect of yourself since the self is also spiraling.

There were woks for sale. Carved Mah jongg tiles. Silk blouses. Ivory buttons. What in life really mattered: a button. A questioning mind.

...We choose for ourselves a limited a future which we think the present always runs to. We say life and death are different, one is before, the other after. But they all come round again in a spiral. Linear thinking prohibits us from seeing a vast array of possibilities in our lives...

"Taxi."

If fat people were outside of people's imaginations, imagine being a lesbian standing outside the accepted norms. Yet, Borrasca's family was accepting of Brenda and Cade's relationship. What did the love of two women for each other mean to them? Their experiences and perceptions did not trap them. Borrasca lived by her own definitions. And Cade presumed to spell out the dimensions on a grander scale. Thank you, Borrasca and Cade. My family never offered me a picture of a woman as a thoughtful creature. I couldn't have known so many insights would result.

The hotel room was sufficient. A dim orange cast to the light. She lay on one of the two neatly made beds with a night stand and a lamp in between, propped up with Cade's book.

Just as the dominant point of view in history is white male--making women invisible, so, too, there is the ignored background of nature, often denied a voice. From whose point of view should a theory of physics or history be written? Novelists use omniscient narrator as an attempt to present all views. To make it appear that objectivity is possible. God is seen as some omniscient force. In fact, god is always a product of vision.

Since history is a conditioned vision set within predetermined boundaries, it takes a supreme effort to stand outside history. The dominant white male culture of America and Western Europe use history to tell their own version of reality. Thus history is the illusion of panorama. If one were to ask people of other cultures, not white, if our version of history coincides with their view of history, the discrepancy becomes clear. More has been left out of history than has gone into it: Other cultures, women, nature are subordinated or omitted. Reality is in danger of being somewhere else than in our experience or our recording of it. With consciousness, one moves out of static written history into a dynamic lived experience.

It takes a minimum of consciousness to remain in history.

Althea underlined that sentence. The world was being framed like a picture she could step back from and grasp. When she pulled back, how quickly the picture shifted--change any one part of the pattern and the whole picture changed.

History is a fiction, and its authors always presume some stance on the periphery. Plot is what we fashion to achieve meaning—does that make the author a fourth point, point D? And isn't God granted some immortal perch with the best vantage point outside, looking down. Are the points limitable? Not so. I'll dance around your god.

Alethea was struck by the acute irony of Cade's adaptable geometry, for she had been point A. Her life these last few months had been contingent on Point B and Point C. Now that she had given up following Borrasca, the pattern would dissolve. When she could let go of Borrasca and Cade, there'd be new points, other ways to be grounded in essential relationship. She had come to know herself in a new light.

In the morning she dialed the Firestones. No answer. No message machine. A reprieve. She took a bus to 125th Street, the *Studio* Museum *in Harlem* and immersed herself in the pictures on the wall instead of the ones in her head. Back in her room, lines replayed from the book. Cade fell. She could not bring herself to go out and eat dinner. She lay on the bed watching the orange light fade into dusk before she managed to take off her clothes and slide under the covers.

Hello. I'm Darlene.

She looked like the fat woman in the circus with a bee bonnet hairdo held stiff by hair spray, except for a few stray locks that dropped over her eyes. She pushed them back around her ear lobes with a pudgy finger. Alethea's eyes widened as Darlene became a three-sided figure, revealing different aspects of herself, like a mirror in a ladies' dressing room offering front, side and rear views. In the first mirror, Alethea saw a woman whose breasts were swallowed in the large body. In her eyes a deep sadness. Her face was disconnected from her body. I am the chubby little girl you were in grammar school, the part of yourself that doesn't like to look in mirrors. Darlene poked at Alethea's body. I'm the part of yourself you can't accept.

The second mirror image appeared. Her cheeks became more prominent. The long bangs on her forehead disappeared. With their protection gone, there was no way to flee the penetrating gaze of loneliness. When all your layers are peeled away, who are you?

Alethea faced the third mirror. Darlene's reflection was serene. Her eyes revealed a compassion born of wisdom. "Do you know beauty when you see it, Alethea? Can you see yourself as what you truly wish to be, a confident, self-directed woman on a path of her own choosing. Love that in yourself. Darlene's luminous eyes were tortoise green. Her hands opened and the palms were cross-crossed with the lines of many lives. She was an old soul. She bowed to Alethea and extended an invitation to dance. They glided around the room, their eyes fastened on one another. She danced with Darlene. With Kate Smith and Ethel Waters. Danced with a new conception of her being.

Alethea fell into the morning light. She was ready to talk to Rose.

"Alethea! You're back. Brenda—is she all right?"

"I think she's okay. I didn't get to talk to her."

Rose heard the intonation. "Alethea's back," Rose called out to Louis. "You'll come over? Yes? Come soon."

Alethea reckoned how disappointed the family would be. She had discovered very little about Borrasca. With her story unscripted, she arrived at the house, happy to see Rose open the door. Alethea felt the warmth of her large frame as they embraced. She hadn't remembered Rose being so affectionate. "I'm so glad to see you, Rose."

"And what about me? She turned to Louis who extended a friendly welcoming arm around her shoulders. "Nu? Talk to us." Mimi bounded into the room, with arms wide open. Her long hug was without unspoken questions. Still, when they separated, the three of them stood waiting for her to talk.

"You expect me to have answers, but I have precious little to report."

"You saw her?"

"Maybe twice. It was hard to tell. Can we sit?" "Of course." They sat at the dining room table across from her. Rose folded her hands.

"The first time I saw her she was moving quickly through a market place crowded with thousands of people. It was my first day there, and I couldn't believe my eyes. She was dressed in white, but so was everyone else. Trying to pick her out among a sea of white saris and dhotis was like being in a desert looking for a grain of sand. By the time I pushed my way through the crowd, she was nowhere in sight. She disappeared just like that."

"So close," said Rose. "And the second time?"

"It was at night during a firework display. I was watching from the street when a flare misfired and headed towards spectators standing on a wall above me. When it burst, I saw her standing there, illuminated in the light. There was chaos as everyone began screaming and running.

"She wasn't hurt?"

"No one was. The firework exploded safely above their heads. I pushed my way through the panicked crowd going in all directions. By the time I got up to the wall, she was nowhere in sight. You must remember New Delhi is a city with millions of people. It was pure chance that I even saw her twice. I can't tell you how frustrating it was not to meet up with her."

Their crestfallen looks compelled her to keep talking. "But she must be healthy to move as fast as she did. I kept going back to the same spot in the market place thinking she'd return. I walked for miles along the streets, checked nearly a 100 hotels. The Embassy. US Express. I don't know why I never got close enough to talk to her. I was so sure I'd come face to face with her."

She went over to Rose who had started crying. "She is never coming back."

Alethea put her hand on her shoulder. "You don't know that. We have to believe that what's happening to her is for the good."

Mimi came around to the other side and enveloped both Rose and Alethea in her outstretched arms. "She's your daughter, Mama. She never forgets that." Louis watched wordlessly.

"I don't want to be insensitive," Mimi said, "but I just got back from jogging, and I have to drink some water."

"We'll talk over lunch."

Eating obscured the need to talk. Alethea couldn't buoy up their spirits with false hope. She looked at the array of food Rose had put on the table. Food as hope. She asked about the food.

"What are these?"

"Potato latkes. Try some."

"Like potato pancakes except more grease," interjected Mimi.

"Shah," said Louis. "Don't be so critical."

"Don't get me wrong, I love them, but I eat them only at home."

"She says at school she eats vegetarian. Nu?"

"To be Jewish is to eat rich food." Mimi offered a humorous commandment.

"Don't insult your mother." Louis' face was red. "Food is part of who we are. Is your family like this, Alethea?"

"You're all quite loving compared to the way I grew up. We weren't a very close family. And Brenda, wherever she may be, is carrying this love with her. I know after I leave, I'll carry you with me like a second family."

Rose studied her. "You're already talking about leaving?" Alethea looked at the three of them and knew she couldn't run off immediately. She was their way of having a bit of Brenda with them. Besides, she cared for them. She shared more of her trip with them, telling the details of her search and offering her impressions of India, even the Taj Mahal.

"You couldn't just play detective," insisted Rose.

"At that point I was very discouraged by not having found Brenda. I agreed to go there with a brother and sister I'd met, Chandi and Lakshmi. They helped me appreciate the differences in the cultures I encountered. It was a way for me to sort out the meaning of my being there. Just seeing myself in the larger context of India gave me a better perspective. I stopped locating my identity in narrow concepts. With all my heart I wish I could have found here for you."

Rose nodded, a hand resting on her forehead. "I don't understand," Rose said. "You want life to be better for your children. After the war, I was sure nothing could ever be so bad again, but now Brenda is gone, maybe forever. I hope there's nothing we did to make her stay away. Brenda and I aren't as close as I'd like, but we're pretty loving—you think so, Miriam?"

"Oh yes. You can't blame yourself."

"This isn't exactly a daughter leaving home. She's deeply troubled," said Rose. "Pain is such a condition of life."

"I'm not sorry you went, Alethea," said Louis. "It was worth it to try, and from what you say, there's maybe still hope, you think?"

"I believe she will come back. I do. And her experiences in India will have mattered. It certainly put me through changes."

"You are different, Alethea," Mimi said.

"How so?"

"Not as timid as you were before."

"Not so much apologizing," added Louis. Rose excused herself from the table. "You'll stay a few days, yes?"

"Yes, "said Alethea touching her arm. A few minutes later she, too, felt a need to stand up. Alethea turned to Mimi. "I think I'll go for a walk." She breathed deeply outside the house and walked briskly in a short burst to the nearest crosswalk. There were less cars than she remembered, even at the mall where she found a bookstore and sat with a cup of coffee in their cafe. Whatever else happened, the search for Borrasca was helping her understand how attached to the Firestones she had become. They felt like family to her.

At the beginning, she had been deluded into thinking Borrasca was only running from the fear of being caught, and Alethea had pursued her like a mystery. But she understood how Borrasca was dealing with the full magnitude of mortality. Until now, death had been at a safe remove. Even when her own mother died, it had felt like it was happening to someone else because she numbed it out.

She walked back, past a block of homes lined with red maples. The family's grief for Cade and their fears for their daughter had put them on familiar terms with Alethea. Death, she saw, was a bond as well as a severance, and Cade's death had begun the whole sequence of events. She was filled with a compassion for the human journey.

With the approach of darkness, she became concerned about turning the right direction towards the house only to find Louis on the corner waiting for her. "I wanted to make sure you were all right." She smiled in relief and put her arm through his. As they came through the back fence into the garden, Mimi was there, her silhouette in the dusk so like Borrasca's. Louis stayed with them, appreciating the sky before he went inside. She and Mimi watched blue dusk give way to the moon which was on the verge of rising, its glow already tingeing the horizon. It would be a luminescent gold sky in New Mexico. She was home. Home was the sky.

She turned her gaze to the manicured yard with beds of early spring bloomers, including a large dogwood tree and a bonsai tree situated in a rock garden for an aesthetic effect. Rose was at home here.

Mimi spoke into the head of the moon that was breaking the plane of the horizon. "You're quiet, but not so much from shyness; it's more interior, like you're absorbed in your thoughts."

Alethea tested the waters. "You know how life can numb people? Well, I think I was like that until I saw two women on a mesa. It has altered my life beyond reckoning."

"You were on the mesa?"

"I was on a mesa opposite them. I called in for help. What I'm getting at is: what happens when you stop watching and become a participant in your own life? All three of us in our reality saw Cade fall. We made a triangle: one on a mesa, one below and one falling. I thought I understood what had happened, but I saw something and assumed it gave me rights of truth like a God—are you following me?"

"Go on." Mimi sensed her train of thought

"I'm explaining it as much to me as I am to you. I stood apart from the incident, like I've been standing apart from experience all my life, thinking my watching was accidental to the reality. That I was a neutral."

"The observer is never impartial," Mimi jumped in, knowing the train of thought was inspired by Cade's book.

"I could never have imagined I'd have some effect on the incident, but I wasn't the only one watching. Nature, who is not just background, witnessed points A, B, and C. We always act as if no one is watching, and when we find we've been watched—as Borrasca did—it throws our notions about life into question."

"You read the book," said Mimi. The moon pushed its way free from the horizon. "Then don't forget God as point G who some people think is always watching. People pray to God, believing he can alter the distance between the points, though deep down many think the points are already cast and fixed. And you, Alethea?"

"I'm re-evaluating everything."

"Brenda used to say that men were always watching, determining the boundaries and distance, watching all women in an effort to control them. She felt the constant presence of their eyes on her when she performed. My sister has been prodding me all my life. I regret to say that there was so much push and pull because I'm indebted to her for seeing the nature of society and the patriarchy in the first place. Alethea, did Brenda know you were there on the mesa?"

"I think it pushed her buttons to discover someone had seen what had happened. I saw Cade fall, but other than that I don't know what really happened. It's changed my life, and I see what it's doing to Borrasca. I was magnetized by what happened. I was like an object drawn to a lodestar. The initial attraction was so strong, I felt compelled, and even now part of me can't resist their pull. I've been a point on the horizon trying to figure out the other points, but when I couldn't meet Borrasca face to face, I began to see that I was also looking for me. I can't define myself in terms of Cade or Borrasca or anyone else."

"I understand, said Mimi. "Brenda is a very forceful being. I've also had to work hard to define myself as an individual apart from her."

Above them the fully risen moon ignited the sky. Alethea was hesitant to explain to Mimi that maybe, just maybe, the attraction to them also came from the magnetic force between her legs. The emotional pull to women was becoming very strong. She knew she wasn't in love with Borrasca. Her heart was with Cade.

"Both of them have come to represent something to me about love. I can't explain it yet to you or me. Cade is dead; yet tonight my heart is with Cade as much as any person I've known."

"Do you know where she's buried?"

"No, but I'm not into another search. I can't keep following them."

"I'm not suggesting that, but going to Cade's grave might help give you closure. And I have another idea—you can reject them all. The Lesbian Herstory Archives is in Manhattan. Brenda was quite impressed with it. You'll find information there about the land where Cade is buried. It might help you make a decision."

Back in Brenda's room, Alethea reflected on a flood of images in her mind, as if she were reaching into an old trunk and pulling out remnants of herself, the textured quality of a person she had previously been. The trunk was older than she was, older than many generations of women. It was trimmed in brass plate and the large lock with the key was in the shape of a large star. A wave swelled inside Alethea. She had lost her heart to one woman falling and the other running. It was recognition of a kinship indwelling. Her journal entry was a letter:

> *Dear Cade,*
> *I write as if I actually knew you. As if you were alive and you are in the way that a woman's spirit empathically lives in another woman. I could not have known you would be a turning point in my life, nor that my voice would one day call out to you. You have given me the gift of myself.*
> *With love, Alethea.*

It was cathartic. With tears running freely, she understood how much she had come to love Cade. Borrasca was more a projection, but Cade's soul radiated love like a light. I, who went searching for the uniqueness that is me, walked through the door of love that is Cade and found the outlines of myself.

TWENTY-NINE

Cade lost track of the seconds
thoughts came now only in random snatches
wind and memory circled along side of her,
moving faster than the body
of death there are many stories
this is a story within the story, and it is Cade's
she knew she was dying even
while writing the book
as if the book were why she had chosen to be born
it was a story a long time in the coming,
the one she started to write year after year
waiting for the right words
while she went about the business of living
for living becomes the breath of stories
meeting Borrasca she found someone notorious
who left a trail of tales spun after her
we came together as strong women
and the power of our passion renewed me,
giving me more time than I might have had.
but Borrasca made the relationship competitive
sizing me up by my degrees and achievement,
she was convinced I was the one with
depth and breadth of being, next to me
and she was only a persona, an image
we carried on, in struggle
I hoped one day women would read my book

its view of the universe would empower them
they'd see their struggles on a universal level
the book would affect the very way they perceived
Borrasca asked what's so god damn holy about being in print?
it was equally uncomfortable for me to enter her world
neither the women on the land,
nor the women in the band validated my work
they gathered as outlaws
on the fringe of the world I described
Nothing either of us did
could get the relationship on better footing:
It was dying. I was dying
it assumed a form in itself
as the book neared completion,
a crystallization occurred
the forms of life and death intersected
I didn't give up on this life
but how to talk to Borrasca about these things?
if women shared the secrets of birthing
why not also share the mystery of dying,
Death, your daughter is a lodestar
and she mother to me.
Lighted circles journeying around one another
and I in the center, a star blazing through me
We are the healing mother lode vein,
the matrix inside the sand painting
the secret inside the seed
where the women birth each other
and death steps back from the ledge.

THIRTY

Nights Borrasca spent in the dark dreaming. By day, the shadows receded. She sought out the light and Gabriele. They developed a relationship with one cornerstone: Gabriele refused to take care of her emotionally. She got up and went to her job, leaving Borrasca to sort out the experience. Their bond as Jewish women, as lovers, maintained them over a difficult period of silence until she was able to talk. Borrasca went out for long walks, drawn back time and again to the cemetery. She shuffled her feet through the leaves looking at head stones. She could face her memories among the peaceful dead, even amid graves marked by metallic crosses.

Growing up had not been easy, not like that of her childhood friends, and more than anything she didn't want to be different from the other children. She had resisted being Rose and Louis' child. What she most recollected were days of walking with Mimi through the halls of a silent house, filled with her parents' unspoken words for which there was no transliteration. She climbed hand over hand towards herself, coming face to face with events through which she had moved unconsciously as a child, strung out on the strands of the repeating dream, the return to the stadium night after night, her body a rubber band twanging as she was wrenched out of sleep, pulled between her world and the stadium. Today in broad daylight, she could not rationally explain the dream, nor the camp experience.

Sima's face appeared before her. "Sima," she cried out loud, as if by calling her, she could assemble the fragmented pieces of her past and they would fall into a cohesive pattern.

She returned for several days to the cemetery, sitting with sun light on her face, until the shock of the camp receded and the beginnings of understanding appeared. She had been exiled from her past and her source of being, but Cade's death had served to throw the order and control maintained by her conscious mind into tumult. From the chaos an inner order constellated, connecting the past with the present. Cade's death had been the opening, connecting her to her roots, familial and spiritual.

Spirituality grew like the roots of huge trees which were gnarled and curled around themselves. Spirit could manifest as the light of auras and high beings, but sometimes it was a dark chthonic force, a hardy root of substance deep in the soul. She had been wandering in the middle of the root stem, stunned at the absence of light, with no sense of the direction of the root behind or before her. Through death came the wonder of how life and death exchanged, as easily as root systems intertwine. So simple it was, and so mysterious, yet not always accessible to logic. Therein lay her problem. She was using logic to understand the camp experience. She might never be able to explain it to others who'd only take it in through the logic of their mind.

Borrasca pulled out her journal, hoping the process of automatic writing would be clarifying. The pen moved across the page, taking her into the world of a poem but now with no music. The singer was gone. Her interior voice needed no accompaniment, rich in itself, born from the fertile place in her being where only poetry expressed the numinous.

To begin to communicate with Gabriele, she brought them back to the cemetery. "It's the perfect place," Gabriele acknowledged.

"You remember the photograph of the stadium in Nuremberg?"

"Yes, I do. I was struck by the brightness of the spotlights which made it possible to take the picture at night."

"I was there. Gabriele, I'm not talking symbolically. I want this to stay very grounded. That photograph was the scene of my earliest remembered experience, one I relived over and over as a child. It was always accompanied by the feeling of my body being stretched like a rubber band as I was torn between my childhood and the scene of the photograph which I returned to every night. For years."

Borrasca kept talking before Gabriele's beautiful mouth formed questions. She recounted the train ride, being hit by the rifle butt, and other details of the camp. Putting the experience out into the world had a light-headed effect on her as the words found a manageable syntax.

"Are you talking reincarnation?"

"Some people want to speak in those terms. That's a trap for me, an idea rather than the particulars of the experience. On some level it was real."

"You're right, I suppose," said Gabriele. "And you can't make it a symbol of your life any more than people can try to make the holocaust a metaphor for different occurrences. It diminishes the experience for Jews that suffered."

Borrasca held up her hand. "I'm still sorting out the experience. It's not a metaphor. It's part of me that I'm coming to terms with. The writer Toni Morrison's word *rememory* is helpful. Several years ago, I had surgery for my shoulder—the same shoulder that was hit by the rifle butt in the camp—I was experiencing discomfort and went for a massage. As the masseuse probed me with touch, I experienced a vague rememory. The masseuse said that we carry knowledge in our bodies. She knew other Jewish woman who experienced a similar phenomenon. I repressed the experience. Now I must find some way to talk to my parents about this. Hopefully it will be worth the painful memories it might revive, for then they'll know that in some way, I've come home to them and myself."

An older woman walked over to the section of the cemetery where they sat, stepping gingerly around the flat headstones. Her hat gave the impression that she was tall, but as she approached a grave near them, she was actually quite short. "Guten Morgan," she said with labored breath.

"Good morning," said Brenda.

She looked over her glasses. "English, are you?"

"American."

Gabriele spoke to her in German and translated for Borrasca. "She says this is the grave of an old friend. Today's her birthday."

One knee at a time, the woman bent down before a barely legible stone lying flush with the ground. Borrasca saw orange lilies growing along the wall and picked a handful. She got down on her knees and faced the woman, their eyes inches away from each other.

"Would she like these flowers?" The woman's eyes brimmed with tears. She brushed off the stone marker and laid the flowers on it. She took Borrasca's hand in hers, praying quietly. From where she stood, it looked to Gabriele as if Borrasca were receiving a benediction. The woman's eyes opened and in the silent exchange, Borrasca experienced a moment of grace.

Gabriele came over and together they helped the woman to her feet. She spoke again in German. "Borrasca, this is Brigitta. She's Swiss but her father was Jewish. He was killed before she was born along with some of his family. She asked if you are visiting someone's grave."

"No. I'm trying to understand my memories of the war even though I was born much later."

Gabriele translated for Brigitta. "Brigitta also has had vivid memories of a camp. She could smell the burning—years later the smell would come to her. There may be no way to understand it, but she knows for her it is true. She says you must do the same. What matters is to trust the truth of your life."

The woman took hold of Borrasca's hand "Good day to you. Guten Tag " She turned and walked out of the cemetery.

"There are no accidents," Gabrielle observed on the way back to her apartment.

The two began living together in a new pattern of intimacy for Borrasca. She was able to be present and go through life at a moderate pace, paying attention to Gabriele rather than getting lost in her head or sinking into her emotions. Admiring how Gabriele would rise early in the morning and began sketching while most of the world was still sleeping. The accumulation of days and Gabriele's gentle affection worked their change. Borrasca finally ventured to tell her about her multiple identities as Bejay Storm and Brenda.

"You're Bejay Storm." Gabriele threw back her head and roared. "Ach mein Gott. At this point, nothing you'd say would surprise me. I almost went to your concert last year. Then I read in *Der Stern* that you had disappeared from sight."

Borrasca inhaled and went on. She told Gabriele about the day Cade flew off the mountain. "I reached for her—too late. I missed."

"Oh, my dear. No wonder you've been overwhelmed by grief," said Gabriele.

"And no time to assimilate it. I ran. From pain, from guilt. From the press and the notoriety that might ensue. Everything began to snowball. I've been flying across the continents, running from pain. Nearly killed myself climbing a mountain in a blizzard to get to a monastery. I've stopped running, but I replay the scene on the mesa. I keep reaching for her, too late."

"It's because it's happening in durational time," Gabriele said. "It endures past the actual event. That's why the Holocaust still goes on for you and your parents. It's why Cade keeps falling."

"Durational time, eh. How do I come to a final peace with it all? I'm trapped in that moment on the mesa, and I can't lay it down."

"I believe you're feeling guilt, not only because you weren't able to save her, but because you weren't the one who fell from the ledge. You feel guilt that Cade is dead and you are still alive. Holocaust survivors feel tremendous guilt at being alive. Even Germans, long after the bombs stopped falling, have guilt replay in their minds.

When Borrasca fell silent, she went on. "I don't know what actually transpired between the two of you—you say you don't even know—but you can't take that heightened moment and carry it around with you all your life. Her death most likely was the consequence of a string of events."

"At the monastery they said that everyone faces a central experience around death which tells us who we are. I came down that mountain as a different being, and I get it that I must transform the pain for the use of life. But knowing that and actualizing it are quite different."

"You might nor find a comforting resolution to it. Only a gradual integration of all that's happened." She put her arms around Borrasca and drew her close. Borrasca relaxed into her. "Tell me about Cade. Describe her to me so I can get a picture of her."

"Well, she was taller than me, and softer, you know, a soft butch."

"I don't know this expression."

"She was just on the masculine end of the butch-femme spectrum."

"Oh, yes. Femme buch."

"She identified as a lesbian, even at the lab, which was brave of her. She wore tailored women's clothes, sometimes men's clothes, but always pants. She would have felt like she was in drag in a dress. Her hair was short brown. It reminded me of a pageboy, cut just below the ears, but no bangs. And she had dark brown eyes with a black rim around the iris. It felt to me like the rim was the edge around a well that went very deep." At that memory she paused.

Gabriele jumped in. "And where did she work?"

"She was a theoretical physicist at Los Alamos—you know, where the bomb was developed."

"What a contrast you two must have been."

"The land women didn't want to hear about a woman working in that nuclear enclave even though her research was for peacetime use."

"What was she researching?"

"Cade was trying to understand the universe in relationship to things like gravity. She felt we needed to know the realities that exist or we don't know who we are. None of the women, not even me, validated her work very much. Can I read you something? She pulled out a letter from a small pocket in her pack.

Dearest B,

It's been cloudy for days, the high desert sky lost from view. This weather reflects my anxieties, so I hibernate and write because it is my one essential cornerstone. And the most unshared part of me. I can't even find a way to share it with you, but there may be a copy of my book ready in time for your birthday. How many women will see you this weekend and desire you. I'm not jealous so much as curious to know how it will affect us. Once I carried a magnetism of my own. I fear it's gone. Last night I had strange flying dreams. I wish I were flying with you.

Love, C

"Wasn't easy being Bejay Storm's lover, eh?"

"No. I had become the object of the fantasies and projections of millions of women. People knew me as an image. They were fooled. So was I. Perhaps I was duped the most."

"Truthfully now, did you drain Cade's energy away from her work?" Gabriele asked.

"I don't think so. I was too caught up being Bejay Storm. Luckily Cade wasn't taken in by the image. And she had her own charisma. She was the first child in her family to go to college, first to get an advanced degree. Her work was studied and widely quoted. When I met her there was a magnetic field around her. The magnet must know when something is being irresistibly drawn to it. My kind of attraction was easy to gauge. Her attraction was more subtle, and more genuine. I was a fast falling star compared to her."

"Two stars drawn to each other. How did you meet?"

"At a party in Santa Fe. Then the band went on the road, and I didn't see her again for three months—until another party. "

THIRTY-ONE

I walked across the *saltillo tiled* floor and reintroduced myself.
"How could I have forgotten you?" was her response. "You're Borrasca. It seems our paths only cross at parties."

"I tend to hide when I'm in Santa Fe."

"I thought it was Bejay Storm that had to hide."

I could feel myself blush. "Was I obnoxious?"

"You put up quite an affected pose."

"I apologize. Thank you for being bold enough to say that. Can we start again. "Let's talk about you. What do you do?"

"Please don't make me answer. You have two sides. I have two sides. I'll relate to you as Borrasca as if I never heard of Bejay Storm, if you'll judge me by who I am right now."

"Is there a mystery to all this?"

Cade watched Borrasca sweeping at her wild bushy hair with a restless hand, a bundle of nervous energy. She was captivated even though Borrasca was not someone she'd usually be attracted to, but there was no accounting for sexual attraction. And no denying it.

"I just want a chance at equal footing with you. Last time the whole conversation was like a fencing match. "

"I take responsibility for hiding behind Bejay."

"Will I like the real you?" The words came out more flirtatiously than Cade expected. She was surprised at the affect on Borrasca.

"I hope." There was tentativeness in her voice—Borrasca exposed her vulnerable side. Cade wanted caution and saw it rush by her as if it were a fleeting thought in the wind. Is Borrasca your real name?"

"It's the name I mostly use. In Spanish, freely interpreted, it means a sudden storm that comes up."

"Bejay and Borrasca. And neither is your real name. Do you come to Santa Fe only when you're not on the road? And do you live nearby?"

"My parents did not give me either of those names. I live just north of town, in La Puebla. Near Chimayo, and Santa Fe is very much my home. What a barrage of questions."

Cade laughed. "Truth is, I'm feeling like an unsure novice."

"Ah! You're talking to Bejay. Of course the star has been around. She sleeps with everyone. The band. Her fans. Just no white men."

Cade smiled at the trademark white man joke. "It won't happen again, but it's a powerful side of you to forget."

"Tell me something about you and we can stop playing a double identity game. My guess is that you're in a long term committed relationship." Sitting on a rug in a corner of Amyneita's house, I became enamored with Cade as she told me about Galen, her former lover. As she talked, I watched her eyes and fell into them.

"We lived together for six years as a married couple in a neighborhood of Los Alamos. There were no Borrascas there. No Bejay. Galen gave me a deep sense of belonging which sufficed for a while. It grew into love and trust, but Galen's commitment was to me, and that was the undoing of our relationship. My commitment was to my work. I told her that you can't just live for another person. Galen agreed, but she couldn't change who she was. It was suffocating me. My need to be free split us apart. When I told Galen I couldn't be in the relationship, there were no harsh words, no arguments. I'm sure Galen never fully understood why I was leaving. I regret that we went from lovers to strangers as soon as my car went around the corner. That was a year ago. Force fields are impersonal things. Some are born with it, others, like Galen, never have it. She couldn't draw people to her so she kept them by her intense concentration on them."

"And others," I asked.

"The connections between two women can be an intense magnetic grounding. Some maintain a hold on you that can be felt miles away. Years later."

Our eyes were riveted on one another. I couldn't get my mouth to work. "Was there was something you were thinking but didn't say, as in censoring?"

"Not censoring. Thinking that you are a woman with an inherent magnetism to draw all manner of things to her."

Cade knew more polite people than blunt ones like Borrasca. "And you are more direct than anyone I've ever met."

"Sometimes I'm too blunt for my own good. I come off as an abrasive New Yorker. I don't want to push you away."

Cade stood up. Borrasca faced her.

"Your magnetism has me a bit flustered right now."

"Should I back off? I don't want you to be uncomfortable."

"Are you going to disappear? Go off on tour"

No. I'm here for a few weeks, and I'd like to see you again. If you don't want to see me, I'll understand."

"I feel like I'm circling a lodestar."

We circled for several days more. Twice during the week we saw each other when Cade got out of work. By the end of the week, the inevitable was drawing closer. We circled up to the last hour, prolonging the butterflies in my stomach. I had brought dinner with me when I pulled up to Cade's house one Friday night.

"Hungry?"

"No. I couldn't eat right now."

Cade drew me in her arms, trying to meet her fears headlong. "Let's hold each other first."

"I didn't know we'd both be so shy," I said into her shoulder, savoring the moment.

"I didn't expect you to be so patient."

Cade nearly had to pull me into the bedroom. I saw that she was nervous, skittish like a horse, and offered, "We can just touch and cuddle."

Cade's mouth came down on mine. "Maybe I needed to hear that."

Cade slid onto my body, wet with perspiration. The edges of skin disappeared.

Cade opened and floated free, only Borrasca's tongue connected her to the earth.

THIRTY-TWO

The earth was home. The people lived in close harmony with their world, shaped by it even as they shaped it. As if they were made of the same substance as the land.

The caves are open, dark mouths, ringed by the socket holes in which the roof timbers once rested. Once, people lived inside these dark interiors. They built their fires and carved on the smoke blackened walls. The caves houses were clustered together. Historians say it was for security as well as warmth. Some say it was their sociable nature.

Over the course of many generations, the people indented the worn footpaths and toe holds into the soft tuff rock. They weaved baskets and made pottery, decorating them with the colors drawn from the clay of the earth.

Around the ruins is the Spirit world, presences that remain to this day, witnesses to life. The natural world goes on, out of the sight of humans who have forgotten their toeholds and the language:

Indian paintbrush

Dwarfed piñon

Yucca

Cane cholla

Crystal mica

Stone mutates

Flakes and pot shards

Milkweed

The prickly pear cactus which, each spring,

blooms into a pale, waxy yellow flower.

Also among these ruins are another language, the petroglyphs. One repeated petroglyph is of the trickster Kokopelli which appears on large boulders. Kokopelli, the hunchbacked flute player, was the 'Casanova of the Cliff Dwellers.' His hump is full of seeds that he scattered on his journeys fertilizing life. He was also a fertility deity and some said he carried unborn children in his hump. His distinctive shape was usually carved into the rock showing antenna that protruded from his head. He had the gift of language and music. Wherever he went he carried his repertoire of stories and played his flute which chased away the winter and brought spring.

THIRTY-THREE

"**D**oes hearing about Cade make you uncomfortable?"
"No. From the beginning I've had a realistic sense of who we are to each other. I never thought to try to make you forget Cade or to take her place."

Borrasca enclosed Gabriele in her arms. "You've helped me reclaim my life, Gabriele. I can't tell you what a gift it's been. I hope I've given some measure of that love back to you."

"You have, believe me."

"I'll have to go soon."

"I know."

"I'm not wanting to leave you, but I'm longing for home. Longing to connect with my family. Will you feel abandoned by me?"

"No, but I'll miss you. You walked into my life out of the blue dealing with Cade's death and the camp experience. But I needed you, too. You helped me see that I also have more emotions to deal with being a survivor's daughter. It was either a political story, or it was my mother's story. I will own it more honestly now."

"I hope I can come back when the rest of this journey is finished. First thing, I'll go see my mother and father."

In the deep sleep of night, Borrasca saw Rose in her garden, surrounded by the Bonsai trees. She was looking forlorn and cold. Borrasca shivered, pulling the blankets around her. As she tried to sleep another image came. It was of Dolna, a little girl from India who had been adopted in infancy by one of the women in Santa Fe. Her original mother had been forced to deliver her at seven months, which they said accounted for her being so tiny. One night Dolna had come to

Borrasca's house along with her mother and a group of friends to play cards. Dolna's mother had given her some crayons and butcher paper so she could draw while they played. The little girl, less than two at the time, whose only memories of her mother and India were those of her first days of life, began making so much noise with the paper that everyone in the room looked over at her. She was wrapping it around herself like a sari. Though she had never worn or seen one, she had an innate knowledge of a sari in her genes and collective unconscious.

Borrasca sat straight up in bed. Her own body and consciousness had knowledge of the camp. This encoded knowledge transcended time and space. Cade had understood that about time, writing about its circular nature. In the peacefulness of the night, Borrasca accepted it. Time, the queer part of the equation, rested easier within her.

THIRTY-FOUR

"Welcome to the Lesbian Herstory Archives." The guide took Alethea and three other women on a tour through the converted limestone townhouse. The library of materials was not to be found anywhere else in the world. Shelves of media, books, newsletters, and non-print materials, including photographs, slides, periodicals, audio-tapes, CDs, DVDS, and copious files, including unpublished papers, and collections of letters between women. On the wall was a poster with a picture of a black woman, Mabel Hampton, and the caption: "In Memory of the Voices We Have Lost."

The archives existed for lesbians who couldn't find their history anywhere else but in this living museum. There were artifacts from women in sports. Women in science. Lesbian comedians. Lesbian musicians. There was a picture of Bejay and an album of the band on display. The existence of such a vast network was astounding to Alethea. It confirmed to her once again the myriad of realities co-existing in the world of which she was only dimly aware. She was going to have to rethink history.

The Cade book of Stella Maris was also there, including several reviews, one quoting a section of the book:

For all I say about change and the realms of the invisible, I crave the physical. I honestly admit I am afraid of death. I of large form and stature want life and love in a physical context. I yearn for a universe where the invisible and the physical can co-exist. When I die, I hope I'm ready. I hope I travel towards a large shining star. I hope what I leave behind is not a dead heart in anyone, least of all myself. I want us to create a better world. I believe women can, if we approach life with new descriptions of reality. Let us not struggle with the old prescriptions. No dead heart in anyone.

Alethea sat for a long time, unconcerned about the tears rolling down her cheek. When she finally stood, she had a keen sense of direction. She found articles written about Morrigan Farm where Cade was buried. Missouri was as good a place as any to begin the next part of her journey.

Rose was the hardest one to say goodbye to. "Everyone leaves too soon," she said. "People return," Alethea responded. "Borrasca will want to see you as soon as she returns to the US."

"Some people leave and never return."

Louis was more positive. "We'll get through this," he said.

"Please write," said Mimi. "And come back."

"I will." She hugged Rose again. "And so will Brenda."

THIRTY FIVE

Alethea took a train from Grand Central and traveled south. Each day was greener, the sky more expansive, though not as enveloping as New Mexico skies. The comprehensive blue after the grayness she felt in New York rejuvenated her.

Overnight the steady clatter on the tracks lulled her into sleep. She stirred when people began moving down the aisle, and she assembled her rumpled self. How far they had come during the night, she inquired of a woman sitting on the aisle, and discovered she was less than three hours to her destination.

She got off at a small dusty stop between north and southbound tracks going as far as the eye could see on both sides. No other buildings. Nothing in sight but dense green trees blocking the horizon. The train left her in a wake of silence. There was no cab, no hint of which way to head. For twenty minutes she chased off flies until a farmer in an old Ford pickup drove up to the depot.

"Hello."

He murmured something that passed for hello. "Came to get my seed." He picked up a large burlap bag and swung it over his shoulder.

"Excuse me, can I get a ride?"

"Yep. Everyone wants a ride from here."

As they turned down a county road, Alethea tried to describe where she was going. He knew the piece of land. From the edge of the property where he left her off, it was still two more miles. The first mile she grumbled under the weight of her bags, the humidity that dampened every inch of her, and the incessant bugs. The last mile was a wonderment. Fields sprung up around her, thick with flowers and grasses. Jonquils and dogwoods. Lush green trees rose on both sides of the road and leaned over to meet in the middle in a high arch above her.

With her head raised to the trees, she nearly stepped on two turtles lying on the road, mistaking them at first for rocks until their markings gave them away. They were ensconced in their shells, and she had to be content to glimpse at their eyes peering out. A few yards further she met up with a long, very long, black bull snake lying lengthwise across the road. She started backwards, spell bound. The snake coiled and watched her without moving until finally it glided its way across the road and into the brush. She briskly passed through that stretch of road, careful now to glance down at her feet.

A weather beaten sign indicated Morrigan Farm. The women's land lacked the crisp upkeep of the neighboring farm which had a carefully managed field with a perfectly painted sign saying KEEP OUT. The main farmhouse appeared roof first, surrounded by several small structures on either side of it. The bright blue trim must have been striking when it was first painted. The house was two stories in a style which someone fancied as Victorian, elaborate in such a remote setting. There was a roughness to the place which she took to after the manicured yards of New York.

Alethea arrived the same day as a raucous van of women, and she appreciated the anonymity it gave her. There was evidently an open door policy, and no one questioned her being there. Everyone introduced themselves three times over, their unusual names tripping over Alethea's tongue. The women were to be there a couple of nights only, and proceeded to make themselves right at home. Alethea marveled at their ease as they walked the land, shirtless. She kept a low profile observing how the women interacted. Her first inclination was to immerse herself in the land not the people.

She walked the green circumference around the farm, which stretched a good many acres, finding small living spaces tucked away that were not visible from the main house or each other. A short distance from the gardens was a parcel of land that had been set aside as a small burial place. She entered the protective ring surrounded by a grove of trees. Singled out from the wild grasses growing all around was a large flat headstone on which the name 'Cade' was carved. She sat before it, lost to time and flooded with a sense of peace. Towards late afternoon, she returned to the main house and introduced herself.

The woman who was cooking walked with a slight limp to her right leg which didn't keep her from managing four pots and one child at the same time. "Hi. I'm Rifka. This is Lisa, Gwendolyn's behind you."

"My name's Alethea. I was wondering if I could stay here a while if I helped with whatever work is needed."

The woman behind her laughed. Alethea turned to look at the tall, copper colored woman who was kneading bread. "Now don't take my laughing wrong." The rolling pin spun out a long rectangular piece of dough. Too long for bread.

"You see, there's always work. And there's always women who say they want to help. When they find out what needs fixing, they disappear." She started braiding the long piece of dough while good-naturedly reeling off a list of chores: the garden, a fence to keep out the rabbits, the ditch. Cut and stack wood. The braided dough was sprinkled with cinnamon and put in the oven, the smell tantalizing her.

Gwendolyn, wiped her hands on a towel. "Don't let the weather deceive you; winter can be pretty cold here. The roofs of three structures are leaking." She went on cataloging the state of disrepair until the braided loaf came out of the oven. It turned out to be a cinnamon roll, not bread after all. They passed around the plate and as she broke off a piece, Alethea laughed, "Okay. I got the picture. I'll tackle that wood pile first thing tomorrow."

They showed her to a large room accessible only by ladder but with a window revealing a wide sky. She crawled in for the night and laughed again. Being on land had not come with a vision of laughter or a yearning on her skin as she watched women touch each other.

In the morning she reclaimed a plumb axe that someone had left in a pile of old rusted tools stacked in the barn. She chopped what she thought would be a week's worth of wood. It disappeared in three days. Chopping wood became her morning ritual, a continuity with her life in New Mexico.

A steady stream of summer visitors arrived. Alethea was excited to see so many other large sized women. When one of them flirted with her, her heart held back, not ready to be open to anyone. One day as she walked across a field, she heard the sounds of a work party playing a tape behind the grove of trees. In mid stride, her walk changed. She stepped into herself as if filling in the outlines of a rough sketch that had been lightly drawn.

Still she kept mostly to herself. They took her reticence for shyness and saw her labor as proof of her willingness to share in their lives. When the days began to shorten, there was a land meeting to see who was staying the winter and how they could live in the limited spaces suitable for winter. Gwendolyn and Lisa, Rifka and her lover Iris. and Zephyr, the one who had inherited the farm through her father, came. Zephyr didn't know how to share well—Rifka whispered this to Alethea—but Alethea knew she could spend a winter with her.

A woman in the corner by the stove had been as quiet as Alethea when she first came. Alethea walked up and introduced herself.

"Victoria—I don't like being called Vickie. Is Alethea your real name? We might be the only two women who haven't changed their names."

Alethea laughed, but was damned if she knew what to say next. How did she move on from what's your name?

"I've been taking photos of women from one end of the continent to the other."

"Country women?"

"All walks of life. Truth is I'm a city girl. I came to take pictures, but after working the harvest, I decided to stay a while. You'll let me take pictures of you, won't you?"

Zephyr called the meeting to order, and after interminable discussion, they decided who would live where and how to contribute expenses. Alethea spent as much time thinking about Victoria as the living arrangements.

"I need volunteers to divert the stream that's sprung up near the well and clear out the mud and debris in the ditch leading from the well to the main garden." Alethea raised her hand. The work would center her. Only one other hand was raised.

The next day she and Victoria lined up with Zephyr on the bank of the stream. They shoveled mud side by side, smelling of sweet sweat until a cloud burst pelted them. Alethea called out through the downpour, "Where's the closest place?"

"My house. If we don't drown first."

They dashed across the garden to the abandoned tool shed that Victoria had converted into a small sleeping space. The room flashed neatness, a honeycomb of shelves and milk crates along the walls were covered with a galaxy of pictures. Clothes and books were meticulously arranged. Alethea felt like a bull in a china shop, but when Victoria brought out her albums, she forgot her self-consciousness. The pictures were as organized as her room, each one labeled and placed according to geography, or theme, or exposure time. They had a special quality of light that captured the character and spirit of a woman.

That had been three days ago. Heavy rains made hermits of them all. On the fourth day of rain they congregated in the main house, the only place left with dry wood. Alethea watched the flicker of kerosene lantern light playing on the indentation along Victoria's cheekbones, highlighting her as if she were a portrait study. She's probably as finicky about her lovers as she is her photographs. It took an effort of will to walk across the room and go over to Victoria who had been doodling in a notebook. Sprawled among the notes, was a hastily drawn sketch of Alethea with her name written several times with flourish. She looked at Victoria, and they both left the kitchen laughing. They walked into the garden, their arms around one another's shoulders. In their shyness, they headed first towards one living space, then the other. Her first kiss with a woman came naturally. Victoria let herself be rumpled and messy, and Alethea let herself be loved.

The seasons went round. Victoria took shots of Alethea in the fall holding large zucchinis. In winter she smiled with mammoth icicles hanging down from the roof after a freezing ice storm. In spring, she took pictures of Alethea haloed in a spray of newly opened forsythia.

"What will I do when you go? Who'll record our pumpkins and chigger bites?" Alethea didn't like that she had resorted to a plea.

"Part of me wants to stay and kiss you with berries in your mouth, but I'm not cut out to be a farm girl. My camera's hungry to take pictures that can't be found here. That's why I came, to take pictures." Victoria went over to the bookcase and handed a leather photo album to Alethea. "I made this for you. Women come and go; pictures stay. It's the only way I could think of to say good-bye. You won't stay forever either. You'll get one chigger bite too many. You'll yearn for coolness. And me. I hope you'll want to see me again."

Alethea wasn't prepared for the hole it left in her heart. She took comfort visiting Cade's grave, relieved that the sky was absent of the woman who used to fall through it.

One afternoon a van drove up to the house. The driver didn't get out right away. Alethea saw her lean back and hesitate before opening the door. Alethea didn't think more about her until dinner. The new woman, like most newcomers, was uncertain how to participate. "Hi, my name is Wind." She kept her eyes behind sunglasses even as she offered fruit to the table.

When the meal ended, the conversation turned inevitably to chores. If there was one thing that would drive Alethea away from the farm, it would be the endless chores. Zephyr, took advantage of everyone being together. "All winter we got rain. Now when we need rain for the garden, there's not a drop. We'll have to divert a channel of water from the well to the garden. Can anyone get into digging a ditch?"

The new woman volunteered, raising a solid arm as if she were in class responding to a teacher. Alethea observed the raised arm, strong, tanned, a little fleshy. She was an abundant woman save for her sparse head shaved close for the heat.

In a mock foreman's voice that was an obvious imitation of Zephyr, Alethea showed her the tools and they worked on the ditch the next afternoon till exhaustion hit them.

"There's a beautiful meadow just over the ridge." Wind nodded. They went through dense woods where alternating bands of striated light came through until they reached the top of the ridge. Alethea saw two birds flying in circles over their heads.

One of the birds was a large, full grown hawk. The other was a baby learning to fly. The mother hawk repeatedly dipped her long brown wings under the baby, gently lifting it along. Sometimes it appeared that she swooped under the baby hawk just in time to keep it from falling.

"She's teaching her baby to fly."

"I thought that came instinctively," Wind called out, her hands cupped around her eyes to see better. The birds made another sweep of the sky, circling back towards them in the early evening light. The baby bird would fly off and then falter. The mother stayed along side it, swooping down as needed, and they'd rise up together. The birds flew off until they became small specks in the sky. "I read somewhere," she said, "that the faster you go, the slower time gets. So birds must have time last longer than we do."

"I've heard that same idea." Alethea jogged her mind to remember where she'd heard it. Off to the left were tiny wild roses, their yellow approaching luminescence in the fading light. They knelt in front of the roses and Wind broke off a stem. She threaded it through the button hole in Alethea's shirt. Alethea was curiously repelled by the electric gesture as much as she was drawn.

The next morning she avoided everyone, stating at breakfast that she was going to check all the fences. It took hours to walk the parameter of the farm, replacing the rotten pieces of wood no longer able to hold up the wire. She piled stones, seeking insights into her uneasiness. Still, it pleased her that Wind was the first one she saw when she returned. "Alethea, were you avoiding me today?"

"I just needed time alone."

"Were you feeling the electricity?"

"I felt something was flying at me as fast as those birds, and I needed to slow it down. Although I guess I'd need it to fly faster to slow time down, wouldn't I?"

"We can move as slowly as we want," said Wind, smiling through her sunglasses.

That week they finished digging the ditch. "We need a rain dance," said Iris. She led the group through the closely planted rows of corn. The tassels brushed against their cheeks. "We often sing this song to the Corn mother." Gwendolyn began and the others followed:

> rainmaker
> ride summer winds
> to cloud people;
> Shawano, Shawano
> corn mother thirsts
> bless these fields we planted.
> Shawano rumble
> climb down those clouds
> shíwana, come to us:
> grandmother waits
> corn mother waits
> four-legged wait
> two-legged wait
> everything waits
> we all await you.

The ritual bonded Alethea and Wind. They wandered off from the rest of the women. When they emerged, their hands were braided together like corn stalks. Before going off to their separate spaces, they kissed under a thin nail of a moon.

The next day Wind found a rose hanging on her door with a note: "Let's meet in the corn under the new moon."

At the first hint of sunset, Wind headed for the field. As she came around the last row of corn, she came face to face with Alethea who was waiting inside the circle, a circular patch of early evening sky above her head. Whatever had propelled her legs now breathed for her. Whatever breathed now loved, in an outpouring of passionate, unlike the small gusts that had come in the playful romping with Victoria. The days of temporizing and waiting churned into desire. Alethea tasted the full-lipped petals of her mouth, felt the warmth massing between their four large breasts, her breath originating from those four directions. She let the length of her body come to rest along side Wind and each carried the other on a light wing, flying in the face of time, birds guiding each other in flight.

They lay in the thicket until evening sent a chill across their bodies. The next few days and nights crowded together. It had been so light hearted with Victoria. When at last she could separate, Alethea left her side one morning to examine the itch that persisted Attracted as she was, an equal and opposite force rose in her. She couldn't explain the it to herself or Wind. Was it the old reflex to monitor life and play it in her head? She remembered how they had fallen asleep last night, and how she dreamed of waking up with her, but at the first light, she had left.

Althea returned to the cabin, tiptoeing as she approached the frame structure, so as to enter quietly if Wind were still asleep. On a sudden impulse she looked in the bathroom window. Wind was standing in front of the mirror, intent on plucking out little hairs on her chin. Her face was turned at an awkward angle, and the silhouette froze Alethea in her tracks. It couldn't be! The possibility rose as a small cry in her throat. Wind saw Alethea's face in the mirror and jumped in alarm.

"Why are you spying on me?"

"I was trying not to wake you." Eyes without their contact lenses stared back at her. "I apologize for invading your privacy." Alethea turned and ran.

Wind tore out of the house after her, chiding herself for her paranoia. She caught up with Alethea and pulled her shaking body against hers. "I overreacted. I'm sorry."

"This is going from strange to bizarre faster than I can reckon with," said Alethea, looking into strangely familiar eyes. "Wind, why did you come to Morrigan Farm?"

"Can we get past this? I'm sorry."

"Why did you come here?"

"Sooner or later every traveling dyke passes through here." Wind hesitated.

"And?" Alethea prodded.

After what seemed an eternity she said, "Someone I know is buried here."

"I can't believe I'm meeting you like this. Are you truly Borrasca?"

Borrasca was stunned to hear her name coming from the woman she had lain with the night before. Alethea grabbed her hand and began running, nearly dragging her along. Though her soul was cringing, Borrasca let herself be led, knowing the direction. They spirited past the rows of corn. Down the embankment dense with cattails that ran alongside the river. Up the other side and across the field. Both were gasping, but there was no stopping until they reached the gravesite. Point A and Point B stood on opposite sides of the grave breathing heavily. Borrasca struggled to catch her breath. "Who are you?"

"I saw you on the mesa with Cade."

"You?"

Alethea nodded, still out of breath.

"You were watching that day—just like you were watching me in the bathroom."

"No. That's not how it was. I was picking wild flowers on a mesa opposite where you were. I just happened to look across with my binoculars to see the two of you on the cliff—seconds before Cade fell. I ran for help as fast as I could."

"What did you see, Alethea? Do you think I pushed her?"

"Oh, no I couldn't say that. It all happened so fast. I lost sight for a split second readjusting the binoculars. Cade was in mid air."

"But you had your suspicions, right? Were you in India or was that my paranoia? Tell me."

"Yes!" Alethea screamed back at her. "And I was outside your dressing room."

"It wasn't total paranoia. You were tracking me down."

It's not what you think. During that time in India I figured out I was really looking for me."

"And you came here looking for me."

"No, I came to see where Cade was buried. And to find out more about myself. I had stopped following you."

Wind began walking in circles. "I got so I couldn't sort out my death trip from Cade's."

"Is that why you didn't you go to her funeral?"

"How could I go?" Alethea heard the tormented anguish pour out of her. "I was sure no one would believe me—I thought they'd connect Bejay and Borrasca and trap me at the funeral. There'd be a scandal. That fear overshadowed the grief I was feeling." Borrasca began to cry and Alethea moved towards her. Borrasca held her at bay with her hand.

"What do you want from me?" Borrasca's voice was rising.

"Please listen," Alethea struggled to speak calmly. "I ran for help and got to your campsite just before the rescue team arrived. That's when I found your journal."

Borrasca's hand went involuntarily to her heart. "I hid it when the rescue team came. For some unexplainable reason, I became protective of you. I never told them I saw someone else on the cliff with Cade. Later I realized the journal was the link between Brenda, Borrasca and Bejay Storm."

"How did they find out?"

"They never did. I'm the only one who knew."

"No one knew." Borrasca walked in a circle repeating, "No one knew." Then she spun around toward Alethea.

"I was pushed by guilt until it threatened to throw me off a mountain of my own making. I believed that when people discovered I'd been there with her, they'd assume I was guilty, especially since we had been arguing that week. It was in my journal. I was obsessed, seeing incriminating headlines. But I was also running from grief."

She began to cry. "I couldn't believe Cade was dead. I didn't give myself a chance to think, much less grieve. Guilt just tripped along side of me waking, sleeping. I imagined people looking for me, wanting answers about life and death. I didn't have any. I panicked. Ran to Tibet. India. Germany. I was carrying enough guilt enough for three: Brenda, Borrasca, and Bejay."

"I didn't recognize you when you first came because your beard and hair were gone. Still there was something about you that was tugging at me. That's why I left the house early, trying to understand what that was."

"So, Alethea, now you can ask me. Don't you want to know if I pushed her?"

The truth Alethea had once been seeking was at hand. "It's not the question any more."

"Good, cause I still don't know the answer. Call it selective amnesia. Call it anything you want. I still don't know what happened that day."

Alethea was dumfounded. Part of the truth did lay with her, not with Borrasca. "Borrasca—I can't call you Wind any more—it's possible that Cade may not have died from the fall."

"How's that?"

"Cade had a disease. I don't even know if I can pronounce it correctly: Amyotrophic lateral sclerosis. A motor neuron disease.

" You never told me you were sick, Cade. I remember that she'd gotten dizzy coming down a ladder at Tsankawi. Even before that day, she had complained of headaches."

"The autopsy results showed that the cause of death was not just the fall, but had been compounded by the disease. Some one else might have survived that fall, but not her. When they did the autopsy, they found her system already so weakened by the disease that, as a result of the fall, her lungs collapsed. They were satisfied that no one else was involved."

"I ran away—crossed the Himalayas, nearly killed myself—thinking I might have been responsible for her death." Alethea watched the core of Borrasca fold up and sit beside Cade's grave. "I'm sorry, baby."

Alethea placed her hands on Borrasca's shoulders. "Please know I never wished you ill, Borrasca. A part of me came to love both of you, even as it became a search for myself."

Borrasca leaned back into Alethea and cried until she could speak again. "I've been coming here nearly every day to talk to her. I still cry, but I've learned to separate myself from her. In a strange way her death has given me a new life."

"As it did for me. Borrasca, there's more to tell."

THIRTY SIX

The intimate bond that existed between Tsankawi and the Ancestral Tewa Pueblo people to whom it was home was an essential relationship that is nearly lost to us. Still its story and ours are intrinsically linked. Early beings left behind a trail we can follow if one is willing to engage with it. Eons ago the natural attraction that connected everything, each to each, was felt as a binding force.

The centuries have left nothing untouched at Tsankawi. Evidence of change is everywhere. Freestanding structures and their roofs with the wood vigas have fallen. Most walls have completely collapsed. What was once the home of the People has been reduced to low mounds of rubble. Only some socket holes used to hold ceiling timbers are still visible. What remains of the kivas are shallow depressions or a low wall covered in crustose lichens. The passing of the centuries has taken its toll. Even the Parajito plateau, which appears solid, shows the wearing effects of time. Part of it, too, is slowly falling into the canyon. Most of the larger piñon trees have worn away from the sides of the receding cliff and fallen, along with the overhanging ledges, into the valley below.

Every step adds to the millions of others. Each person is part of the erosion process. Each animal. Each gust of wind. The curling tree roots. Winter run-offs and spring rains. Freezing and thawing expand and contract the molecules. The volcanic tuff reacts chemically with rainwater and breaks down the rock into white ash soil.

On the mesa itself, other rocks prepare for their falling. One particular block of the mesa extends far out like a long platform. A tree's root on one stretch of the mesa grows down into the cleft in the rock. Little gaps have appeared between the extended platform and the rest of the plateau. Grass and the roots of tiny cedar trees have sprung up in the gap expanding it. The gaps have become fissures. No human ever sees the full progression. Few witness the actual separation when in a few seconds the edges of the mesa fall away in a timeless world.

THIRTY SEVEN

"Borrasca. I also met your parents." Borrasca blanched as the revelations kept coming.

"Seeing you on the mesa triggered unforeseen changes in me. You were larger than life, a mirror in which I could see myself in a new light. I believed if I found you, I'd find the answers to my own life. I saw the address in your journal under Brenda Firestone and found myself on a plane to New York. I had never done anything that bold before. I really liked them and they were very loving to me. Mimi, too."

"The ironic thing is that I never had a chance to explain who I was. Just as I got there, Mimi arrived with a letter from you. They were so excited to hear from you that she read it right then and there. The four of us were drawn together by your letter, and one thing led to another. They wanted to protect your privacy as you had requested, but they were very concerned about your safety. Your father understood why he as a parent shouldn't go, but he thought that if I went to India, they could still honor the intent behind your wishes, and find out if you were safe. I couldn't say no to them."

"I slept in your bedroom, wore your clothes." Alethea went on, anticipating an angry reaction. "I read my way into consciousness reading your books and Cade's book.

It was incredulous to Borrasca.

"Have you been home?"

"It was wonderful to see them. I told them I wasn't ready for any questions about Cade. I still didn't know how to talk to them about what had happened. My father cried as soon as I came in the door. My mother opened her arms and embraced me." Tears filled Borrasca's eyes. "Holding my mother after that long ordeal was sweeter than I can describe. The need for explanations didn't impose itself right away. That first night my mother and I curled up on the couch after dinner. I remember the comfort of her stroking my hair. I should have been holding her for the months of uncertainty I put her through. I fell asleep with her combing my hair with her fingers as if she were looking for lice. Finally I was able to talk to them about what had happened and what I had been through. It was a healing time for the four of us."

"Still, after Mimi went back to school, the pattern of an adult child living with parents set in, the three of us walking around each other in that big house with long lapses of silence. They understood I couldn't stay. I came here to be with Cade."

"It's hard to believe you were looking for yourself in me. You're not the groupie type. Groupies are scary. They have no self-concept. They mimicked me, or whoever was lighting up the charts"

"I wasn't trying to lose myself in you, Borrasca. What I saw in both you and Cade were active women with genuine substance unlike anyone I'd known. You both helped me find my own inner strength."

"But that's where I went wrong," Borrasca offered. "I was so misled by the outer trappings of my public persona that I lost my identity. Cade never knew which of me would show up at her door. It was my inability to be comfortable with my inner self that caused us difficulty. She was the most genuine person I had ever met. Maybe that's why without her, I felt unreal for such a long time. I don't blame myself anymore. That's who I was. I can love that person now, but I'm grateful I've changed. Major differences between Cade and me resulted in difficult times which is why we decided to go off by ourselves camping that weekend. You romanticized that episode on the mesa until we became larger than life figures. What do third parties ever know about what happens between two people?"

"The bonds between us were intense; nothing else existed sometimes. The myth of lesbians always being in bed is a distortion of that bonding: You walk around carrying your lover with you all day.

When I left Cade's bed, I felt the invisible strands connecting us miles away. That's how it can be between women. But when the energy shifts—if one of you falls in love with someone else, or if one of you dies—there is a terrible wrenching. A vital center is disturbed."

"In our case our differences were intensifying, and we were starting to drift away. We were on that mesa hoping to find a way to bridge our differences. Our work and our needs were taking us away from each other in time and space. And from the natural world which we both loved so much."

THIRTY EIGHT

"Hi, Cade. It's me. I've been missing you." "Hi, love. I've missed you, too."

"Can I to see you tonight?"

"I can't."

"What am I getting stood up for this time?" Cade paused before answering, wanting to distract Borrasca from her sarcasm without a confrontation, once again having to figure out Borrasca's mood.

"I'm in the middle of an experiment that I began early this morning before I knew you were back in town. It won't be finished until close to midnight."

"I see."

"Do you?"

"Of course. I just really want to see you."

"Can you come up here?"

"No way. I can't bear the lab, you know that."

"Just thought I'd offer. Are you in town for a while?"

"For a couple of days."

"Let's spend the night together, Borrasca, even if it'll be late. I have to warn you I might be exhausted. My headaches are back."

"I just want to hold you into sleep."

"How can I refuse?"

At midnight she drove up to Cade's house. Their bodies came together tensed, weary. Longing was secondary to a comforting reunion. By 1:00 they were both asleep. At dawn, their bodies began seeking each other out. Their hands fanned out over their bodies, but there was a desperation to their lovemaking. It rose in waves only to subside. Hands and tongues yearned to create sparks, but nothing could break through the barrier of skin. The soft breasts and folds of skin nestled in the secret places waiting for the wonderment that never materialized. Desire went slack; their bodies unwound, and they rolled away from each other like uncoiling springs. "We can't take this personally," tendered Cade. "We're both under a great deal of pressure."

"Right. It's not happening to us—has nothing to do with us. We can't make love, but everything is all right."

Cade put a hand over her eyes. "When did this pattern begin?"

"What pattern?"

"Damn it, you know what I mean. The sarcasm. We stick each other with little barbs. I'm not trying to find blame. I just want to understand what's happening between us."

"I don't know where the sarcasm comes from. It's my first line of defense. The words pop out before I can stop them."

"Have you been seeing Calypso?"

"You mean sleeping with her? I told you it was over months ago."

"It's hard not to imagine every woman in America wanting you. I'm jealous, or maybe it's lack of confidence, mine's at an all time low."

"Don't get down on yourself. Maybe I appear confident to you, but it's lonely traveling from hotel to hotel to concert. Many fans and few friends. I couldn't wait to see you. Just to talk to you."

"I get that. There are few who can relate to me on an equal basis. Fewer still who want to share my world."

"I want to share your world, Cade.

"Do you? I keep thinking music is your whole life."

"We've had this conversation a hundred times. I love my music and I love you. I don't want them to be in competition. I don't know how to change this cycle either."

"Let's change the scenery!" Cade sensed the idea was right immediately.

Borrasca rolled over and saw her eyes were on fire.

"Let's go away for a few days. Not be at your place or mine where one of us is always feeling powerless and out of their element. When I get depressed my first urge is to go somewhere high in the mountains. She sat up. "I want to be close to the sky. I've been missing it."

"We could go up to Bandelier. Better yet Tsankawai," said Borrasca remembering the quiet mesa, the cave dwellings, the cliffs lined with ribbons of orange like blankets.

From the moment they left town, their serenity increased as the car inched up the mountain toward the Pajarito Plateau. They parked the car and packed in their supplies until they found a place to set up a base camp before hiking along the high mesa. When Cade tired, they rested in wild grasses, the wide expanse of sky enveloping them, reciting the Spanish names for all the herbs and flowers they could recognize: chamisa, las flores de la quebrada, yerba de la negritude. Cachana. Canaigre. Escobar. Cade jumped on Borrasca who yelled, "Don't tickle me." Cade pressed her mouth against Borrasca's. They threw off their clothes and rubbed sparks across their bodies, rising until gravity came to meet them. The soft meadow grasses were feathers against their bare skin until they were unable to sort out whose tongue was whose. Afterwards they lay peacefully, the sharp edges had vanished.

So as not to break the interlude, they silently put their clothes on and walked with their arms around each other above the rest of the world. Along the edge of the plateau, Cade stumbled and Borrasca caught her. Cade put her hand on her forehead. "I'm a little dizzy."

They knelt together, listening to noisy blue jays until the headache was gone and the jays had flown away. The peacefulness between them stayed with them all evening. Stars spun brilliantly through the sky, a backdrop against their two forms seated around the campfire. Borrasca looked across the fire and saw the black sky with white stars haloing Cade. There was a reflective aspect to her face, but Borrasca refrained from asking any questions that might disturb the peace.

After dinner, Cade pulled out a crumpled Tarot card from her backpack. She held it out for Borrasca to see in the light of the fire. It was the gaily colored Fool who walked on mountains shaped much like the Jemez surrounding them here, but in the card it was bright sunlight and a dog accompanied the Fool who was hovering along a ledge.

"I've been carrying this around with me for a week now. Do you know what a spiritual double is, Borrasca?"

When Borrasca shook her head, Cade explained. "There's an ancient legend that says everyone has a spiritual double, a soul which exists at a safe remove, not afflicted by the losses or injuries of our present, physical body. I found this quote:

My death is far from here and hard to find, on the wide ocean. In that sea is an island. A green oak tree grows there. Beneath the oak is an iron chest. Inside the chest is a basket. In the basket is a hare. And in the hare, an egg. Who finds the eggs and breaks it, kills me.'

Borrasca didn't know what to make of the story, so eerie did it feel in the telling. Cade was speaking of death, but without morbidity, only a sense of the ineffable. She offered no other comment. In the serenity which expanded into the night, Borrasca could find no words for the questions inside her.

In the morning, silliness returned. They sang old 50's Motown songs while they drank coffee. Still humming, they descended the mesa and hiked to the cave dwellings, surrounded to the west by the Jemez mountain range and to the east by the Sangre de Christos. At one point, they had to climb down a wooden ladder built by the Forest service for safe descent. Cade started down only to stop midway, holding on to the rung above her. "I'll just stay on this rung for a minute. It's probably just the altitude."

Borrasca joined her at the foot of the ladder and gently rubbed Cade's forehead until her equilibrium returned. She put her arm around Cade's waist, and they walked side by side until the footpath restricted their movement. It was barely wide enough for them to squeeze sideways through the narrow opening between two boulders. On one of them was a petroglyph of Kokopelli cut into the stone. They followed a toehold trail that someone hundreds of years before had used until they came to the cluster of honeycombed caves they had visited many times. Above each cave, were the remains of socket holes where roof beams had once been. They crawled inside several caves looking at the petroglyphs that were still visible: a deer, a streak of lightning, spirals, a wave of water, and in one cave where the roof had been blackened by hundreds of years of fires, a long serpentine figure had been carved.

Borrasca crawled inside one of the caves and sat on the powdery tuff floor. When she looked out through a round opening cut out in the rock face, she saw Cade outlined against the sky. Cade turned and saw Borrasca who grinned through the opening. Cade came inside and they sat with their shoulders leaning together, embracing the magic of the moment in the dark, ancient place.

As they climbed back up to the campsite, Cade began a round of teasing when she saw Borrasca's fro matted with grasses clinging to the tight curls.

"It's a walking bush," Cade exclaimed, grabbing for her hair.

Borrasca ducked. "I am the queen clown."

"Ah, ha! A Fool to my Fool," cried Cade.

"A Fool. An outlaw," chorused Borrasca. "Outhouse."

"House mother. Mother Nature," Cade sang and danced off in mock retreat.

She pirouetted away. Borrasca playfully reached for her as she backed up. The leaping left foot came down and twisted on a cactus nestled near the edge of the earth. Cade's abrupt movement jarred the outlying rock platform. She spun on her ankle and arched in the air for one graceful second, as if there were full intention of the moment. And then she fell towards the grasp of gravity.

THIRTY NINE

"Alethea, I reached for her and missed. I missed! I kept reaching for her, too late. I myself was at the very edge. She flew away. "There's no way to describe the unreality of it."

"I remember screaming. It was as if we had been abandoned by the forces. I left my body in a way quite unlike Cade. I couldn't go or stay, be or unbe. The world was in flight. I'd try to run for help. And she would fall, and I'd come rushing back to stop her from falling. She fell for excruciating minutes. For months. I was spinning on my own downward spiral. Always it came back to me the same: her body flying in mid air. The effortlessness of her body floating in the air.

Alethea put her hand on Borrasca's shoulder. "All this time, for me as well, the sky's been a woman falling through it. I don't obsess with it as much now. I replay my climb down, running for help, my return to the top. I expected you to be there with full explanation. I was dismayed to find only the sky met me, though your face hovered around the site. Her body appeared to me over and over, arrested in mid air. Cade appearing in the round eye of the binoculars changed my whole life. At first I thought you had all the answers, so I was compelled to find you. But it became something else for me, just like it led you to other understandings. I never knew what I'd say to you if I met up with you. But the questions changed. I no longer needed to ask you anything since I was really trying to find me."

"The two of you were a magnet drawing me, and the matter of desire caught in the attraction cannot stay immobile."

"You read her book."

"It gave me a clue about who Wind was—something you said about the birds—The faster one flies...the slower time goes."

Borrasca laughed. "I didn't really want to take on another name. Cade also said each of us gets to dance within the energy field for a longer or shorter time. It's nothing personal. We get larger or smaller magnetic fields, depending on chance and probabilities. The danger is in being so ego involved, we're sure meaning is tied up with our perception."

"The irony of meeting like this," mused Borrasca. "How different we perceived this whole thing. Stranger still that we're sitting here besides her. I carried her with me. And you were carrying us both."

"Are you still carrying her?"

"Differently now, Alethea. Cade's fall sent me on a path I'd never have taken if it weren't for that day. Her death began my understanding about grief, about myself and my history." I began the slow process of integrating my personal pain with the pain that I carry as the daughter of survivors. As a Jew, I found that the collective memory of death and pain persist long after the experience, longer than a generation. Memory cannot be obliterated nor repressed."

"You were the quarry at first, Borrasca, but the original questions changed. I read Cade's book and began to see how truth was a function of my perceptions. We both changed."

"Maybe all three of us."

"And, Althea confessed, you both had an erotic pull on me. After all, the sky became a woman falling through it rather than men and planes. Cade especially imprinted her image on me. It was the first time I really loved someone. This probably sounds strange to hear me say it, but I opened my heart to her, even wrote an imaginary letter to her. It was then that I was able to understand your loss and anguish. To be able to feel compassion is no small gift."

"Possible only after we've learned to love ourselves," said Borrasca. Alethea reached for her and felt Borrasca's body pressing against her, but the attraction had ceased. She had given one her heart and the other her fiercest devotion. The spell was broken. She was free.

In the place of passion Borrasca found a keen tenderness. "I saw an obituary written about Cade before I came here. They said her book was a correlation of her life and death as if she had lived out all her theories. I don't myself believe there's a simple cause and effect, though I'll never know for sure what role her illness, fate or the mesa itself played in our lives. It was synchronistic."

"In my personal obituary for her, I'd say: "Once upon a time there was a warrior named Cade who resisted the deadly atrophying of the world. To those who say she has no voice, I say we are her voice."

They held hands and circled around her grave. "This circle reminds me of a postcard Cade sent to me. In it, two bears are dancing alone in a forest under a crescent moon. In the background are tall spruces outlined in the moonlight. One bear is shorter than the other; she has her right hind paw slightly elevated as she reaches up to the other bear in a loving nuzzle. On the post card, Cade wrote me a note that's indelibly etched in my memory:

"I don't know if anything I do will make a difference in the world, but I have to live as if it will. I will never fall prey to the disease of the world which runs hopelessly towards destruction, all the men's stories tragic. I will live as if love can make a difference, for I see that to live that way will surely make a difference."

"As Brenda, I could only see the effects of Jewish history on my life and my personal relationship to pain. As Bejay, I set myself apart from others and played into the world view which sets people apart. Now, more than anything, I want to feel my connection to the world and be part of the stream of women nourishing life."

"A web of women connected by love," Alethea affirmed. "All the web connected by the spark. A telegraphed love, an abiding affection."

FORTY

Cade knew she and Borrasca
were permanently connected to each other,
but on the way down,
her self, feathered in flight,
framed her world
she was dizzy from the spinning and spiraling
finally she stopped resisting
and let the forces carry her off.
She floated free above her body
becoming a part of the sky,
even as the earth got nearer.
Borrasca, are you flying with me
Is anyone flying with me?
Cade had several trails to take
though it appeared she was only falling.
She saw how the journey
was the passing of one another
through the corridors:
some on the future stem of the spiral;
others on a return loop to the past.
The difference between past and the present
was the thin gauze separating them
as they passed in the spiral.
Soon the thoughts resolved into white
like a painting she had seen
where the canvas opened and flowered in white

and was both earth and horizon.
It was her view, past the cliffs
into the light of an intense afternoon sun.
She started to go head first
through the spiral.
flying in the face of everything
Flight now her most recent memory,
she a star unto herself.

ABOUT THE AUTHOR

At heart a poet, Sandia Belgrade has taught writing at UCSC and creative writing workshops. She has published *At the Sweet Hour of Hand in Hand* (Naiad Press), a translation of Renée Vivien who was part of the vibrant community in Paris in the 1920's. Fire Bear Press also published *Children of the Second Birth*, a collection of her poetry. Sandia was one of the winners of the 1998 Anna Davis Rosenberg Poetry Award. A third poetry book, *The Running Shape of Wisdom* will be published in 2013. She has also written a libretto on Sor Juana Ines de la Cruz. Sandia has been published in magazines and anthologies including the inspiring anthology. *Sisters Singing*. You can follow her work at:

http://www.firebearpress.com
https://www.facebook.com/FirebearPress.SandiaBelgrade?fref=ts

24001192R00151

Made in the USA
Lexington, KY
01 July 2013